MW01016103

Hugs

LAWRENCE WILLIAMS

BALBOA.
PRESS

A DIVISION OF HAY HOUSE

Balboa Press books may be ordered through booksellers or by contacting:

Balboa Press
A Division of Hay House
1663 Liberty Drive
Bloomington, IN 47403
www.balboapress.com
1 (877) 407-4847

Print information available on the last page.

ISBN: 978-1-5043-8595-4 (sc)
ISBN: 978-1-5043-8597-8 (hc)
ISBN: 978-1-5043-8596-1 (e)

Library of Congress Control Number: 2017912112

Balboa Press rev. date: 08/15/2017

This book is dedicated to my incredible wife, who does all the heavy lifting, my two daughters whose daily interaction with Tyler has been consistently spectacular, those family members, friends, and health care professionals, doctors, dentists, and therapists who have touched us so deeply through our son. And especially, to Tyler, who has taught us so many valuable lessons. For those of you who may not have understood, you were instantly forgiven.

"I am your father. You are my son.
We are best friends. I will love you forever."

Contents

Chapter 1

Damn, that one hurt! They didn't used to hurt so much. At first it felt like a pinprick, something easily ignored. Gradually, it became a sharp stitch like when you were a kid and ran too far, too fast—just a little jab in the ribs. That had been nothing to fret about; the pain was gone in an instant. Now it hurt deep, somewhere near where he imagined his soul to be located. And it lasted a long time, driving him to his knees. He bent over, wanting to vomit; it was that kind of pain. It would last several minutes—more than twelve minutes, if the last one was any indication. They had increased in intensity and duration and were almost unbearable now, closing in on that last hug. He had to judge it just perfectly. If he died during one of these episodes, Taylor would never forgive him—not to mention his wife, Gina. She begged him not to do it for anyone, not even Taylor. He rolled over on the cool stone surface of the bathroom floor, praying for some abatement, some surcease of the excruciating pain. *Endure, just endure. It won't be much longer. Just endure.*

He was sweating profusely. Beads of salty moisture erupted on his brow, and rivulets of perspiration trickled down his spine. His body was wasting away, some forty pounds lighter than his normal 190 pounds. He lay back on the floor, panting, trying to recover his breath. *Oh, God, help me!*

Gina came into the bathroom, looked at her watch, and hit the timer. She wanted to see how much longer it would take him to recover and compare it to the last episode. They seemed to be increasing in severity and length. She didn't speak. She didn't trust her voice. She just looked down at Steve and shook her head in exasperation. This situation had

1

become unbearable. She had a difficult time accepting the terms of this arrangement, this aberration of everything she thought was true. She sat down on the closed lid of the commode and watched the seconds tick away. She knew there was nothing she could do for him—nothing but wait for the inevitable.

She opened the curtain and looked outside at the family whose son Steve had just treated. The father was sobbing, holding his son at arm's length, staring at him as though he was seeing him for the first time. Gina thought, *He really is seeing him for the first time—his potential, his future—a future that held some promise.* The little boy returned his father's smile, perhaps for the first time in his life—at least, that's what Gina imagined. She didn't know who they were or where they came from. The identities of the children they treated were intentionally withheld from them. That was part of the protocol of these trials. Neither she nor Steve would have prior knowledge of the nature and severity of the child's affliction or even if the child was truly autistic. But Steve knew with 100 percent accuracy if the child was autistic as soon as they met. He'd proved it countless times, but Dr. Jacobs still inserted an occasional impostor to confirm Steve's ability. He identified every normally developed child immediately, so Gina felt confident what she witnessed outside was an authentic miracle of recovery.

The entire family was outside now, weeping together. The father, mother, and an older teenage girl let loose an unbridled waterfall of emotion. Their lives would be different now—no more special schools, short buses, biting, pinching, and screaming, or embarrassment. The formerly autistic eight-year-old little brother joined in, even though he didn't know what everyone was crying about. He hugged each of them as though it was the most normal thing in the world, although he'd never hugged any of them before. And that just made them cry even harder. The more he hugged, the more they cried. For the unidentified family, the future had some hope.

Gina turned away from the window and consulted the timer on

her watch to discover they were already past the twelve-minute mark. She watched as her husband sat up and smiled as he always did after he recovered. She wondered if she would ever experience the joy she'd witnessed outside the window with their son. Hope was her only friend.

Chapter 2

Steve and Gina pored over the family photo album. The big, heavy, leather-lined affair was awkward to handle without loosening the binder that held the pictures together. They sat on the overstuffed L-shaped sofa, their hips touching, while Steve turned the pages and Gina looked on.

"Oh, God, remember that one?" Gina asked. The photo was of their son, Taylor, only one-year old at the time. It showed him racing after his older sister, Alexis, seventeen months his senior, his face a mask of pure joy as he pursued her through the kitchen. His mop of light brown hair, punctuated with blond streaks only a child's hormones could produce, bounced off his forehead as he chased his raven-haired sibling, who remained just out of reach.

"Yeah, that was the happiest time. The world was full of promise. We thought we had it all," Steve said.

Gina laid her head on his shoulder in a gesture of comfort. "I still wouldn't change it for anything."

Steve shifted to put his arm around her and said, "Me neither."

He turned the page and saw an entirely different picture, one of his son at two and a half years old, his eyes diverted downward, away from the attention of the camera, a look of utter confusion painted on his face. He couldn't look at Gina. Steve turned another page.

"The kids sure changed things for us, didn't they?" Steve commented.

"It seems like our life sped up to warp drive after we found out about Taylor," she replied. "It feels like just a blur now."

"Yeah, there was never enough time for anything after that."

"Do you remember that first meeting with Dr. Billings?" she asked.

"How could I forget?" Steve said. "I didn't even know what autism was. No one did back in the eighties. We had to go to the library—no Google then."

"I remember he said Taylor might just be a slow developer, not to worry. God, I wish he'd been right," Gina said.

"Me, too."

"You know what always puzzled me?" Gina asked.

"What?"

"How fast his words went away," she said. "One day, he could say *mom-mom* for me and *daa* for you, *les* for Alexis, even *og* for the dog. Then, as if by magic, they disappeared all at once. How does that happen?"

"I doubt we'll ever know."

"It's a shame your parents never got to meet our kids," Gina said. "They would have been great to have around at the time."

"My mother would have insisted on a Catholic baptism for them and worn out her knees in prayer over Taylor," Steve commented wryly. "But she never would have given up hope, just like you."

Gina smiled up at him. "They didn't get to see their little boy get married either. I bet they would have made such a fuss over you."

"My mother would have. My dad would have acted properly aloof until he had a few cocktails. Then the lid would have come off." Steve said, "That drunk driver took that option off the table for us." His parents had been T-boned by an intoxicated truck driver and died before Steve proposed. He and Gina opted for an elopement in Carmel, California, shortly thereafter.

"I didn't know I was pregnant already," she said. "And nine months later, along comes Alexis."

Steve said, "Yeah, and she came out with a full head of jet-black hair and porcelain skin, just like her grandmother—must be the Japanese heritage. It sure didn't come from me."

"Well, seventeen months later, your son came out with very little hair that sprouted into a blond bush, just like his dad at that age. I thought he looked like a blond stalk of broccoli."

"Don't remind me," Steve said, brushing his thinning pate.

"I wonder if Dr. Billings had any idea Taylor was autistic after that one-year checkup?"

"I doubt it," Steve said. "He seemed genuinely surprised when we returned at fifteen months. I think he suspected it then, but still, he wouldn't give us a diagnosis. I remember he asked us to wait for the nineteen-month visit. That was a long four months."

"It sure was," Gina said. "I remember every detail. We were so naive."

Their ruminations transported them back to 1989.

When Gina and Steve returned to see Dr. Billings, he took his time eliciting responses to a variety of stimuli from their baby boy. When he lifted Taylor up onto the examination table and set him on the fresh paper covering, Taylor reacted by plugging his ears with his thumbs and screwing his eyes shut against the crinkling noise the paper made. The doctor frowned. Steve and Gina traded a worried glance. "Have you seen this reaction before?" Dr. Billings asked.

"No, this is the first time," Gina said.

"Well, we know he can hear. Let's try something else." The doctor abruptly snapped his fingers in front of Taylor's face, only inches away from his eyes. Taylor ignored him, as though he didn't hear the snap or see the movement.

Dr. Billings maneuvered behind the toddler, produced a tambourine, and banged it against his hand, mere inches from the boy's ear. Taylor did not react.

He poked and prodded, used a rubber mallet to check involuntary responses, and spoke to Taylor in different degrees of volume and emotion, all to no avail. Taylor did not respond to anything except the crinkling of the paper.

After twenty more minutes of testing, Dr. Billings asked the family to join him in his office. Gina and Steve exchanged a concerned glance and followed him in. When he closed the door, Steve knew he was about to learn something awful. He was right.

Dr. Billings settled behind his desk and said, "Taylor does not respond to any stimuli in a typical way that I would expect most young toddlers would. He has no startle reflex. I don't have any other way to say this, but I strongly suspect he's autistic."

"What's that?" Steve asked.

"It's a behavioral disorder that interferes with normal development in young children, predominantly boys," the doctor said. "There are varying degrees of severity. Over time, the severity of this diagnosis will become apparent."

"Is he in any danger?" Gina asked.

"No, not physically," Dr. Billings said, "but his development will not be typical. His social behavior, speech, and emotional responses will all be very different from his sister."

"How so?"

"Well, we don't know yet. He may improve; he may get worse, lose any desire for human contact. We just don't know enough about autism yet to predict an outcome."

Gina looked to Steve for an answer. He offered a blank stare.

Dr. Billings said, "I'll leave you in my office for a few minutes. There is some literature I want to get for you." He left the room and closed the door quietly behind him. Taylor just sat on the floor, staring at the pattern in the rug, blissfully unaware of what had just transpired.

Gina began to cry, softly at first, and then the sobs escalated into a full-fledged crying jag. Steve went to her and knelt in front of her chair. He patted her knee, massaged her shoulders, and finally, just held her. He was lost. He didn't fully understand what the doctor had just told him about his son, what it truly meant.

"I always knew something was wrong," she managed between sobs.

Chapter 3

"Where are you going? Home is that way," Gina asked.

"The library," Steve said. "I need to know what this is. These brochures are useless."

"Take us home first. I want to get Taylor settled."

Steve pulled a U-turn and headed for home. He dropped off Gina and Taylor. "I'll pick up Lex from preschool on the way back."

"No, take your time. I'll get Alexis. Bring back anything you can find."

"Okay," he relented. "I shouldn't be long." He kissed her goodbye and sat in the car while she retrieved Taylor from his car seat in the rear compartment.

When he entered the library, Steve went to the information desk and asked, "Can you tell me where to find books on autism?"

The librarian, a middle-aged woman sporting the requisite reading glasses suspended on a thin silver chain around her neck, replied, "What is that?"

"Autism. It's a brain development disorder." The woman recognized the look of concern on Steve's face and said," Come with me. I think I know where to look." She escorted him to the psychology department and then to the child development area. "Let's look here," she said.

She scoured the shelves and retrieved two books that appeared to have never been cracked. "I'm afraid that's all we have," she said.

Steve took the two books and settled down at a table to read. The session was informative, not because of the information Steve gained from the written materials, but because of the lack of it. These were the only two books on the subject, both written by medical doctors whose exposure to their topic was third party at best. There was no concrete information contained within, only academic speculation. They were also written in an antiseptic jargon reserved for other health practitioners who would be writing future papers, continuing the lack of personalization he discovered in the texts. He was looking for something more personal, perhaps written by parents of similar children—a how-to-fix-it manual. He couldn't even find a what-the-hell-is-this manual. Frustrated, he read through the pertinent material in both books.

Two hours later, he was even more frustrated and a lot more worried. No one had isolated the cause of the affliction, or recommended a specific line of treatment, drugs, or anything that suggested Taylor would get any better. He left the books on the table and drove to the local Barnes & Noble. Surely, he would find something there.

He fought the shadow of depression that was gradually creeping into his thoughts and following wherever he went. He was not about to give in to that. That would help no one. He found the mental health section of the store and began his search. The more he searched, the stronger the feeling of desperation grew. And then he found what he was seeking: one book. It was written by a behavioral scientist, a discipline Steve had never needed to recognize as something that existed in the world or, at least, in his world. Once again, he sat down to read.

The first thing he learned was that there was a lot more to learn. No one had a handle on the cause or treatment of autism. There was a sliding scale of severity that ranged from savant to incapacity, genius to idiot. Recommended treatment varied in length and approach, and the only consensus appeared to be intervention on every possible level—education, exposure to stimuli, behavioral intervention, speech therapy, physical therapy, occupational therapy; the list went on and on. He brought the book to the front counter.

The checkout clerk read the title and asked, "Are you a doctor?"

Steve reacted as though he'd been slapped, then recovered quickly. "No, I'm just doing a little research."

"I've never seen this subject matter before," the man said. "Autism...." When he looked up and discovered Steve's pained look, he realized his miscue. After that, he couldn't maintain eye contact with his customer; he looked everywhere but at Steve, the first of many such reactions the young father would experience.

"Me neither," Steve said.

Depression, his new friend, followed him home.

Chapter 4

"**D**id you find anything?" Gina asked as he walked through the door. "I found this book at Barnes & Noble. There's not much else at the library or anywhere I can think of. I want to look at the *Physicians' Desk Reference* book. Where is it?"

"Right here," she answered. "I already read it. Good luck."

They exchanged reading materials. "Where are the kids?" Steve asked.

"I put them down for a nap. Alexis is probably reading her children's books or anything else besides sleeping."

"Okay, I'll go read in her room. Why don't you look at this book and we'll talk later?"

"Okay."

Steve went to Alexis's room, and as predicted, she had her nose buried in a Disney book. She'd learned to read as well as a third grader by the precocious age of three and was never without reading material. He secretly applauded the situation and said, "Lie down, honey, and I'll read this book to you. You know the drill. I read as long as your eyes are closed."

"Deal," she said. They bumped fists to seal the deal, and she closed her eyes. Steve began to read aloud.

Only four minutes later, her eyes still closed, Alexis asked, "Is Taylor artistic? Is that why he won't talk to me?"

Steve let out a chuckle, despite himself. "No, honey, I'm reading about an autistic, not an artistic. And I don't know why Taylor doesn't speak to you, but we're going to find out. This is the start of it, the research. Do you remember talking about research?"

"Yes."

"Well, that's what we're doing now."

"Then will Taylor talk to me after that?"

Steve almost choked on the emotion that reared up and short-circuited his vocal chords. He hesitated until he could modulate his voice. "Yes, sweetheart, that's the goal."

"Okay then, Dad" she said. "Keep reading."

After Alexis fell asleep, Steve read some rather disturbing information. The *Physicians' Desk Reference* book cited a "cold mother syndrome," the inability of some mothers to bond with their children in the early development stages, as a possible cause. Now he realized Gina had just finished reading this nonsense.

Steve stayed in Alexis' room for over an hour, alternating between watching her tiny chest rise and fall, and contemplating his next course of action. They needed to contact a professional, a behavioral scientist, a neurologist, someone. But first they needed to talk.

Chapter 5

Steve returned to the family room and asked Gina, "Did you read anything there that you want to discuss?"

"I don't know where to begin. I'm just as confused as I have been since the diagnosis. We need to talk to someone who deals with this daily and find out what to expect, how to deal with it."

"The cold-mother-syndrome thing didn't bother you?"

"Of course, it did," she said. "But I'm not ready to discuss it."

"You know that's nonsense."

"Yes, and I still don't want to talk."

"Okay." He knew now was not the time.

Steve pulled out the list of references they received from Dr. Billings. "There's a behavioral therapist he recommended highly. Let's see if we can contact her. It says Kristine Quinn. She's at Children's Hospital."

Gina took the proffered business card and said, "I'll take care of it."

Two long, nerve-racking weeks passed before they could go to their appointment. They brought Taylor to the hospital and searched everywhere for Suite 136 until they thought they had the wrong hospital. Finally, they stopped in the General Information Center and asked how to find Kristine Quinn.

A cheerful, gray-haired woman in her seventies found her for them. "You exit these doors and turn left. Go past the parking garages and turn right for one more block and you'll see a collection of temporary trailers in the lot there. Kristine is in one-thirty-six. It's right behind the West Wing. You can't miss it."

Once again, they exchanged an exasperated glance, thanked the woman, and followed her directions out the door. They continued and found the trailers ten minutes later. There was a handicapped ramp leading up to the light blue wooden structure. It looked like those temporary classrooms in the underfunded junior high school where Steve had worked as a teaching assistant while in college. It had dark blue trim painted around the windows and doors. That's where they found the placard that identified the trailer as the office of Kristine Quinn.

Inside, they found bedlam. There were three sets of parents sitting in plastic chairs. Their children were playing on the floor with toy cars or different colored plastic rings. None of them were interacting with the aides assigned to them. They were simply playing in the same area as the adults as if they did not exist. Steve and Gina were already familiar with that routine. These kids reminded them of Taylor. One little boy attempted to bite his aide when she removed a toy from the collection in front of him. The aide did not respond other than to keep her distance. The other aides took notes on their writing pads and checked off behaviors as they observed them. The parents stared off into space. Gina dubbed it the "thousand-yard stare." The parents saw everything, and they saw nothing. They were just there.

Gina signed them in while Steve situated Taylor on the floor, away from the biter, with a set of multicolored rings of various sizes that he was supposed to stack on a graduated cylinder in order of size. Taylor looked at it for a moment and stacked them perfectly in three seconds, his hands a blur. Steve looked up at Gina and smiled at his obvious intellect and dexterity. Gina smiled back. Then Taylor took it apart and put it back together again. Steve smiled. Gina did not. She knew what was coming. Taylor did it again. Steve still smiled at his antics. Then he did it again and again and again and again. The smile disappeared.

Forty-five minutes later, they were admitted into Kristine's office for an evaluation. "Mr. and Mrs. Wilson?" the receptionist called out.

Steve collected Taylor and carried him to the door. Gina followed. Inside, Kristine greeted them. "Hello, I'm Kristine Quinn. Nice to meet you. Have a seat." She indicated two more plastic chairs arranged in front of an overloaded desk that threatened to collapse under the weight of its burden. She was brisk to the point of curtness.

"I'm going to play with Taylor for a while before we speak, so just relax for a while," she instructed.

Steve and Gina took their seats in silence.

Kristine assumed a position on the floor opposite Taylor. First, she examined him for any physical defects and then for any startle reflex. She played with him on the carpeted floor for twenty minutes, teasing him with new items with bright colors to elicit a response—first offering them and then snatching them away. It looked almost cruel to do that to a two-year-old. There was no response. Taylor reached out to take the offered toy, and when it was taken away, he simply went back to what he was doing. He didn't cry, yell, or show any emotion. He just ignored it.

Kristine returned to her desk and sat down. She pulled out a prepared packet of written material and slid it across the desk. "This is a list of recommended therapies—speech, physical, behavioral, and occupational. You need to get Taylor into programs for all of them as soon as it is possible. You also need to prepare for his 'special education' needs. There is a list of preschools that will accept a child like Taylor. I'm afraid it's a very short list. However, there are buses available for those in need, and you'll find those numbers in here as well—"

"Wait, wait a second, Dr. Quinn," Steve interrupted. "Can't you tell us what the diagnosis is and how to treat it first?"

Kristine directed her gaze toward Steve and blew off her face a strand of hair that had invaded from the bunch tucked behind her ear. "I'm sorry, Mr. Wilson, it's been a long day. Let me explain what we do here. I'm not a doctor. I'm a behavioral therapist." She pointed to the diploma behind her chair. It read Master of Children's Behavioral Science. "I'm working on my doctorate, but I'm not there yet. As to the diagnosis, Taylor is autistic. On a sliding scale of ten, I've evaluated him at a seven in severity; it's not good, but it could be worse. He may also be developmentally disabled. It's too early to tell yet. He may never attain speech. He will never attend regular schools, or play sports, date, or drive a car. He may never recognize his name. He may have to be institutionalized. Your life just changed forever. I'm very sorry."

Steve just stared at her. He felt like he'd just gone one round with Mike Tyson. In fact, that would have been preferable to hearing this.

Kristine, a veteran of many such encounters with newly diagnosed parents, softened her approach. "Look, I know this comes as a shock to you both. My job here is to hit you over the head with a two-by-four. Mr. Wilson, you need to understand the severity of your situation. I can't stress the importance of early intervention enough. You must accept your son's disability and get started on mitigating his behaviors. They will likely grow worse."

Gina took it all in without protest. She was already in crisis mode. Steve just hadn't recognized it. He also realized this two-by-four approach was intended for him. Gina had already accepted Taylor as he was. He still had hopes of fixing him. Both women somehow knew that.

Once that realization took root, he said, "Kristine, thank you. I do understand. But I will not accept this as Taylor's fate. He will talk. He will learn his name. He will go to school. He will learn. Or I will die trying."

"Then let me refer you to someone who may be able to help you with that," Kristine said. "This is the number of the childhood development section at the university. Dr. Lara Jacobs is the head of the department there. I strongly suggest you make an appointment to see her."

"Thank you," Steve said. He picked up his son and left the office. Gina followed without a word.

They walked across the parking lot, and Steve couldn't help himself. He blurted, "We're screwed."

"What?" Gina said. "Why did you say that?"

"Come on, Gina. Our total resources are composed of a woman with a master's degree in child psychology or something, and her office is a trailer. Not a lot of hope there."

"None of that matters," she replied. "We will figure it out. You just told that woman that Taylor will talk. I will hold you to that."

Steve nodded his assent, properly chastised by the quiet woman who did all the heavy lifting.

Chapter 6

Steve called the medical distribution business he'd founded ten years earlier and spoke to his personal assistant, Cecile. "How are things going?" he asked.

"Fine, Steve; what's up?" Cecile had been with him for most of the ten years of the business's existence and knew when he was making small talk.

"Uh, I'm going to be out of the office for a while and I wanted to let you know. Taylor needs some special attention, and Gina and I are going to be busy for a while."

Cecile was already aware of Taylor's peculiar habits and knew just what to say. "Good, maybe I'll be able to get something done around here if you quit bothering us."

"You're way too funny, Cecile," he replied. "We have some appointments to set up to find out what's going on with Taylor, and it'll take some time. Call me if you need anything."

"That's unlikely, but if it will make you feel wanted, I'll call occasionally."

Steve smiled on his end of the phone. If there was a light at the end of the tunnel, it was that their business was flourishing and Cecile could run it with little supervision. Steve distributed medical supplies in Southern California and had established a small, but profitable business that allowed them to afford resources that most parents of autistic children could not.

"Okay, smart-ass; I'll call you when we know something. Bye."

"Bye, Steve. Tell Gina I'm thinking of you guys."

Next, he called the university and secured an appointment. Through some basic research, he learned the department utilized an army of grad students who required practical experience to acquire their master's degrees in the behavioral sciences. The psychology department, headed by Dr. Lara Jacobs, specialized in autism and offered a program that paired aspiring students with autistic children, once she had met the child and developed a program designed to meet his or her needs.

They arrived at the university full of hope. They located the doctor's office with little trouble and were seated in the waiting room. Taylor played with blue and yellow blocks, lining them up on the floor, eschewing the other colors. Steve and Gina sat down and mentally prepared to answer the myriad questions they couldn't hope to anticipate.

Dr. Jacobs appeared and greeted them, shaking hands with each. She was a small woman with curly gray hair and a huge smile, dressed in blue jeans and a loose T-shirt. Her energy was infectious. It immediately infused the room with a positive atmosphere. "Hi, I'm Dr. Jacobs. Call me Lara."

Steve introduced them. "Hi, I'm Steve and this is my wife, Gina."

"And this must be Taylor," she cooed. "Can I sit with him for a moment?"

"Of course," he said.

She did not attempt to establish contact with Taylor. She simply sat down next to him and observed his actions. After a few minutes, she asked, "Does he prefer blue and yellow to other colors?"

Steve hadn't the faintest idea. Gina said, "Yes, he does. He seeks them out first."

He was still trying to figure out how she knew this when Dr. Jacobs asked, "And does he like to line things up?"

"Yes." Again, he wondered how Gina knew this. But he should have known she would spend an inordinate amount of time with Taylor and catalog his every move in preparation for this meeting. Duh!

"Is this typical behavior for an autistic?" Steve asked.

"Yes and no," she answered. "Unfortunately, every autistic child is different. There are so many different presentations that no one behavior is unique and no one behavior is totally different."

"Let me see him walk," she said.

Steve knew from experience that calling his name would produce no reaction, so he went over, picked him up, and brought him to his mother. He immediately turned around and did what they called his "Charlie Chaplin walk," sort of on his toes, without his heels touching the floor.

Dr. Jacobs nodded as if to confirm something. "Does he always walk like that?"

"Yes," Gina said.

"Does he flap his hands like this?" She flapped her hands back and forth like the homecoming queen on a float.

"Yes," Gina replied, "just like that."

"Does he ever look directly in your eyes?"

"No, he never looks directly at us, but I know he sees us by how he reacts," Steve interjected.

"What do you mean?" she asked.

"Well, if I throw a ball at him, even if he's not looking directly at me, he reacts as though he did see it."

"How does he react? Does he try to catch it?"

"Yes, not well, but he tries. He puts his hand out. Then he goes and gets it and hands it back."

"He doesn't throw it back?"

"No, he walks over and hands it to me."

"Which hand does he attempt to catch the ball with?"

"His left," Steve stated with confidence. "I always thought he was a lefty like his mother."

Dr. Jacobs nodded noncommittally again.

"You're right-handed, I assume?"

"Yes."

"Throw it to him again, this time with your left hand," she said.

Taylor watched the ball sail past him and then got up and retrieved it. He handed it to his father but with his right hand this time. Steve noticed the difference immediately. "Does that mean something?"

"Many autistic children learn through mirror imaging. If you use your right hand, he will most likely use his left to imitate you, like viewing himself a mirror. He doesn't have the ability to turn it around in his mind and then imitate you with the same hand. I was curious, is all. I want to assess him further. Can you stay for three more hours?"

"Yes," they chorused.

"I'd like to take Taylor back to the playroom without your presence. You can observe through the one-way glass, but I do not want you to interfere in any way."

"Let's get started," Gina said. Finally, a ray of hope had appeared.

Chapter 7

Two weeks later, they had a program designed for Taylor. They hired a supervisor, Becky Robins, and two therapists, Pam and Patricia. Pam would focus on speech therapy, and Patricia would focus on occupational therapy. One would work on developing the muscles necessary for speech, and the other would concentrate on everyday behaviors. Simple actions like buttoning buttons or zipping up zippers, unsnapping snaps, eating with a spoon instead of his hands, using the toilet, and brushing his teeth were all major challenges for Taylor. The list was impossible to anticipate. Most children learn their behaviors by osmosis—that is, by observing their parents and modeling after them. Taylor didn't observe others' behavior or model after them. He lived exclusively in his own world.

Armed with a list of physical therapies Dr. Jacobs had suggested might help Taylor progress, Steve drove off in the Suburban and visited with a wholesale distributor of gymnastic equipment. He met with the owner, Ingrid, and explained his family circumstances to her. She was only too happy to assist him. "Come along with me," she said.

He followed the athletic young woman down a long hallway and into a warehouse only an aspiring Olympian could have dreamed up. Brightly colored mats covered the floors. Every gymnastic training aid imaginable hung from the rafters. Exercise balls of every size, racks of free weights, kettle bells, dumbbells, medicine balls, skip ropes, and gymnastic apparatus lined the outer walls. Steve was obviously overwhelmed with his choices. "Wow!" was all he could manage. "I don't know where to begin."

"Let me see your list," the young woman said. She pored over the papers and then said, "Look, let me have a few hours to gather what I think you need and then I'll give you a call. If anything does not work out, for any reason, just return it and we'll start over. Do you mind if I contact this Dr. Jacobs?"

"Not at all," Steve said. "In fact, that would be great." He wondered if his relief was that obvious.

"Okay, you take off and I'll see you bright and early tomorrow."

The next day, Steve returned at eight in the morning. Ingrid, her flaxen-blond hair pulled into a long ponytail and wearing stretchy athletic clothes that displayed her muscular form, greeted him at the door. "Come see what we put together," she said. "I spoke with Lara yesterday, and she was rather enthusiastic about our new project. I may go see her next week to talk about setting up something at the university."

"Great," Steve responded. He followed her into the warehouse.

Overnight they had set up a physical therapy section in the warehouse. It was covered in brightly colored, three-inch-thick mats to reduce the impact in case of a fall. They'd hung a bolster, a padded log really, from two bolts secured in the ceiling by each of the long ends, so when the bolster moved in an unpredictable arc, or bucked like a bronco, Taylor would have to adjust his movements involuntarily to remain aboard while playing on it. This would stimulate his proprioceptive ability that most children typically gain from simple movement. She showed Steve another piece of equipment that was destined to become Taylor's favorite. It was a child's safety swing seat designed with leg holes to envelop him and prevent him from falling. It also hung from the rafters. But instead of a sturdy length of rope, the seat was attached to the ceiling by a thick bungee cord. This moved in an even more unpredictable motion—like a rubber ball attached to a paddle by a rubber band—also designed to stimulate the physical response required to remain upright. She'd also hung a simple trapeze from the ceiling that would stimulate Taylor's grasping muscles, something he struggled with.

Ingrid showed him an exercise ball, the type used in a public gym for doing wall squats or crunches. It was bright green, about two feet high, and made of soft, pliable rubber. She suggested Taylor could be hoisted up on the ball and held in precarious positions until he slid off onto the mats. She patiently demonstrated each piece of equipment with the ease of a former gymnast as they spoke.

After the demonstration, Ingrid invited Steve to her office. "This is the equipment Dr. Jacobs suggested we start with, and I agree with her. As Taylor progresses, we can trade out for other things as required."

"Ingrid, I can't thank you enough for all you've done. What do I owe you?"

"This is on the house," she answered.

"I can't accept that," Steve said. "You have costs associated with all this."

"My equipment manufacturer donated the equipment, and my employees donated their time. Matthew and Thomas will be installing the equipment in your garage tomorrow. I've already made arrangements with your wife for tomorrow morning."

"You can't do that," Steve protested.

"I'm afraid I can," she answered. "Thanks to you, I have a new department in my business that will keep us busy for some time. Go home and play with your son, Steve."

"You're amazing" was all he could manage.

Ingrid stood and gave him a quick hug. "Take care, Steve. Matthew and Thomas will see you tomorrow."

He fought back tears as he drove home.

The next day, as promised, a pair of athletic young men installed the equipment in one bay of the Wilsons' garage in no time at all. They refused any attempt to compensate them for their time and left as soon as they finished. Steve was still shaking his head at the generosity of strangers.

Gina and Steve gathered the two kids and brought them out to the garage. Alexis responded with open-mouthed wonder, but Taylor didn't respond at all. He just sat on the mat and inspected the texture of the floor coverings.

Gina took over. "Come on, Alexis, let's try it." She hoisted her daughter up into the bungee swing and positioned her legs through the holes. She pulled her back and pushed the swing out in a circular arc.

Alexis bounced crazily in unpredictable patterns until Gina grabbed her and spun her again. Whoops of laughter erupted from their little girl and immediately infected both parents.

Then their first little miracle occurred. Taylor stood up and raised his arms to be held. At first, Steve didn't react. Taylor had never initiated an activity before. "Pick him up, you idiot," Gina said, laughing. "He wants a turn."

Steve couldn't stop grinning. He picked up his son and held him as Alexis bounced all over the garage in wild abandon, laughing uncontrollably. Then Taylor leaned away from Steve to capture the gyrating swing. Gina said, "Okay, Lex, it's Taylor's turn."

The parents swapped kids, and Gina put Taylor into the toddler's seat. She bounced him gently at first to get him accustomed to the movement, but when he responded by jumping up and down to get the swing moving faster, she accommodated his wish and swung him just as she had Alexis. As he bounced about the garage, he let out a loud, unadulterated squeal of laughter that delighted all three family members. Steve hugged his wife and daughter. "Looks like he's having fun!" Steve laughed.

Gina indicated the supersized grin on their daughter's face. "I'm not sure who's enjoying his turn more, Alexis or Taylor."

Steve swooped up his daughter and hugged her to him. "You're the best sister a boy could have, honey! I'm very proud of you."

"Did you hear him laugh?" she responded. "Push him higher, Mom!"

That evening was one of the best times the family had shared in a long time.

Taylor didn't understand the objective of this new activity. He just enjoyed being swung around on this new phenomenon in the garage or bouncing around on his ball. For the first time in his life, he was engaged. He was being physical. He enjoyed it, particularly the bungee swing. The next evening, Taylor approached Steve, who was sitting on the couch watching the news, and took him by the hand. He began pulling him, trying get his father to stand. When Steve did so, Taylor led him to the garage door. "Honey, look! Taylor's asking me to play with him!"

Gina grinned from ear to ear. "Then let's go play! C'mon, Lex," she said. She dropped the dish towel she was holding and followed them to the garage gym with Alexis in tow. Both parents were thrilled. This was the first time Taylor had initiated a form of play with another playmate.

This led to another lesson: taking turns. Taylor had no concept of sharing. He either had something or he didn't. Each child playing with the same object and taking turns was not part of his emotional vocabulary. So, they invited Alexis to join them in the garage for these sessions. Steve would push Taylor on the swing, then remove him and push Alexis. Gina restrained Taylor on the mats while Alexis got her turn. He invariably struggled to escape and get back on the swing. He did not understand why he had to wait for his turn.

"How come Taylor doesn't want to let me have a turn?" Alexis asked.

Steve felt a twinge of guilt for his daughter. She was so loving and protective of her little brother but received no reciprocal treatment. "He just doesn't understand how to share, sweetheart. That's what we're trying to teach him now. He'll get it soon. You watch and see. He'll get it."

After a short time, the children traded places once more. It took several weeks for Taylor to understand the concept and stop struggling, but he finally got it. He would sit quietly on the mat until Steve removed Alexis and then pop up instantly when she vacated the swing.

The next exercise was designed to simulate typical play among children. They put both children on the bolster together and rocked it gently to force the kids to grab on to something to maintain their balance. "Hold on to Taylor, honey," Gina instructed. "Let's see if he holds on to you, too."

Sure enough, once Taylor realized his sister could use him to maintain her balance, he imitated her by grabbing her upper arms for support as Steve manipulated the padded log. Soon the two siblings were clutching one another and laughing in unison, a sound that brought tears to Steve's eyes.

"Are you crying, Dad?" Alexis asked.

Steve wiped the moisture from his eyes. "No, Lex, I'm just happy. You've made me very happy." He smiled at his beautiful daughter.

The garage play became a several-times-a-day activity. Taylor could not lift himself up high enough to sit in the bungee swing, so he learned how to use other people to get something he wanted. This led to leading his mother, or anyone else available, by the hand to the refrigerator or the pantry for a snack. Visitors and relatives who were subjected to this behavior felt complimented when Taylor took them by the hand to the refrigerator and thought they were the lucky ones who provided a breakthrough with Taylor. He obviously wanted their companionship. They didn't realize Taylor saw them as a tool, something to use to get what he wanted like a doorknob or an "on" button. But it was progress of a sort.

The speech therapy was another matter. It seemed impossible to elicit any sound or form of communication that would qualify as speech. The tedious chore of holding Taylor's face and forming it into a usable configuration capable of speech appeared draconian at best. Pam would make the requested sound while holding his face in the required position, let go to elicit the same sound, and then repeat the procedure. After months of this therapy, sounds began to emerge—not words exactly but voluntary sounds. It also led to a newly discovered level of frustration as Taylor approached four years old: screaming.

Chapter 8

Over the next several years, the challenges in their lives mounted. Steve had never imagined this level of depression and frustration would enter his life. Like most successful people, he expected life to proceed in an orderly fashion while he toiled away at his business to provide a good life for his wife and children. God laughs while man plans.

The parade of benchmarks that most parents look forward to witnessing was quite different for the Wilsons. In Taylor's third year, they began potty training. Of course, there was no language communication to explain to the youngster why it was important to do his business in the toilet. Lara Jacobs provided the strategy to train Taylor through her graduate students. Whenever Taylor dirtied his diaper, he was taken to the toilet, had his dirty diaper pulled down and back up, and then returned to his prior activity, usually watching a Disney video. This routine was repeated three times until it made even Taylor uncomfortable. It took six months of dogged determination by everyone in the household to teach Taylor to use the bathroom. To his credit, that was all it took. Once the habit was formed, Taylor faithfully became a toilet user. One day he stopped watching a Disney video right in the middle of it and walked to the powder room off the kitchen, pulled down his diaper, and sat on the pot. Gina and Steve shared a silent high five while they watched from the doorway. "I'll be damned. It worked," Steve said.

"Watch your language or that'll be his first word," Gina replied.

Taylor was sensitive to many sounds and sensations. Brushing his teeth was akin to a wrestling match. He would squirm every which way to avoid the scrub-brush feel of the toothbrush on his gums and teeth. He would contort his lips or close his mouth to prevent any contact. After one such session, Steve asked, "How did it go?"

"He wears me out sometimes." Gina blew a strand of hair out of her face. "Now he turns into a noodle each time I try to stand him up on his stepstool to look in the mirror. I have to pin him against the sink counter with my hips to hold him there while I brush his teeth."

It took four months to achieve a modest amount of cooperation.

Baths were easy because Taylor loved the water. When Steve picked him up and headed to the tub in the master bathroom, Taylor instantly became compliant. Occasionally, he would leave a present in the water; Alexis would shriek and immediately vacate the tub whenever he got that strange look on his face that predicted the appearance of a floater.

Steve was reading a paperback while the kids played in the oversized tub when Alexis stood up and said, "Dad, he's got that look on his face again. He's gonna go!"

Steve grabbed his son and placed him on the toilet just in time. Alexis was becoming so attuned to Taylor, she could predict a wide range of behaviors before they occurred. Their growing closeness gave their parents a glimmer of hope for the future. It occurred to Steve that his son had not learned to generalize his need to use the potty under differing circumstances—one more thing to work on.

Haircuts were painful, for Taylor and for Steve. Taylor recoiled at the snip of the scissor or the buzz of an electric shaver. He would flee whenever Elena, a family friend and hairstylist, entered the house. He knew that awful sound and sensation was about to happen. Steve would position him on his lap facing one another, so he could restrain Taylor as Elena quickly cut his hair. Taylor's response to being physically controlled was to grab a couple of inches of flesh around Steve's love handles and twist until he raised bruises. The first time Elena saw the marks as Taylor climbed down from his lap, her eyes clouded up. "How long has that been going on?" she asked.

Steve wasn't sure how to answer, so he went to the standard reply. "He's getting better each time. It looks worse than it feels." At least on the outside!

Naps or bedtime was another adventure. Taylor simply did not understand the concept. He just fell asleep whenever and wherever he felt the need. Structured times for this activity did not compute. Someone had to stay with him in his room, on his bed, to get him to sleep. Unfortunately, when he was required to stay in bed, he just got up and left. Steve would find him wandering around the house at night, alone.

One summer evening, in the middle of the night, Gina shook Steve awake and whispered, "I hear someone in the house." Steve grabbed a Little League baseball bat and padded silently to the children's rooms, with Gina close behind. Alexis was fast asleep in her bed, blissfully unaware of any potential threat. Taylor's door was wide open, and his room was empty. "Stay with Alexis," Steve said. He tiptoed through the house on bare feet, trying his best to do so in complete silence. When he entered the kitchen, he saw a light on in the pantry. He crept up to the doorway and risked a quick peek around the doorjamb. There was Taylor, sitting cross-legged on the floor and eating directly from a Fruit Loops cereal box. Multicolored nuggets littered the tile floor around the little boy.

Relief flooded Steve's system as the pent-up adrenalin sought release. He called to his wife, "It's all right. Taylor decided to have a midnight snack."

Gina arrived, picked him up, and held him. "You scared us, little man. Come on, let's go to bed. I got him, Steve. Go back to bed."

"Yeah, that'll happen." There was no way he could sleep now.

The solution was to reverse the locks on Taylor's bedroom door to keep him inside overnight, so the rest of the house could sleep, too. Steve got to work on the door the following morning.

When Taylor erupted in a fit of frustration, Steve and Gina were at a loss about how to stop his behavior without employing a physical restraint that might harm him. Dr. Jacobs had impressed upon them the importance of not reacting physically; spanking or rough treatment of any kind would be interpreted as acceptable behavior that Taylor could learn and utilize in the future. Steve and Gina had agreed before their marriage that spanking any child was unacceptable, let alone a learning-disabled one. They learned from their army of saviors, the graduate students, how to restrain Taylor by crossing his wrists over his chest from behind, so he couldn't bite or pinch himself or one of them, and hold him like that until he gave up, exhausted, and went to sleep.

One afternoon Taylor became frustrated because he could not make Steve understand which Disney video he wanted to watch. He fell to the tile floor, screaming and biting his own wrists. Gina rushed to comfort him before Steve held up his hand and said, "I'll do it this time. You relax."

Steve rolled up Taylor in a ball and picked him up by placing one arm under his knees, with his son's wrists secured in that same hand, away from his teeth so he could not bite them. The other arm was behind his upper torso, effectively folding him at the waist. He carried him into the master bedroom in that position and sat in a lounge chair to watch an NBA game while Taylor shrieked as though he was being tortured. As he fought to escape and attempted to bite Steve or his own wrist repeatedly, Steve restrained him gently, keeping his teeth away from both. He just held him rolled up like a roly-poly bug. Steve tried desperately to ignore his son's attempts to injure them both as Taylor contorted his little body to reach him with his teeth or escape. Sometimes the wrestling match took twenty minutes. Sometimes it took two hours. It was an enormously gratifying experience when Steve felt Taylor's little body go limp, a signal he had given up the fight—a reward of sorts. Steve would remember that relinquishment as one of the most satisfying times spent with his son. It was such a rare pleasure to feel his tiny boy fall asleep on his chest in peace, almost like a typical child.

Steve and Gina tried every home remedy they could dream up. They installed a zip line to develop Taylor's grasp muscles. The little guy loved to watch Alexis zip down the makeshift play equipment. He jumped up and down, waving his hands in a fit of glee, as she glided down the span of wire. Steve lifted Taylor up to grasp the handles in the hope he would emulate his older sibling's glide. He lasted for only a span of five feet before he had to let go.

"Doesn't he want to do it, Dad?" Alexis asked.

"I think so, honey. He just doesn't know how yet." He tried hard to conceal his disappointment at another failed experiment from his daughter. "Why don't you do it for him?"

"Okay, Dad," she said.

They built an elevated wooden playhouse connected to a swing set and monkey bars. Taylor loved to climb. He climbed the monkey bars. He climbed to the canvas roof of the playhouse. He climbed the length of the support to the swing set. He climbed anything he could, most of them dangerous to his health and well-being.

"What are we going to do?" Steve lamented.

"Watch him carefully, I guess." Gina laughed. "He's learning to grasp things. Isn't that what you wanted?"

That led to another incident when Taylor was three years old. Steve and Gina went to his bedroom one morning and unlocked his door only to find him gone. The bedroom door had been locked, so he had to be inside somewhere. When Steve opened the walk-in closet to look for him, he heard a crackling sound that could only mean broken glass. He found Taylor asleep, clad only in a diaper, among scattered glass fragments. He'd climbed the closet shelves, closed the door, and dislodged a large, glass picture frame stored there. It broke into dozens of small jagged pieces when it fell. There was not a mark on him. Steve stepped carefully around the sharp edges and scooped him up without waking him. He deposited him back in bed, wondering how long he had been in the closet. Without a word, Gina collapsed into his arms and silently wept in frustration at the near disaster.

They found Taylor loved to be pushed in the backyard swing. Unfortunately, he also liked to intentionally launch himself out of the swing at the top of the arc to propel his little body through the air and land on his hands and knees like a monkey. The first time he did it, Steve reacted. "Whoa, Taylor, no no no!" he blurted. "Don't do that."

After the second jump, Steve fashioned a safety bar around the seat to prevent him from flying off and used their time together to sing nursery rhymes to his now-captive son, incorporating his name and address. "My name is Taylor Wilson, and this is where I live ..." Steve repeated his name and address repeatedly until Taylor would hum the ditty, not well, but it was a type of imitation. It was a sound. It was progress! It was a success!

The swing set led to the installation of a thirty-foot-long rope swing secured high in a eucalyptus tree. They attached a wooden slat to form a substantial seat so Taylor could sit on Steve's lap to introduce him to this new activity. After giving Alexis a ride, he picked up Taylor and seated him on his lap so they were facing one another. They took off from the elevated brick veranda in the backyard and swooshed through the air for some fifty feet before the centrifugal force dissipated and they reversed course.

Taylor screeched in sheer delight! "Aaaahhh! Aaaahhh!" he yelled. The family laughed with him. He loved it! Soon he could grasp the rope in his little hands and sit on the swing on his own. The travel length of the swing delighted Taylor. Gina and Steve suspected that the centrifugal force generated when he released the little guy from the elevated porch height gave him a sense of freedom and movement he couldn't generate on his own. Or maybe he just liked it!

Gina hugged Steve and Alexis. "Success," she declared. "Finally, a success."

Learning to ride a two-wheeled bike was another adventure. The concept of braking was difficult to explain to a nonverbal six-year-old. First Steve put Taylor on his shoulders and rode him around the driveway on an adult bike to acclimate him to the movement. That simulated the same welcome sensation Taylor got from the rope swing, a natural progression. But when Taylor was seated on his own twenty-inch bike with training wheels, he could not grasp the concept of pushing the pedals to produce forward momentum. Steve would push him down a slight decline in the driveway, and Taylor would extend his legs like airplane wings to keep his balance. The pedals were useless to him.

"I'm not sure this one is going to work," Gina said.

"Wait. Watch him for a moment. I'll be right back," Steve said.

The solution was duct tape. Steve taped his feet to the pedals and slowly pushed the bike around the oval drive until Taylor became accustomed to the feel of his legs moving in a circular, pistonlike motion. After a few weeks, he began to apply pressure to the pedals on his own and a monster was born. You couldn't keep him off the bike after that revelation. He could go fast on his own!

Unfortunately, the other concept, stopping, had eluded the lesson plan. Taylor refused to learn what the brakes were for, and Steve could not develop a method to make him understand. Taylor solved the problem by dragging his sneakers along the cement to slow his speed or intentionally riding on the grass to retard his progress. Shoes did not last long, nor did several strategically positioned bushes. Taylor used them to crash into when he needed to stop. Gina turned to her husband with a wry grin. "Why else would someone plant a bush where he rode his bike?"

Steve shook his head. "Thank goodness we have a circular driveway," he said.

The feeling of forward motion was attractive to Taylor on a very basic level. He liked it. This led to an unusual and unexpected development. The exercise ball they had introduced him to in the garage became a means of locomotion. He used the ball as a seat while he watched his Disney tapes. The Wilsons encouraged this behavior because it strengthened his core muscles and balance. Soon, he was raising up and scooting the ball forward with his hands, while he jumped forward to get closer to the television, and landing in a seated position upon the ball without obvious effort. At first, they feared Taylor would fall and hurt himself while not paying attention to what he was doing, but after several weeks of observing his new method of locomotion without one mishap, they were confident he had more coordination than they had thought.

Taylor soon used the exercise ball to get around. He could take it anywhere in the house by bouncing off the ball and scooting it forward by hand as he jumped forward and landed on it in a sitting position, generating enough forward momentum that Steve and Gina had to trot to keep pace with him. Then he took it outside and bounced around the oval driveway. The friction against the coarse cement burst the ball on occasion, but that did not deter Taylor from repeating the behavior as soon as Steve purchased a replacement. It was his new means to travel. And, boy, did he travel!

One Saturday morning, while Steve was coaching Alexis's soccer team, Taylor slipped out of the house on his ball. He stood on it to release the latch installed at the top of the gate to prevent just such an occurrence. He proceeded to bounce his way out of the residential streets to a two-lane road with a forty-five-mile-per-hour speed limit, and then up the centerline of the busy avenue with a twenty-degree incline for half a mile.

When Gina discovered that Taylor was missing, she contacted Steve by calling a neighbor and asking her to find Steve while she searched the area near the house. Dina, who was a dear friend, found Steve and said, "Gina called. Taylor got out of the yard. He's missing. She needs help."

"Could you watch Alexis?" he asked.

"Of course," she answered. "Go, go; I got her."

Steve sped away from soccer practice, leaving Alexis in her care. He was almost in tears when he spotted the green ball and the flashing lights of a police car in a busy intersection. He pulled over in a panic to discover Taylor sitting quietly in the rear seat of the police cruiser, staring at his green ball, which had been confiscated and left outside the vehicle.

Steve pulled off the asphalt road and parked. He rushed to the police car. "Is he okay? Is he okay?"

A highway patrolman stopped him and identified him as Taylor's father. Steve choked back tears as he explained Taylor's challenges. "He's autistic. He doesn't understand language or the danger he was in."

Steve received an admonishment to keep a closer eye on his son in the future, and Taylor was released to his custody. Steve drove Taylor and his ball home, still fighting back tears of relief. How many cars had passed his son at high speed before a Good Samaritan had the courage to stop and come to his aid? If only the officer realized his child-rearing sermon was easier said than done.

When they arrived home, Gina was in tears. "I'm sorry, Steve. I was putting the wash in the dryer and he just disappeared." She hugged her son fiercely. "I'm so sorry."

Steve held his wife and son together. "Are you kidding? This is no one's fault. It's our life. I should have installed a lock on that gate, not just a rope. There's more than enough blame to go around. It was not your fault."

"Could you put a lock on it right now?"

"I'll get on it." Steve left to secure the gate.

One important physical milestone was a welcome development. The Wilsons were fortunate enough to have an in-ground swimming pool in a fenced area of the yard. Steve was a strong swimmer, and when he introduced Taylor to the pool at the age of three, it was like a mother duck leading her offspring to the most natural behavior in the world. Steve carried him piggyback style to the pool and waded in. When Taylor made enthusiastic sounds of approval, Steve moved out into the deep end and swam with his son clinging to his back. More approving sounds emanated from Taylor, so Steve was encouraged to dive underwater for only a moment. When they surfaced, Taylor was enthralled. He was making sounds of pure delight, kicking his legs into his ribs and steering Steve by the hair grasped in each hand as though he were a horse.

Gina laughed from the sidelines. "Apparently, that's how our forebears learned to ride a horse."

After wearing out his father, Taylor taught himself to swim. Style and technique did not matter; all that mattered was remaining afloat, staring at the bubbles he created by moving his legs and hands around the warm water. The visual stimulation was the focus. Swimming was the way to create the stimulation. He had no fear of drowning. Panic would never enter his mind. That concept did not occur to him. Swimming was just as easy as walking. He would agitate the water, dunk his head with his eyes open to watch the bubbles form, and then disappear. He spent hours, then days and weeks, engrossed in this activity. He could fashion a water cannon, with his hands clasped tightly together, and shoot a stream of water twenty feet by the time he was five. Anything to create bubbles!

When Alexis was ten years old, she and a friend were required to pass a water safety test administered by a qualified swim instructor to be accepted into Junior Lifeguards. Taylor could not be kept out of the pool when anyone else was swimming, so Steve and Gina let him play in the pool while the girls treaded water for the required twenty minutes. They didn't pay any attention to Taylor floating as though he were taking an upright nap behind the struggling swimmers. He was as relaxed as an otter.

When the test ended, the instructor approached the parents. "Is he going to qualify for Junior Lifeguards, too? I don't have any paperwork on him."

The Wilsons got a welcome laugh at that thought before they replied.

"No, Taylor is autistic and simply loves to swim," Gina explained. "He swims as well as he walks."

"Well, he impressed the heck out of me," the instructor said, laughing with them.

Taylor's physical development was not typical of other little boys, but nonetheless, progress did occur. His intellectual and emotional development was another matter.

Chapter 9

Holidays were a nonevent to Taylor. There was no way to communicate the joy of Christmas, the spookiness of Halloween, or the rebirth celebrated at Easter. Church, or any form of religion, was not a part of his life. Steve attended midnight Mass at Christmas and Easter vigil alone. The couple's largest concern was the impact on Alexis. They resolved to make her world as normal as possible while attending to Taylor's unique needs that they struggled to become familiar with; thus, holidays were as much a source of nervous frustration as they were cause for celebration. Steve and Gina feared for Alexis's emotional well-being as much as Taylor's.

On Easter morning, Gina decorated the house in gay colors, replete with bunnies, colored eggs, and candy. The couple hid scores of plastic eggs all over the house and yard to normalize the holiday for Alexis and stimulate some response from Taylor. Alexis attacked the egg hunt with joy and enthusiasm. Taylor watched. Steve took him by the hand and led him to an egg secreted in a bush. He put his hand over his son's and grasped the treasure in his hand. He opened it to discover his favorite treat, Skittles. Taylor sat down on the grass and ate the candy. The hunt was abandoned. The connection between the discovery of the egg and the reward was not understood.

Gina laughed at them. "I guess he's into immediate gratification."

"You're too funny," Steve replied. "How are we going to get him to understand there are more eggs to find?"

"Hey, it's his first time. Give him some time."

Alexis retrieved all the eggs and surprised both parents as she divided up her loot and deposited half in Taylor's basket without being asked to do so. The simplest act of kindness brought tears. Steve was immensely proud of his young daughter. The couple vowed to repeat the process each year until Taylor made the connection.

On Halloween, Taylor was dressed up like a pirate and taken, along with Alexis and several neighborhood kids, out for trick or treat. He didn't understand exactly what the holiday meant, but receiving candy when he went to a house thrilled him. He would try to eat each offered morsel before moving on to the next house until Steve took charge of his bag and kept him moving. They got through the evening without a meltdown and returned home relieved. The next evening Taylor appeared, carrying his pirate outfit with him. Apparently, it was time to go trick or treating again.

"Go ahead and get him dressed," Steve said. "I have an idea."

They laughed together at their solution. Steve took him outside and rang the front door bell. He cried, "Trick or treat," when Gina answered the door and deposited some of the previous night's candy in Taylor's bag. Then Steve led him to the side door where the process was repeated. They performed this routine several times until their son was satisfied with his haul. Taylor celebrated four more Halloweens that week until Gina hid the outfit.

Christmas was a huge disappointment. Taylor didn't want to decorate the tree, sit in Santa's lap, or open presents because the tearing of wrapping paper hurt his ears like the paper on a medical examination table. Tinsel, however, fascinated him. He "stimmed," a repetitive manifestation of autism the family discouraged. Taylor dropped the shiny strands, allowing the tinsel to descend through the air and stooped to follow them until they hit the floor, his face pinned to the carpet. It was painful to witness. The tinsel disappeared from Christmas.

Sitting on Santa's lap led to an investigation of the texture and tensile strength of his beard. This also led to the inadvertent exposure of a clean-shaven face to the waiting children and their parents. Taylor had dispelled the myth of Santa Claus to dozens of open-mouthed children and their irate parents in one fell swoop. Steve observed the reaction of the people waiting in line and said, "Time to go, guys." They picked up their kids and left the mall.

On Christmas morning, Alexis fetched Taylor from his room and brought him into the living room where the tree was located. The lights and music and the joy in the air delighted him. Steve and Gina were elated with his response and the upbeat mood. Both children seemed infected with the ambiance of the holiday. Smiles erupted all around.

Unfortunately, it didn't last. When Steve put him on his lap to open a few presents with his hand over Taylor's hand, he had a meltdown. He shrieked and then tried to bite Steve's hand and escape from his lap. Steve controlled him with techniques he learned from the grad students, quickly opened two gifts, and then released his son to his own devices. There would be more Christmases, more opportunities to improve. He and Gina shared a moment of despair and then made yet one more effort to restore the joyful mood for Alexis's sake.

"Next year will be better," Steve promised. "Let's see what Santa brought."

Chapter 10

The search for a remedy for Taylor's condition was the focus of both parents over the next decade, but Gina took over the heavy lifting. In addition to dozens of doctor's visits, Gina investigated every avenue that presented even a shred of hope.

While Steve stayed home with Alexis, Gina took Taylor to St. Louis for auditory training, a method that isolated specific sounds in headphones supposedly to help him concentrate and improve intellectually. When she returned from the trip, Steve asked, "Well, how did he react to the treatment?" Gina, exasperated, shook her head and said, "A colossal waste of time."

She pleaded with every doctor she knew socially to obtain a rare, expensive, intravenous drug that promised the same improvement in focus. She arranged the transfusions, drove Taylor to the hospital for the weekly infusion of this miracle drug, and held him while they performed the required functions. After several weeks of treatment, she told Steve, "This isn't working. There's been no change in his receptive or expressive language. It's not the remedy we were hoping for."

She tried facilitative learning techniques that taught Taylor to communicate by typing his responses to spoken questions as though he understood the questions. When a more scientific method, a double-blind test, proved the technique to be an unintended hoax—facilitated by the handler's subconscious desire to answer the question accurately and, thus, direct the child's hand without realizing it—the parents abandoned the practice.

Gina helped to develop a picture exchange communication system for Taylor with Dr. Jacobs's interns that consisted of pictures of activities he needed to perform, such as dressing, brushing his teeth, and bathing. This provided the family with a system of communication that Taylor responded to positively. He performed the required function pictured in the graphic with assistance from a therapist, pulled the picture from the to-do list, and attached it via Velcro to the finished list. She hugged Steve. "We have a breakthrough! He understands the pictures. It's a start!"

She took him to physical therapy, occupational therapy, the dentist, the family doctor, neurologists, hearing centers, and speech therapists, and drove him to six different schools that were more appropriate for his development as he grew. Nothing could dissuade Gina from building on their one success.

She took him to the Helen Woodard Animal Center for therapeutic horse riding, where Taylor promptly fell asleep in the saddle. She took him on playdates to expose him to other, more typical behaviors. He played alone. She purchased every educational device and toy that promised enjoyable play while simultaneously teaching daily living skills. No connection occurred. She took him on daily excursions to expose Taylor to different stimuli—Disneyland, Legoland, Sea World, the zoo, and the Wild Animal Park—and kept a journal of each attempt and its result, or lack thereof.

Steve watched his wife go through every possible remedy, one at a time. There were even a few witch doctors mixed in somewhere. They tried everything. She never quit. She never complained. She never got down in front of Alexis or any of their friends or relatives. She plodded on. She endured. She was a saint.

But each excursion, each failure, took a toll. There were inevitable down days for both parents. It seemed that all the hours, all the spent resources, all the prayers were for naught. Taylor continued to present social challenges that were never anticipated. Every outing was structured. Every outing was complicated. There was little room for spontaneity for fear of a public meltdown. If Taylor was attracted to a favorite ride in an amusement park, someone in the family went on that ride repeatedly to accompany him. Inevitably, Alexis and one parent went their own way.

Bathroom breaks were also eventful. Taylor needed an extraordinary amount of time to accomplish that task, much to the dismay of others waiting to use the facilities. When Taylor had a meltdown, or made strange noises of enjoyment, people stared. The family became immune to these episodes, or so they thought. But each one silently took a piece of their soul away from them and wore them down.

They worried every day for young Alexis. She didn't deserve to be exposed to this level of embarrassment at such a young age. When she was eight years old, she asked Steve, "Have you ever been ashamed of Taylor?"

"No, never," he replied. The question set him back. It implied Alexis did suffer shame on occasion, so Steve followed up. "But I've been embarrassed many times by his behavior. There's quite a difference between the two. You see, I could never be ashamed of either of my children. I love each of you too much, equally but differently, simply because you are my children. You each need different things from me. But I could be embarrassed by inappropriate behavior from either of you. Do you understand?"

"Not really," she said.

"If you sassed your mother in public or used bad language, I would be embarrassed by your behavior. I wouldn't be ashamed of you. You should be ashamed of yourself, though. In my mind, shame is reserved for the person who behaves poorly, not the one who observes it."

"I think I get it," Alexis said. "Thanks, Dad."

"You're welcome." He hugged his little girl. Things were complicated.

Alexis deserved some of what her parents called "normal time." In her case, that meant going on excursions with one parent while the other stayed home with Taylor. When she was in a school play, one parent attended. When she played sports, one parent attended. When she received academic honors, one parent attended.

Gina took Alexis on vacations alone. She took her to plays and movies alone. She took her shopping alone. She took her to school alone. Steve played catch, tag, and rode bikes with her alone. He took her on ski trips alone. He took her to sporting events alone. He coached her in soccer or basketball alone. The family was apart. Each of them was alone.

The family suffered in other ways too painful to articulate. No one could understand how pervasive and destructive this disorder was to the family unit. In approximately 85 percent of marriages that involved an autistic child, divorce ensued. In most instances, the father left, unable to endure the emotional pain and embarrassment of raising an autistic son. And sometimes the mother departed without a backward glance, emotionally bankrupt and clinically depressed.

The Wilsons were aware of those awful statistics. They would not apply to them. They would fight that spiral of depression. They would endure for Taylor, for Alexis, and for each other.

Chapter 11

Human beings are adaptable creatures. For their marriage to survive, Gina and Steve created individual coping mechanisms without consciously realizing it. Gina created remarkable crafts, pencil drawings, and watercolors as a method of creating an alternative universe, one in which there were no meltdowns, no parade of doctors, and no stares in public. She was talented. She enjoyed her alone time with her art. It recharged her; it gave her the energy to once again wear the mantle of mother, caregiver, and family therapist.

Steve coped by going away on "boys" trips. He went hunting for deer or elk with his brother each October. They rode horses deep into the Sierra Mountains for a week at a time. He went on a two-week ski trip each February by himself and pounded the slopes until he was worn out. He went on fly-fishing trips to Colorado. He went to Maui each March for his medical device distribution business and spent a week on the ocean. He took up golf. He joined a gym. He ran five miles every lunch hour. After he had worn off the resentment and the depression through physical exertion, he was once again motivated to resume his role as a father and provider. Life, as unusual as it was, went on.

What no one realized was Steve was not running away from something; he was running to something. The places he went were the best cathedrals in the world to pray in. The grandeur of the mountains in winter, the placid beauty of a fly-fishing stream in the early morning, the massive power of the ocean felt through a paddleboard; each was a point of introspection he tapped into. It gave him peace. It also made him realize how insignificant he truly was, how small the challenge of

Taylor really was when he was surrounded by these masterpieces of nature. In the grand scheme of life, his tenure was a blip on the radar screen, here for a moment and then gone. He found solace in the prayers he offered up—not a prayer for his son to be healed, not for his family to be normal. It was to express gratitude for the gift of Taylor and the lessons in humility, patience, and strength he brought with him; for the gift of an incredible wife and a strong sibling for his son. These were the precious gifts he thanked God for when he left. And he felt a physical sensation, almost a shudder, when he truly conveyed his gratitude to that higher power. It was a drug for him, the constant search for that feeling of peace, a reconnection to something greater than mankind.

Steve also incorporated this coping mechanism into his daily life. He began to pray every day. He was raised as a Catholic and began to carry a rosary with him always. When he was depressed, he took out his beads and said a rosary for his son's progress, his family's health, and his performance as a father. He also attended Mass every Saturday evening alone. Gina had been raised as a Buddhist and held no belief in an existential being that ruled her life. Steve prayed there was just such an entity that existed and would provide him with the grace and strength to endure. It seemed natural to carry a rosary while he ran during his lunch hour. Each mile provided enough time, seven minutes, to say one rosary. Five miles equated to five rosaries. Five lunch-hour runs equated to twenty-five rosaries per week. For years, Steve applied both disciplines fervently. He never missed a day.

Thirteen years passed. The family coped with their unique situation and remained a family. Alexis flourished in school and sports and seemed to be a contented teenager. She was a fierce defender of her brother and included him in any activity she could.

There was an instance when Alexis noticed two girls sitting behind little Taylor at the beach, imitating his strange noises and flapping their arms when he did. Alexis rushed to his side before Steve could get up, faced off with the two girls, and said, "You think you're funny?" Steve snatched her away before the situation escalated and said, "No, Alexis, that's not how we settle these things." He glared at the two adolescents,

46

picked up Taylor, and returned to their blanket. Alexis was visibly upset as the two girls sauntered away.

"Dad, that's not what you did in Maui when that old man was harsh to Taylor," Alexis challenged him.

"I know, honey, and I was wrong. I should have ignored him. Confronting people like that doesn't accomplish anything." When an ignorant tourist had snapped his fingers in Taylor's face to stop him from making unusual noises of excitement in an ice cream parlor, Gina had to physically restrain Steve from retaliating. Steve hugged his daughter and whispered in her ear, "But I'm proud of you." Then in a more normal tone of voice, he said, "Come on, let's swim."

Gina and Steve came to accept their life with Taylor and its limitations, fashioning a life together that was complicated but also rewarding and positive. They made the best of it.

Gina continued creating incredible pieces of art, and Steve continued taking his boys' trips. One trip changed their life forever.

Steve, his older brother Tim, and a lifelong friend, Mark, went into the mountains on their annual deer-hunting trip. They drove up Highway 395 through Adelanto, Big Pine, Independence, and Lone Pine. When they reached Bishop, they headed west up into the mountains. At the end of a gravel road, they came to a series of fly-fishing lakes that fronted the pack station they had been frequenting for ten years. The horses and mules were already saddled for the five-hour trip over Paiute Pass and down into the valley situated almost dead center between Fresno and Bishop. It was some of the prettiest and most remote country in California.

Mike and Robert, the brothers who owned the pack station, greeted them with the ease of old friends. "You gonna fill your tags this year, boys?" Mike teased.

"We're gonna try," Tim said and laughed. "How are you doing, Mike?"

"If I was any better, there'd be two of me," he said.

Both pairs of brothers, and Mark, shook hands and clapped each other on the shoulder, pleased to be together again. Mark was considered one of the Wilson brothers and fit in as though born to it. They caught up on the local gossip regarding the location of the biggest bucks in the Sierras and the spots they intended to camp while they loaded their gear in the panniers, and hoisted them up on the mules. In no time at all, they were riding through the fluttering gold of the aspen trees and climbing past the boulder-strewn landscape above the timberline. Three hours later, they crested the pass at eleven thousand feet and rode across a barren moonscape dotted with shallow alpine lakes. After a few miles, they descended into a densely wooded valley below Pilot Knob, where they would make camp.

They decided to erect their campsite at their usual spot, one hundred yards off the trail, next to a flowing creek. The site gave them access to French Canyon to the northwest, Pilot Knob on their northeast, and Honeymoon Lake to the southeast. That way, each of them could hunt for sign in every direction before they decided where they would have the best opportunity for a successful group hunt. Steve was already in the clutches of that familiar feeling of peace the mountains held for him. He was happy.

They unloaded their gear and set up their tents, and then they said goodbye to Mike and Robert. "See you in four days, boys," Mike called as he moseyed off, leading the string of mules. "Mind the weather. It feels like a storm brewing. My bum leg says so."

"Now you're talking to your leg," Steve chided him. "Next you'll be talking to your horse."

"I been talkin' to my horse for years, Steve. He's the only one that'll listen to me."

"Have a safe ride, boys," Steve called after them.

The brothers waved a goodbye without turning in their saddles.

"Mind the weather," Mike called out.

"Yup," Mark answered. He turned to Tim and asked, "Do you think he's serious about the weather?"

"The forecast said there was a slight chance of showers tonight, but clear for the rest of the week. He's just joshing us. Besides, it's not like we haven't been caught up here in the snow before."

That comment recalled the year they woke up to eighteen inches of unexpected snow and found all their gear buried in piles of the heavy wet stuff. It also prompted them to tell worn-out tales of past hunts each of them had heard from one another countless times before. Steve smiled at the thought. He was in his beloved mountains and had a great brother and a wonderful friend with him. What could be better!

They gathered wood, constructed a privy, set a fire, had a meal of steak and beans, passed around a bottle of Scotch, and then banked the fire and retired to their tents. The hunt would start at first light.

Chapter 12

After a quick breakfast, Tim asked, "Which way do you want to go?"

"I'm headed to French Canyon," Mark said.

"I'll take Honeymoon Lake if that's okay," Steve replied.

"Okay, I'll work the Knob," Tim said. "I'll see you guys back here before dark. If you get anything, fire two shots and we'll come help."

Each man headed off in a different direction. Steve had to cross a swollen stream nearby, so he walked along the bank until he found a fallen tree he could use as a footbridge. He shouldered his rifle and walked the timber as though it was a tightrope. If he fell, the wet and cold would force him back to camp before he even got started. After he gained the other side, he located the familiar game trail that led up to Honeymoon Lake and started to climb. As the sun rose and lit up the valley on the opposite side, he noticed the clouds scudding in from the west and piling up against the peaks behind him. No worries, he had rain gear in his backpack. He could wait it out if necessary.

Steve saw a lot of deer sign as he trudged up the steep incline, but he never saw any animals. They probably knew where he was long before he approached. But that didn't matter. This was just a reconnaissance mission, unless he got lucky. Tomorrow, the serious hunt would begin. After a two-hour climb, he spied the reflection of Honeymoon Lake shimmering through the pines. The sun had risen above the jagged peaks and dispersed the clouds to reveal its treasure. He unconsciously increased his pace as he threaded his way through the remaining trees. Steve always felt a jolt of wonderment each time he came here.

He emerged from the trees and stopped to admire the tableau before him. The lake, thirty acres across, was nestled in a high alpine bowl that resembled a volcanic cone. A two-thousand-foot wall of snow-capped granite peaks rose behind it to form a half circle that framed the still water from northeast to southeast and protected it from the weather. The west side of the lake swelled up and funneled out to spill over a series of small, rocky waterfalls until it formed a rapid stream that flowed through the trees and raced to join the larger stream in the valley below. The ground on this side of the lake was soft, mossy grass dotted with stunted pines and boulders expelled from the peaks above. It was a perfect cathedral that only God could erect, far better than the most elaborate churches built by man. He felt that welcome shiver tickle his spine.

Steve shrugged off his rifle and backpack, leaned the weapon against a tree, and laid the pack on the soft ground to use as a backrest. He took off his down vest and spread it next to the pack and sat on it to recover from the thin air and arduous climb. He relaxed and let the sun warm him as he stared at the placid water. The wall of granite behind the lake guarded it from the wind to form a perfect, still canvas that reflected the jagged peaks in an upside-down mirror image of itself. As if on cue, a red-tailed hawk swooped down from the trees and snatched a small trout from the lake, only twenty feet from the shore. Steve let out a whoop of joy at his own personal National Geographic moment like a kid on his first trip to Disneyland. He so wanted Gina to see this.

For reasons he would never comprehend, Steve felt an urgent need to express his gratitude to the only God he was taught to worship at a young age. He doffed his hat, retrieved his rosary from his pocket, and knelt in the mossy grass. He fingered the plastic beads and began the familiar mantra, "In the name of the Father …"

When he finished his prayers, he fluffed up his pack for a pillow, lay down on his vest, and felt the sun caress his face. He pulled the brim of his cowboy hat down to shade his eyes. He hadn't felt this content in a long time. He relaxed into the warm sensation.

An hour later, Steve bolted upright, clutching at his torso as a peal of thunder reverberated through his chest cavity. It sounded as if it were right above him, close enough to touch. It was cold. The sky had darkened to an angry purple and gray; the massive clouds, swollen with moisture, butted up against the granite peaks. He knew he had to get out of there, down to the shelter of the trees in the valley below and away from the lightning that was sure to follow. He stood, pulled on his vest and backpack, donned his hat, grabbed his rifle, and headed back to the trail. Going downhill would be much faster than climbing up.

As he traversed the slope, he noted the giant slabs of granite on his left that had shorn off the mountain like gargantuan bread slices. The sight reassured him. He was halfway to the camp. He remembered thinking he was going to make it without having to resort to his rain gear when it happened.

He was walking quickly down the trail next to a large granite slab when the world exploded in a blinding ball of light. He felt his world burst apart, and his last conscious thought was *What will Taylor do without me?*

Chapter 13

He felt warm, comfortable, bathed in an eerie light. It wasn't bright. He didn't have to squint. It was a perfect light, designed for ease and clarity of vision. It was a quality of light he'd never experienced. It soothed him. It was welcome. He wasn't afraid. In fact, he felt a perfect sensation of joy, of serenity, of peace. It was magical.

And he heard a voice speaking to him in the most calming tone he'd ever heard. No, it wasn't a voice. He didn't hear words. He just heard something in his head, some profound message that he knew had changed him forever. There was an instruction contained in the communication he couldn't decipher, something important. He grasped at it. He needed to capture it. It eluded his efforts, as though he was not worthy of holding it in his hands. It stayed just out of his reach. He redoubled his efforts until he felt the strain—his muscles tearing, his breath leaving his lungs, his legs failing to respond. He had to reach it. Maddening!

He bolted upright for a second time that day. Sweat poured off his brow, his breath came in ragged gasps, and his joints felt like lead. He hurt all over. He lay back and gathered his wits. Something had happened, something momentous. He just didn't know what it was. He surveyed his surroundings. His backpack and vest were still on him. His rifle was lying at his side. His hat was twenty feet back up the hill as though some unseen force had blasted it off his head. The ground around him was undisturbed.

At first, he thought he'd been hit by lightning, but the evidence around him didn't support that theory. He wasn't burned. There was no more pain. His hearing had returned to normal. His body didn't ache any longer. Birds were chirping. Squirrels scampered up in the trees. The sky was bright blue, freckled with clouds. Everything was as it had been before the light hit him, before he woke next to the lake.

He wasn't frightened. A veil of serenity descended over him. He felt better than he could ever remember. He sat up with ease, picked up his rifle, and retrieved his hat. He sat down on a small boulder to collect his thoughts. When he looked around the forest below, he saw the largest buck he'd ever seen just a hundred yards distant, a magnificent creature adorned with a massive rack. And even though it was an easy shot, it just stood there, looking back at him, calm. Steve knew he couldn't shoot him. The buck sensed he wouldn't be shot. Then he slowly meandered along the trail through the trees until he disappeared. Steve felt like he'd passed some sort of test. He didn't know why. But the sensation was as real as anything he'd ever felt in his life.

Steve resumed his downward trek to camp in a strange mood. He knew something had happened—something he couldn't explain. He also knew with a certainty that whatever it was would be revealed to him in time. He already possessed that knowledge. He just couldn't find words to adequately express what he knew. He reached camp an hour later.

"Hey," Mark called out to him as he approached, "what took you so long?"

"What do you mean?" Steve replied.

"It's almost dark, Steve. We were beginning to worry," Tim added. "Supper is on the fire. Come on, lend a hand."

Steve came to his senses in a hurry. "Sorry, guys. I didn't mean to worry you. I just got caught up in the day, you know?" Somehow, he'd lost several hours and couldn't account for it.

"Did you see anything?" Tim asked. "Any sign?"

Steve hesitated before he answered. "No, no deer and very little sign. And what there was of it was very old. How about you guys?" He didn't know why he lied, why he couldn't tell them.

Mark rose from his seat on a stump and approached Steve. "I saw plenty of sign up in French Canyon. We could try there in the morning. It looks promising."

He stared at Steve. Tim came over from the fire.

"What?" Steve blurted.

"Are you alright?" Tim asked. "Did anything happen up there?"

"Why are you questioning me? What's gotten into you two?"

"You just seem different," Mark said.

"Different? How?"

"I don't know, just different," Mark said.

Steve's brother, Tim, just stared at him. He said nothing. He knew his brother well. Something happened he didn't want to talk about. He returned to his duties at the fire.

"Hey," Steve called out from the trees as he unloaded his rifle, "did you guys run into any weather up there?"

"No, it was nice all day in the canyon," Mark said. He and Tim exchanged a puzzled look.

"Nothing up on the knob either," Tim said. He turned and looked out through the gloom to see an outline of his brother. "It was nice all day. Come on, the stew is ready." Something was wrong. Steve was concealing something from him.

The trio ate their supper. Steve did the dishes and rinsed them in the stream, taking a long time in the process to be alone and think. He wasn't ready to talk. They'd think he'd gone crazy. They stood around the fire and shared a few tales from the day and drank a few beers.

To deflect their curiosity about his day, Steve said, "I saw a hawk swoop down and take a trout out of the lake right in front of me. It was amazing to see. It was only twenty feet away."

"I'd have liked to see that," Mark said. "Maybe I'll hike up there tomorrow."

"I thought we were going to hunt French Canyon tomorrow," Steve replied.

"Yeah," Tim added, "that's what I thought, too."

"Okay, okay," Mark relented. "French Canyon it is."

Steve sensed Tim had come to his rescue. He also knew his brother well enough that he was not fooling him. "Well, I'm heading for bed. I'm bushed."

"Me, too," Tim said. "It's been a long day."

With that, they all retired to their individual tents to prepare for the early morning hunt. Steve was relieved to be alone with his thoughts. He didn't like the idea of holding out on his brother or his best friend.

Chapter 14

Mark bagged a nice-sized buck the following day in French Canyon, an eight pointer that dressed out at 150 pounds. Tim shot his buck the next day up on the Knob. Steve never fired his rifle.

On the fourth day, as they were breaking down camp, Mike rode into the clearing leading a string of six mules and three saddled horses. "Looks like you filled some tags, boys," he said as he dismounted and approached the hanging carcasses. "But there's only two. Who's the unlucky one?"

"That would be me," Steve said. "I didn't see anything worth shooting. I guess it wasn't my week."

"Win some; lose some," he said. "Let's get packed up. I want to be home before dark."

They loaded the mules with the gear and the two animals, and began the long ride out of the mountains. Steve couldn't help thinking this was his last hunt. He didn't know why, but he was sure of it.

They loaded the SUV, tied the deer on the roof to drop off at the butcher in Bishop, and said their goodbyes with a promise to return next year. They drove down the mountain, dropped off the animals at the butcher shop, and started the seven-hour drive home. Steve sat in the back. Mark drove, and Tim sat shotgun.

About halfway home, Tim turned to Steve and said, "Do you want to talk about it now?"

"Talk about what?"

"Whatever happened up at Honeymoon Lake," he said.

"Nothing happened, Tim. I wish you'd lay off."

"You're not kidding anyone, Steve," Mark said without taking his eyes off the road. "We both know you too well. When you came back to camp the first day, you were different. I can't put it into words, but you were changed somehow."

Steve stared out the side window at the high desert scrub and the mountains beyond it. He came to a decision. "First, tell me how I was different. Give me something."

Tim took over the conversation. "You had a glow about you."

Steve snorted.

"No, I'm serious, Steve. You looked different—peaceful, content. It permeated the camp. Mark felt it. I felt it. Don't tell us you didn't feel it. We talked about it when you were out of camp."

"Bullshit."

"You may call it bullshit, but when you get home and Gina sees you, you'd better have a good story prepared because she's going to notice a difference, and she's going to stay on you until she gets an answer."

Steve continued to stare out the window at the passing landscape. He felt confused. He felt dishonest. He wasn't sure what to say. "I love you guys. You know that. Please don't laugh at me. You're right. Something happened. I'm not sure what."

"We're not going to laugh, Steve," Mark said. "We're just concerned. Whatever happened to you affected us, too."

"Are you serious?"

"I've never been more serious. We felt it, too."

Steve couldn't look at them. He stared out at the passing scenery as he explained, "When I was up at Honeymoon, I saw that hawk, like I said. Afterward I said a prayer of gratitude for the day, the hawk, your friendship, the beauty of the mountains. I just felt blessed, you know."

He hesitated again and then went on. "On the way down, near that massive outcrop of granite, I was hit with a powerful light. I blacked out. I thought I was hit by lightning. That's why I asked about the weather when I came into camp. When I woke up, there was no damage. I was sore, as sore as I've ever been. And then, when I was fully awake and sat up, I wasn't sore at all. It was like I was miraculously cured of everything. I felt clean, strong, at peace with the world. It was the most awesome feeling I've ever had. I don't know how else to put it into words."

No one spoke. It was as if all the oxygen whooshed out of the vehicle, dead silence.

"You don't believe me."

Tim took the lead. "It's not that, Steve. We know something happened to you. This is just so hard to comprehend. We don't know what to think. You don't either. We're not laughing at you, and we know you're serious. We just have to digest this a little at a time."

"There's more," Steve said. Now that he'd started, he wanted to air it all out—get some perspective before he faced his wife. "I've been hearing voices. Not voices, really, more like a presence passing along knowledge, a powerful presence. Something not human, something I've never encountered. And it's important, extremely important. And I don't know what it is. It's like I'm gaining more knowledge each time I go to sleep. I almost had it last night, but it escaped my grasp, like I'm not ready yet."

Tim was turned in his seat, observing his brother while he talked. Mark drove slowly, concentrating more on the conversation than the highway. Neither man interrupted him.

"I know I'm supposed to do something. I don't know what it is yet, but I'm sure it's something that will change everything—my marriage, my family, my relationships with everyone, you two included."

Tim reached back and patted his brother on the knee. "Whatever it is, Steve, we'll be with you. Maybe we don't understand this now, but we'll stick with you."

"Both of us," Mark added.

Steve was near tears. "Is it okay if we don't talk about this anymore? I just want to think about it for a while." He couldn't pull his gaze away from the window. He knew he'd lose it if he did.

"No problem, brother. Get some rest." He and Mark exchanged a look of concern.

Chapter 15

It was late when Steve finally made it home to San Diego. The house was dark except for a light in the kitchen. He left his gear in the garage because it reeked of campfire smoke, unwashed body, and horse sweat. Then he peeled off his clothes and left them on the garage floor before he entered the kitchen. When he stepped through the door, Gina was standing there with a big grin on her face. She looked him up and down, amused at his nudity.

"Apparently, you couldn't wait to see me," she teased.

Steve put his hands up in mock surrender. "Guilty as charged," he said. "Let me get into the shower first and then we'll talk."

She pinched her nose with a finger and thumb. "Good idea, cowboy. I can wait."

As Steve passed her by without a kiss, she detected something different, something foreign. She looked after him, puzzled. "Steve?"

"Let me get a shower first," he called. "I'll just be a minute."

He spent a long time in the shower. He shaved off his six-day beard even though it was a tradition to leave it for the winter months. He brushed and flossed his teeth. He delayed every way imaginable so he wouldn't have to face his wife. Reluctantly, he turned off the taps and toweled off. He put on boxers and a T-shirt and went to their bed. Gina was sitting up with the lamp on, waiting. Her arms were crossed and that look was on her face, the one that said, "This better be good."

Steve sat on the edge of the bed, facing away from her. "Could you turn off the light, please? I have something to tell you."

She complied without a word.

With the light out, Steve fluffed up his pillows and sat up like his wife. The moonlight filtered through the venetian blinds, casting alternating bars of light and dark across the bedspread. They reminded Steve of a prison, though he'd never been in one. Somehow the image seemed appropriate.

"Where do I start?" he said. "You're going to think I'm crazy."

"Just start, Steve. Whatever it is, I can take it."

"First, did Tim call you after I left him in Orange County?"

"No, he didn't. And I don't need your brother to tell me when something is wrong with you. I knew it the second you walked in the door."

Steve nodded his head as though she had confirmed something.

"Something happened in the mountains, something strange, something impossible to explain," he said.

"Try me," she said.

"Okay, okay," he began, "just let me get it all out before you say anything."

"Okay."

"Do you remember me telling you about Honeymoon Lake, that place up in the mountains I'm always drawn to? Well, I went up there like I always do, and it was just as special as it's always been. In fact, it was more special this time. It was so beautiful. The weather was perfect, sunny with a few clouds. The temperature was in the fifties. The lake was beautiful, still, with the snow-capped peaks behind it. I even saw a hawk snatch a fish out of the lake right in front of me."

He took a moment to gather his thoughts before he continued. "I said a prayer to thank God for the day, for you and Alexis, for Taylor, for everything. Then I fell asleep. When I woke up, there was a gathering storm brewing right above the lake. Dark clouds had bunched up against the peaks, the wind picked up, and there was loud thunder that was so close to me, I got scared. I grabbed my gear, and I hightailed it out of there as fast as I could. I got halfway back to camp and something happened to me."

He paused, searching for words. "I was struck by a bolt of light out of the sky. I blacked out—for hours, I guess. I didn't realize the time had passed until I got back to camp and Tim and Mark were worried. Anyway, when I woke up, I was bathed in this light, a perfect light that I wanted to stay in forever. Then I was aware of excruciating pain, something I don't want to feel again. I hurt all over like someone beat me up. Then, when I sat up, the pain disappeared like it was never there. It was replaced with a sensation of peace, calmness, and serenity. I felt as strong and as capable as I ever have. I sat down on a rock to recover and saw the biggest buck I've ever seen. He just stared at me. He wasn't spooked in the least. It was like he was making sure I was all right. It spooked me even more."

He knew his wife was looking at him in the dark, but he couldn't return her gaze. He stared straight ahead and continued. "When I got back to camp, Mark asked me out of the blue what happened to me, like he knew something. When I said nothing, he said something to the effect that I wasn't kidding anyone. He asked me again. I told him I was fine and to lay off. Tim didn't say anything, but he knew. He knew. "On the drive home, Tim asked me what happened up at Honeymoon. He said he and Mark felt it, too—the change in me, I mean. They had discussed it while I was gone from camp. They knew something had happened before I told them. I was afraid to answer their questions, but Tim wouldn't let it go. So, I told them what I'm telling you now."

Tears were spilling over and coursing down his cheeks without Steve being aware of it. He was just sitting there in misery, afraid everyone he loved thought he was crazy. Gina picked up on his train of thought immediately. She took his hand in hers and said, "Lie down, honey. You've had a long day. Let me talk for a while." She handed him a tissue to clean up with and pushed him down to recline on his back, staring at the ceiling.

"First, I don't think you're crazy. That is what you're worried about, isn't it?"

"Of course," he replied. "Tim and Mark probably think so, too."

She shushed him. "I doubt that, Steve, because I felt it, too, the minute you came through the door. I was sound asleep, but I knew you were in the house. I felt you here, with me. And when I saw you, I knew you were different. I can't tell you how. I just knew."

"Do I look different?"

"No, you don't look different. You feel different. Like there's a glow around you. I mean, I don't see a glow; I sense it. You had all this dirt on you. You smelled horrible. But you glowed, right through all of it. You glowed."

"That's the same thing Mark said to me. I glowed."

"You see, darling? We all felt it. You're not crazy. Or maybe we're all crazy. At least you'll have company at the asylum."

"There's more, Gina. I feel something when I sleep like someone, or something, is teaching me something—like they're imparting some deep knowledge, an awareness of something I should do, something I don't know yet. It scares me," he admitted for the first time. "It scares me."

Gina snuggled against him. "You don't need to be scared. I'm right here beside you, where I'll always be. Sleep now, honey. We'll talk more in the morning."

She positioned her body alongside him, her hand on his chest and her cheek on his shoulder. "Sleep now, honey. We'll figure it out tomorrow." She looked at him and realized he was already out, deep in slumber. Perplexed at how fast he fell asleep, she molded his body to her and tried to sleep. Tomorrow would be interesting.

Chapter 16

When Steve woke up, the house was empty. It took him a moment to realize it was Monday and Alexis was already in school, and Gina had driven Taylor to his school twenty miles away. He had the house to himself. It was better that way. The nighttime visions had returned, revealing even more absurd messages. He couldn't deny it had happened. He felt refreshed, strong, positive he had a purpose he didn't have before the hunting trip. He was certain of it. But it was still just out of reach, beyond his ability to grasp what it was. He knelt beside the bed and prayed for clarity. He needed to understand what had happened. He needed to know he wasn't coming unhinged. He buried his face in the disheveled bedclothes and focused on his plea.

An hour later, he had no answers, but he knew one thing with certainty. The episode in the mountains and the recurring dreams had something to do with Taylor. He didn't know what the message was, but it did concern his son. He was not alarmed at this revelation. On the contrary, it gave him a semblance of peace, an assurance that he would eventually comprehend the message. He was refreshed once again.

He ate a hard-boiled egg, a banana, and an apple. He sprinkled granola over Greek yogurt and covered it in honey. He ate it all and washed it down with a pint of tomato juice as if he had been starving. He was still ravenous when he finished. Rather than dwell on the incidents of the past five days, he busied himself in the garage. He opened the gun safe and retrieved the rifle he'd taken on the trip. He cleaned it meticulously even though he hadn't even fired it, anything to stay busy. He spread his tent, sleeping bag, and pads out in the sun to dry and air out. He cleaned his hiking boots, polished his rifle scabbard until the leather shone like new, and replaced his unused ammunition in the factory box. He deposited his soiled clothing in the washing machine and started the load, stored his unstamped hunting tag and license in the home office, and returned to the kitchen just as Gina entered.

She stopped abruptly as she spied him. "What?" Steve blurted.

She smiled. "Nothing, it's just that this is going to take some getting used to."

"What is?"

"You are. You're different somehow. I thought when I got back and saw you in daylight, this would all make some sense. It doesn't."

"You ought to experience it from my perspective," Steve joked.

"No thanks. One weirdo in the family is enough." Gina immediately regretted her remark. The look on Steve's face was one of pure astonishment like she'd slapped him for no reason.

"Honey, I didn't mean it that way—"

"No, no, it's all right," he interrupted. "This is going to take some getting used to for both of us. I'm not offended."

Gina went into his arms and held him. "Still, I'm sorry."

"Don't be. It's nothing." He hugged her closer.

"Are you going in to the office?" she asked.

"No, I want to see the kids when they get out of school. The office can wait."

"Do you want to pick up Alexis from school?"

"No, I think I'll pick up Taylor instead."

"You never pick up Taylor. Are you sure you know where his school is?" she kidded.

He kissed the top of her head. "I'll manage, smart-ass."

Gina said, "Let's sit at the table and have some coffee. I need a shot of caffeine."

"Okay."

She poured two cups and they sat down. "Did you have any more visions last night?"

"Not really," he began. "They're not like visions that I can recollect.

I couldn't describe what I saw. They're more like impressions, ideas that won't coalesce into a clear picture. Am I making any sense?"

"Nope." She smiled at her husband. "Is anything becoming clearer?"

"Well, one thing became clear last night." He hesitated. "It has to do with Taylor. But don't worry. It's something positive. But it's also complicated. I just don't know what it is yet. It's driving me crazy."

"You may not want to use that word when describing your dreams, honey."

"Wow, I thought you'd be alarmed when I mentioned Taylor. And you're making jokes about it."

"You always said when Taylor did something embarrassing, we could either laugh or cry and pick one and move on. I choose laugh."

He gazed at the woman he loved more than breathing. "You're amazing!"

"Yes, I am." She laughed.

"And you do believe me?"

"I believe something happened to you up there. Apparently, Tim and Mark do, too. But, honey, this sounds a bit incredible—the flash of light, being enveloped in a warm light, all of it. It sounds like those kooks you see on television who claimed to have seen God."

Steve stared at his coffee cup. "I know. It sounded plausible last night when I was exhausted from the horse ride, the drive home. Now it sounds like I made it up, even to me."

"So, tell me again. Don't worry about what I think. Just tell me."

He went through the story again, trying to make some sense of what he was saying, but it remained a fantasy, something he made up. Instead of convincing Gina he'd had a magical experience, he was slowly convincing himself he was delusional.

After he'd recounted the tale in detail for the third time, Gina said, "Tell you what, why don't we just sit on this story for a while? Maybe some explanation will emerge over time, Steve."

"Maybe you're right. Besides, I don't like the way you're looking at me now. I didn't like the way Tim looked at me last night either. I don't know what to do, Gina."

"Do you mind if I call Tim? Maybe if we talk, something will become a little clearer."

"No, go ahead. I just don't want to be here when you do. I've had enough."

He got up from the table. "I'm going out for a while. I'll pick up Taylor at two thirty and then I'll be home."

Chapter 17

After Steve drove off, Gina sat at her desk and called his brother, Tim. They exchanged the usual greetings and then Tim said, "I figured you'd call sometime today."

"You did, huh?"

"Yes, and if you hadn't, I would have called you."

"What happened, Tim?"

"I don't know, Gina. Steve came back late to camp the first day, and then everything got weird. He looked different. No, I take that back. He didn't look different. He felt different. I knew something happened right away. He wouldn't admit it, but I knew. I could feel it."

"Me, too," Gina said. "I was fast asleep when he got home, but I came fully awake when he arrived. I mean, I didn't hear him come in. I just felt him there. I knew he was home."

"Did he look different to you?"

"No, he felt different. He had this sort of glow about him, something not quite right. You know what I mean?"

"Yeah, it struck me the same way. I told him that, that he had a glow about him, the exact same words."

"Did he tell you his story?"

"Yes. It didn't make any sense then, and it still doesn't. Do you think he's all right? Did anything happen to him lately?"

"Do you mean like a bump on the head?" She laughed.

"Yeah, I guess."

"No, no bump on the head. This all started when he came back from your hunting trip. I was hoping you could explain some of this."

"Let's compare what he told you to what he told me. Maybe we'll figure this out for him."

"Okay." They each verified the tale Steve told them and found no inconsistencies. Steve had relayed the exact details to both—the trip up to Honeymoon Lake, the hawk, the storm, the burst of light, and the serene feeling he acquired as a result. There were no differences, none.

"Did he say anything about hearing voices in his sleep?" Gina asked.

"Yes, but he said they weren't voices, more like subliminal messages that he couldn't decipher. He was agitated about that. I could tell. He couldn't figure out what it meant."

"He told me the same thing. And I agree, he's upset about it."

"Did he mention seeing a large buck after the light hit him?" Gina asked.

"No, he didn't. He told us he didn't see any deer and no recent sign. Hmmm ... that's odd. Now that I look back on it, it's almost like he didn't want us to go up there. We both filled our tags elsewhere, so there was no reason to hike all the way up there. It didn't dawn on us to go up and have a look-see. I guess we should have."

"Tim, don't beat yourself up. There's no playbook for this."

"No, I guess not."

They continued exploring every possible explanation, and once they'd exhausted any new information, Tim said, "I'm not sure what else to say. Please keep a close eye on my little brother, Gina. Let me know if I can help in any way."

"And you call me if anything else occurs to you," Gina responded. "I'm worried."

"Me, too," he said. "I'll keep in touch. Bye."

"Bye."

Chapter 18

Steve drove to the beach and walked along the deserted shore. In addition to his experience in the mountains, he had a disturbing message the previous night that implied a warning about his son, Taylor. He couldn't interpret the language associated with the message, but he knew he needed to be careful when he saw Taylor, as if something bad would happen to his son or himself if he didn't comply. He didn't mention it to Gina because he didn't understand it himself, and relating an amorphous warning to his wife would have worried her even more. It was maddening. He felt like he was going insane. Nothing was any clearer than the day before. He sought out one of the places he went to for a perspective check: the ocean.

He walked south along the sands of Del Mar, with the rising sun off his left shoulder. The day was shaping up to be one of those warm, fall days that felt more like summer than fall because of the Santa Ana winds that blew offshore and cleared out the smog. The view over the Pacific was so acute you could see the Coronado Islands in stark relief. He sat down, tired of thinking, and gazed out at the sparkling water, which the sun's reflection had burnished into a liquid field of sparkling diamonds. He sat there for a long time, allowing the combination of salt air, sand, sun, and water to alleviate his inner struggle. He went blank.

When Steve reclaimed reality, it was hours later, already early afternoon. The beach was dotted with sunbathers. His nightmares had become daydreams. He knew now he'd been given both a gift and a warning. The messages were becoming clearer, and they involved his son. It had to do with the sense of touch, and the warning implied it concerned Taylor. He returned to his car, determined to decipher the mystery. He headed north to pick up his son from school. He knew this was the next step he was supposed to take; he just didn't know why.

He arrived at the junior high school ten minutes before the dismissal bell and parked in the visitors' lot. The school housed a large contingent of disabled students ranging in age from five to eighteen, and it was a center of learning for these challenging students because of its resources and the dedication of its staff. The teachers here faced difficult odds every day, struggling to engage the students and give them a sense of self. Most of the curriculum revolved around teaching daily living skills, so the educators were more like a family than an outside influence. They were the best of the best, preparing their charges for life outside the home.

Steve stood outside his car, enjoying the warm afternoon temperature and the constant breeze. He noticed a small boy, perhaps eight or nine years old, walking alone outside the security fence designed as the primary barrier between the highway and the natural curiosity of children who had no sense of danger to themselves. The boy was jumping up and down on his tiptoes and flapping his hands each time a vehicle whizzed by, mesmerized by the rapid movement. To Steve, this was clearly the self-stimulating behavior of an autistic child that was usually discouraged by parents and educators alike. He instinctively walked toward the child as any father who understood the situation would.

As he neared the boy, he took note of the dirty blond hair, the mismatched shorts and T-shirt, and the battered sneakers that were telltale signs of an autistic child who had little regard for appearances. Taylor, at thirteen years old, was the same way. If you allowed him to choose his clothing for the day, the results would be entertaining: plaids with stripes, odd colors, and long pants with a sweatshirt on a ninety-degree day. All were within the bounds of tasteful dress.

Steve increased his pace without breaking into a run that might startle the boy and cause him to dart into traffic. He was already off the curb as Steve approached. He maintained an angle that concealed him from the child's field of vision and closed the distance between them. He was ten feet away when the boy jumped into the first lane to greet the oncoming traffic. Steve ran into the street and grabbed the little guy just as a dilapidated van screeched to a halt with its horn blaring and slewed sideways to stop before it ran over them. Steve snatched him up and cradled him in his arms, hugging the boy to him as he lunged to the safety of the sidewalk with no room to spare. It was close, as close as he ever wanted to be to getting creamed by a speeding vehicle.

Several things happened at once. A string of cars hit their brakes, adding to the blaring cacophony of the van. The driver spewed a string of curses directed at Steve, shaking his fist in a fit of rage caused by the near miss. "Keep your goddamned kid out of the street, you idiot!" he screamed.

Steve paid no attention to the irate driver because the little boy had sunk his teeth into his trapezium muscle and bit down, breaking the skin. He pulled Steve close in a bear hug that surprised him in its strength and intensity, and Steve reacted by squeezing the boy to him to gain release without wrenching him away and incurring any additional damage to his shoulder. He felt a sharp jab in his kidney area when he clutched him to his chest as though someone had stuck him with a pin. What came next was a complete surprise.

The child eased his hold on him, sat back in his arms, looked him directly in the eye, and said, "I'm sorry, mister. I didn't mean to bite you. I just had to, you know?"

"No, no, it's okay," Steve said, still holding the child in his arms. "I thought you were a disabled student."

"I am," the boy said.

Before he could say anything in reply, several adults raced over to retrieve the child. One large young man, built like a refrigerator, approached, bristling with anger. "Put him down. What are you doing, pal? Why are you here?" He pulled the boy out of his grasp and handed him off to another woman.

"Wait … wait, John. I saw the whole thing. This man saved Jeremy from getting hit by a car. He ran into traffic and grabbed him in the nick of time," a young teacher intervened. She turned to Steve. "Are you Taylor's father?"

"Yes." Steve was too shaken to say more. Something important had happened, something he didn't understand. He sat down on the grass, unconcerned by the stares he received from the school staff. He was exhausted and didn't know why.

"Are you okay? Were you hit?" the young woman asked. "I'm Miss Stafford. I was Taylor's speech therapist last year."

Steve just stared up at her.

"You weren't hit, were you? Are you injured?"

Steve shook off his confusion and said, "No. No, I'm fine. How's the boy?" He looked around at the gathering crowd as though he noticed them for the first time. He was about to stand up when the boy squiggled through the adult legs and approached Steve, now at eye level, still sitting on the grass.

In a clear, enunciated voice, he said, "Thank you, mister. I feel better now."

Everyone turned at the sound of the boy's voice and stared. Steve was growing more confused by the moment. "You're welcome," he managed.

The boy turned to leave, his obligation fulfilled, and then turned back to Steve. "And thanks for the hug. That felt great."

Steve had no answer to that. He was stunned. Something had become clear to him in that instant. The boy had done something to him. And it hurt. He wasn't sure how, but it left a profound impact on him.

Miss Stafford, the woman who had introduced herself, knelt next to him. She was looking at him with a mixture of awe and concern. "Are you sure you're okay? You look a bit dazed."

Steve rose unsteadily and brushed the grass from his trousers. He reached up to massage his muscle where the boy had bitten him. He pulled his shirt away from his neck to examine the wound only to find no marks on his skin. He was sure the child had imbedded his teeth in a fit of rage and broke the skin, but there was no blood. He recalled the pinprick in his back, held his shirt away from his back, and contorted his body to look for any sign of a wound there—nothing. He'd acutely felt both insults to his flesh, but there was no evidence that either had ever happened. He realized everyone was staring at him like he was from another planet. He surveyed the crowd as though in a fog.

Miss Stafford broke the impasse. She took Steve by the arm and led him away. "Come with me, Mister Wilson. I'll take you to Taylor."

Steve allowed himself to be propelled away, numb. She accompanied him to her office, placed a call to someone, and directed the person to bring Taylor Wilson to her office. While they waited, she asked, "Do you remember me?"

Steve looked at the woman. She was about thirty-five or so, with short brown hair and an engaging smile. She wore a practical white blouse tucked into jeans that hugged a generous figure and sneakers—a practical uniform for a teacher who probably experienced daily physical outbursts from her students when she challenged them to form words. She looked familiar, and Gina would have recognized her anywhere, in any setting. Steve was having difficulty recalling when they'd met. "It was at Taylor's annual IEP meeting that we met," she said.

"Oh, the goal-setting deal we attend every year," he replied.

"Yes."

"Okay, now I remember. How are you?"

"I'm fine. I'm more concerned about you. Are you feeling all right?"

"I'm fine."

"Would you like some water?"

"Yes, please."

She handed him a bottle of water from her desk, and he drank half of it down in one swallow. He looked at her and said, "What? Why are you looking at me like that?"

"Mr. Wilson, Jeremy is profoundly autistic. He does not have speech motility. He cannot form words. Or he couldn't before today."

"Do you mean the little boy in the street?"

"Yes, that was Jeremy."

"He spoke to me. He seemed normal."

"I know," she replied. "Can you tell me what happened out there?"

"Well, I was standing by my car, waiting for school to let out, and I saw the little boy, Jeremy, I guess, walk out into traffic. I wasn't thinking. I just reacted."

"I saw that part. I was watching from the playground. I think one of

74

the maintenance staff left the gate open. That got my attention. Then I saw you, what you did."

"Then you already know what happened." Steve was becoming increasingly nervous.

"That's not what I meant. And I think you know that."

They were interrupted when the office door opened and Taylor appeared, escorted by the same large young man who had confronted Steve outside. His demeanor was quite different now, almost deferential. He extended a hand the size of a catcher's mitt to shake. "I want to apologize for my behavior out there. I didn't know who you were. I'm Jeff."

Steve shook the proffered hand and said, "Not at all. I'm glad to know someone looks out for these kids." He retrieved his hand and turned to Taylor with his hand extended upward for a high five, a ritual they shared each time they met. Taylor slapped his hand in a Pavlovian response and said in a halting voice, "Hi ... Dad." His pronunciation was faulty, and there was a several-second delay between the *hi* and *dad*. It sounded more like "daid" than dad, but the intent was clear. That was their usual greeting.

"Hello, Taylor, how are you?"

"I am fine." Taylor hesitated for several seconds while he preprocessed the next expected response. "How are you?"

"Fine," answered Steve. It was the rote greeting Taylor had learned for his father, although the fact that Steve hadn't seen him in five days really didn't register. Either his father was present or he wasn't. The passage of time held no meaning for Taylor.

Steve took advantage of Taylor's presence to leave. "Come on, buddy, let's go home."

"Wait, please," Miss Stafford said. "We need to talk."

"I'm sorry, Miss Stafford. We should get going. My wife is expecting us." He took Taylor by the arm and walked to the door, the water bottle still in hand. "I'm sorry," he repeated. "I need to think about this." He tipped up the water bottle and drained it in one long gulp. He was still thirsty.

He dropped the empty bottle in the wastebasket and hurried out of the office, leaving two very confused educators in his wake.

"You saw what I saw, right?" Miss Stafford asked Jeff.

"Everybody did," he said.

"How do we explain this to Jeremy's parents?"

"I have no idea," Jeff said.

Chapter 19

As they drove home, Steve was struck with an almost unbearable urge to stop the car, get out, and hug his son to see what happened. But every time he checked his mirror for a break in traffic to pull over safely, a deep sense of foreboding took over. He was overwhelmed with a horrible feeling of dread every time the desire surfaced. It scared him. He drove on, his knuckles white on the steering wheel.

Gina held the interior door leading to the garage open before Steve even turned the ignition off. She already knew. Steve exited the car and went around to fetch Taylor, his classic stalling technique. Alexis stood behind her mother, eager to greet her father. He escorted his son to the door and leaned down to embrace his daughter. Alexis hugged him before he thought to prevent it. "Hi, Dad. How are you?" she said. "Did you shoot anything?"

"No, honey, not this time," he said. He studied his daughter for any sign of impact from the hug—nothing. And he felt nothing like what he'd felt with the little boy. A wave of relief washed over him, one hurdle down. Now he was sure. He wasn't worried about hugging his daughter. And hugging was not one of Taylor's favorite activities. Steve would avoid that sort of contact until he understood what was happening. He hid his concern and released her. "Uncle Tim got a nice buck, and Mark got a trophy, for sure."

Alexis scrunched up her face to indicate her disapproval of hunting in general and Steve's use of the word *trophy* to refer to one of God's creatures. Steve ignored her.

"Alexis, would you fix a snack for your brother and make sure he uses the bathroom? Your father and I need to talk."

"Okay, Mom."

Gina crooked her finger at her husband to indicate he should follow her out to the yard. He trailed behind her retreating figure, trying desperately to figure out what to say.

When they were out of earshot of the house, Gina spun on him. "I got a call from Barbara Stafford at the school. She told me a fantastic story about a little boy you saved from being hit by a car." She was staring intently at Steve as she spoke, as though she expected to find something different in her husband than she'd seen before. "She said the boy spoke for the first time in his life after you picked him up. She said he's acting as typical as any normally developed eight-year-old. She was so excited she could hardly speak."

Steve returned her gaze, unable to find his voice. He stood there mute.

"Steve, are you alright? You're scaring me."

The question jarred him back to the present. "Honey, I'm fine." He wasn't sure how to convey his next message, although he'd thought about it all the way home. He thought he was prepared for this moment; he wasn't.

"Things are becoming clearer, Gina. I know I had an unusual experience when I picked up that little boy, something not normal. I'm not scared anymore, honey. I'm just confused. There's more I don't understand, but something happened. I felt it."

"Felt what?"

Steve pulled his shirt off over his head, mussing his long hair. "Do you see any bite marks on my shoulder?" he asked as he turned around.

Gina examined his right shoulder. "No, there's no mark."

"Is there a pinprick on my back, by my left kidney?" He indicated the area with his hand.

She bent to inspect his lower back. "No, nothing's there either. Why?"

"When I picked up the little boy, he bit me on the shoulder, hard. And I felt a sharp stab of pain like someone had stuck me with a pin or a needle." He put the shirt back on.

"Is that what you said you felt?" she asked.

"No, I mean I felt that, too, but that's not what I meant. I felt a connection with the boy. And then I felt tired, very tired. I sat down on the grass, exhausted. And I don't know why, but it's connected to the boy."

"Let's sit down, Steve." They sat down on the grass and she held both of his hands in hers. "I'm worried, honey. This is spiraling out of control."

"What do you mean?"

"Miss Stafford is in a tizzy. The entire staff of the school is talking about this incident where a little boy was instantly cured of autism, profound autism. This isn't going to stop, Steve. You have to realize that."

"Do they think I did it?"

"They don't know. But they do know you had something to do with it. And now you say you were bitten, and there's no mark. This is crazy."

"There's more, Gina."

"What?"

"I'm not supposed to hug Taylor," he said. He held up his hand to cut off her reply. "Just listen to me. All the way home, I had the impulse to pull over and hug Taylor as hard as I could. I nearly did several times. But something held me back. Every time that thought entered my head, a deep feeling of dread came over me; something powerful reached out telling me not to do that, telling me to resist."

"What do you mean 'telling you' … in words?"

"No, I don't hear words. I hear a message, some form of communication, but not words. It's hard to explain. It's just there."

"You hugged Alexis."

"I know. It scared me after I realized what I'd done. But I didn't feel anything. And I didn't get that same feeling of dread before I did it. I think that part is fine. I'm not worried about that anymore."

"Thank God," she said.

"I thought you didn't believe in God."

"Not your version, anyway. Besides, if such a God exists, why would he do this to Taylor, to us, to anyone? That's the God you want me to believe in?"

"I have to believe in something. This world didn't just explode into existence from an unexplained mixture of gases that could not have existed on their own. Where'd they come from?"

"I don't know and I don't care. That's just as good an explanation as some all-powerful heavenly being floating around the ether that looks after all of us. That sounds more like Peter Pan. Why does it have to be explained? Why can't we just accept life as it is? Why not just take care of each other, get on with our day? Why do men go to war over these questions and kill each other? That's what you want me to believe in?"

"You have to believe in something. Where did we come from? How did we get here? Where are we going? You don't want to know?"

"I believe in the here and now, and doing the best I can with what actually exists in my life. Maybe you have time for theoretical questions," she said. "I have to get up every day and deal with the reality of Taylor. So far, your God hasn't shown up to help."

"Really, Gina?" he commented.

"Steve, I was raised in a Buddhist household. We have some weird practices that people make fun of—the chanting, the robes, the incense. But we also believe in treating everyone, and everything, with kindness and respect. I don't need anything else."

Alexis came out to the yard. "Are you guys okay?"

Gina answered for them. "We're fine, Lex. We'll be right there." She got up and extended her hand to Steve. "Come on, let's go." She pulled him up.

"Hey, Gina," he joked as she retreated." Do you want a hug?"

She almost laughed but then checked her response. "You're not funny, Steve."

Chapter 20

The phone was ringing when they entered the kitchen. Gina picked it up and said hello. Then she listened for a moment before saying, "I don't know what you're talking about. You have the wrong number." She hung up. The phone rang again.

"Don't answer it," Gina said. "Let it go to voice mail. Steve, let's go in the other room."

"Wait a minute," Alexis protested. "Aren't you going to tell me what's going on? Stop treating me like a child. I'm fifteen years old."

Taylor, oblivious to the conversation, continued to eat his apple. Steve turned to Gina. "She's right, honey. She's part of this family, too."

Gina relented. "Come on, Lex. Let's sit down." The phone rang again. "Just a minute," she said. She adjusted the answering machine so it would not ring to announce another call. It would go straight to voice mail.

"Steve, you're the one who should explain."

He began, "Alexis, something strange happened to me in the mountains …" He recounted the story, ending with the day's event regarding young Jeremy, and answered the inevitable questions as best he could. He finished by saying, "Honey, I don't know what we're going to do. This is as odd for me as anything I've ever encountered."

And out of the mouths of babes came the best suggestion yet. "Call Dr. Lara," Alexis said.

Steve and Gina exchanged a familiar look. "Thanks, Lex; we will."

Gina went to the house phone, noticed the green light that indicated it was engaged, and grimaced. "I need my cell. This phone is going to be useless for a while." She went to the bedroom to place the call.

She returned fifteen minutes later and said, "Dr. Jacobs is going to call Miss Stafford at the school and then call us back."

"How did she take the news?" Steve asked.

"She was skeptical, as I expected. If she wasn't, I'd be alarmed. You'd better get used to that reaction, Steve. It will be the new normal."

"I guess so."

Thirty minutes later, Gina answered her cell. She spoke for a few minutes and then said, "She wants us to come to the university lab, all of us. I said yes."

"Then let's go," Steve said. "Alexis, please get Taylor ready."

They gathered their things and piled in the car. Their home was guarded by an electric gate they'd installed to contain Taylor, and as they approached the barrier, they saw the street was full of vehicles. Several were from local news stations, replete with an array of antennae and small dishes mounted on the roofs. There was a police car parked in the drive with the blue lights revolving. The officer was out of his car attempting to corral the gathering crowd that was eager to discover what was happening in their neighborhood.

Steve maneuvered the car around the crowd, ignoring the shouted questions, and sped away before anyone could react. He took the turn at the bottom of the hill and made it to the freeway before a pursuit could be mounted. He peered at the rearview mirror until he was satisfied no one had followed in his wake.

Twenty minutes later, they parked in the university's behavioral sciences lot and walked into Dr. Jacobs's lab. Lara greeted them warmly and then ushered all of them into her private office. "I spoke to Miss Stafford at Taylor's school, and she convinced me that I should meet with you as soon as possible. A certain amount of credibility comes with that suggestion because Miss Stafford, Barbara to us, was one of my most dedicated graduate students. I've known her for over ten years."

"That's a relief," Steve said. "I was afraid you'd have a rubber room ready for me here."

"Mr. Wilson, we don't use rubber rooms anymore. We bludgeon all false prophets into submission when it comes to the health and welfare of our clients. There is enough false information out there in the public arena regarding autism without our adding to it." She paused for a moment and then went on. "Now, I'd like you to recount exactly what happened to you in the mountains and what occurred at the school."

Steve repeated his fantastic tale once more, but this time Dr. Jacobs did not interrupt him as the others had. She listened intently, took notes for later questions, and maintained a neutral posture that did not indicate any evidence of belief, or lack thereof. Steve finished with a description of the crowd that had gathered outside their home. "By the time we got the kids in the car to come here, there were already over one hundred people milling around outside our gates. It was crazy. I've never experienced anything like it. I got out of there in a hurry. There was a police car parked in my driveway, or else the crowd would have invaded our yard. I drove around the cop car and over the grass to escape before anyone could stop me. I got on the freeway before anyone could follow us, I think."

"Let's hope so," Lara said. She went straight to the obvious. "Why don't you hug Taylor then? That should prove something."

"I'm not supposed to," Steve said.

"What is that supposed to mean?"

"I don't know. I just know I'm not supposed to."

"Did this strange voice tell you that?" Dr. Jacobs asked.

Steve was having difficulty maintaining a civil tone. "I told you, it's not a voice. I just know somehow."

"Uh-huh," she replied. "Well, I have a likely candidate in the other room. Would you agree to give her a hug?"

"Who is she?"

"That doesn't matter. She is a clinically diagnosed, nine-year-old, autistic female child. She has very limited communication skills, and I prefer that you do not know who she is and no one knows who you are. This needs to, at least, resemble a double-blind test. No one else in this lab even knows you're here or has gotten wind of these recent developments. Do you understand?"

"Yes."

"And do you agree to this test?"

"Yes."

"Come with me. Gina, Alexis, you can watch through the one-way glass." She pulled a curtain aside to reveal an adjacent room where a young girl played with a wooden puzzle on the carpet while a grad student took notes.

Lara Jacobs entered first and spoke to the student. The young lady left, and Lara sat down on the carpet to talk with the child. After a few minutes, Lara left the room and returned with Steve.

Steve looked at the little girl. She was beautiful, with long brown hair and a spray of freckles across her nose and cheeks. Her large golden-brown eyes, devoid of guile, flickered up at Steve, dismissed him, and returned to her puzzle. Steve was quite familiar with the lack of interest. He'd experienced it so many times with his own son. He was aware he was sweating, nervous. He was afraid to experiment with this child, and yet he had to. He had to know. He took a seat.

"Janet, look at me," Lara said.

The little girl hesitated, inserted another puzzle piece, and then looked up at Dr. Jacobs with a blank but compliant look.

"Please say hello to Mr. Wilson."

The girl studied Steve for a moment, approached him, and held out a limp hand to shake. Steve took it in his and said, "Hello, Janet."

The little girl did not reply.

Dr. Jacobs said, "Please give him a hug."

Again, she hesitated and then came forward and leaned in timidly with her arms opened slightly to offer a hug. Steve shifted in his seat and gently surrounded her with his arms. Her reaction was immediate. She hugged him to her little frame with such force that Steve was taken aback. She held on so tight that he felt his face turn bright red. He hugged her back. He felt the same jab in his back, this time on the right side, and then the feeling of weakness took over. He felt like he would keel over off the chair. Janet, the little autistic girl, released him and said, "Thank you, Mr. Wilson." Steve fell sideways out of the chair.

If Dr. Jacobs hadn't been sitting on the floor already, she would have fallen out of hers. In forty-plus years of practice, she'd never witnessed anything like this!

Gina and Alexis rushed into the room and went directly to Steve;

they knelt beside him and pulled him upright. "Steve, are you alright?" Gina cried. Alexis clung to her father without speaking. She was scared. Taylor stayed in Lara's office with a grad assistant. He continued to play with his blocks.

Steve noticed the stricken look on his daughter's face and reacted as any father would. He sat up on his own and said, "I'm fine, Lex. I just have a funny reaction when I do this. I just need a little time to recover." He reached out and pulled his daughter to him. Gina did not comment, but Steve knew she was not pleased.

Janet, the little girl, stood next to them. She said, "Mr. Wilson?" to gain his attention.

"Yes?"

"Thank you for the hug. It felt good. I hope it didn't hurt you too much."

Steve managed a smile. "No, Janet, it didn't hurt at all."

"Not even your back?"

Steve experienced an epiphany at that moment. She felt it, too. She knew! He couldn't let the opportunity be wasted. "Did you feel it, too?"

"Yes."

"What did it feel like to you?"

"It felt like a little piece of you broke," she answered.

Dr. Jacobs recovered from her astonishment and took charge. "Janet, look at me." When the little girl complied, the professor asked, "Can you explain what that means? How did it break?"

"I don't know, Lara," the girl said, using the only name she had been taught to refer to Dr. Jacobs. "It just felt like a little piece fell off Mr. Wilson. Will he be okay?"

"I'm fine, Janet. I don't hurt at all." It was Steve's turn to interrupt. "Will you do me one favor?"

"Yes."

"Would you give me another hug?"

"I don't want to hurt you."

"I promise, you won't hurt me."

Janet did as he asked and gave him a hug. She was tentative at first, but as soon as she realized she would not hurt him, she hugged him fiercely. "Thank you, thank you, Mr. Wilson. I can talk now. I can speak to my mom. I'm not afraid."

Steve held her at arm's length. "You do that, little one. You talk to your mom. You tell her how much you love her."

"I will, Mr. Wilson. I will."

Gina and Alexis had tears in their eyes as they watched the exchange between their loved one and the little girl, Janet. Steve used the nickname, "little one," he'd anointed Alexis with when she was young. They knew what Steve was feeling.

Dr. Jacobs took over the meeting. "Janet, I'm going to call your mother to come and get you, but I need to talk to her first. Mr. Wilson, will you wait in my office? We need to talk."

"Of course," he replied.

The family exited the room, arm in arm. No one knew what to say, what to think. Gina and Alexis were just as numb as Steve. When they rejoined Taylor, he was sitting on the floor, rearranging a set of building blocks into perfect rows. It felt like a body blow to Steve. He shook his head in dismay.

Gina noticed. "What, Steve? What's the matter?"

Steve continued to stare at his son. "I learned something else in there," he said. "I need to think about it for a while before I say anything. I have a feeling you're not going to like it."

Chapter 21

Lara Jacobs returned within thirty minutes. She explained that she needed to talk with Janet's mother and reassure her they'd made a significant breakthrough, but cautioned her not to make any of this public until the university could verify the results. They would need weeks to ensure this was a permanent development. She wisely left Steve's role out of it and elicited a promise from the overwhelmed and delighted mother to keep this matter confidential until Lara could confirm a permanent diagnosis. Thus, they had a few days to come up with a plan.

Dr. Jacobs said, "I have to admit I was skeptical, even after speaking with Barbara. Now I've seen it with my own eyes. What I asked of Janet's mother, I must ask of you. This phenomenon needs study. There are a host of protocols to be followed to verify the results. These children need to be studied. There's so much we need to do!" The enormity of this situation was beginning to dawn on all of them, all of them except Taylor. *Overwhelming* was not a strong enough word to describe the atmosphere in the room.

Then she rested her eyes on Taylor. "Mr. Wilson, I have to ask you the obvious question again. What about Taylor?"

Steve replied with no hesitation. "I told you. I can't hug Taylor."

"Why not?"

"I don't know the reason. I just know I won't be able to do this anymore if I hug him."

"But how do you know that? Was there a message you didn't relay to me?"

Steve looked exasperated. "No, I suspected it before. It was confirmed in there"—he pointed to the therapy room beyond the glass— "when she hugged me."

"You felt something?"

"Not like that. It just came to me. I know it for a certainty. If I hug Taylor, he will be cured. But that will be the end of it. I know it. I don't know how I know it. But I know it."

"And you're sure of this?"

"Positive," Steve said.

Dr. Jacobs took a moment to digest this new information. Then she said, "Tell us about the pain you felt. Janet said it felt like something broke in you."

Steve knew she was deflecting the news regarding Taylor, and he was grateful for the reprieve from the subject. He said, "That's an accurate description. I was surprised when Janet put it into words like that. Because that's what it felt like—like something was diminished somehow, something inside me."

"Is it a physical sensation that you can describe in detail?"

Steve thought about it and said, "When I grabbed that little boy earlier today, I felt something like a pinprick in my back, on the left side, down low. Then I felt tired, like I needed to lie down. In fact, I did lie down. I had to ... like in there, when I fell out of my chair, the same thing."

"What about this time, with Janet?"

"I felt the same pain but maybe a little more intense. It still felt like a pinprick, but this time it was a little harder, and it was on my right side. But it went away immediately."

"Can I see your back?"

Steve stood up and pulled his shirt over his head. He backed up to Lara's chair. She produced a magnifying glass from her desk drawer and examined his back. She took a long time before she suggested he put his shirt on and sit down. "I can't find anything—no marks, no bruising, not a scratch."

"I know," Steve said. "It heals right away."

"What?" Dr. Jacobs said. "What do you mean?"

"When I picked up the little boy, he bit me, hard, on my right shoulder. I was sure he broke the skin, but when I looked at it, there was no mark, nothing. But I know I felt it. I thought I was bleeding."

An awkward silence descended on the room. No one wanted to speculate without benefit of more information. Dr. Jacobs was a person of science. This situation had escaped that realm already. Finally, Gina broke the impasse. "What now, Lara? What do we do?"

"I don't have a clue other than to suggest more investigation. I am very interested, to say the least. Will you work with me?" the professor asked.

"Steve, what do you say?" Gina addressed her husband.

"I need some time to think this over. I know Dr. Jacobs is our best resource for the moment, but I need to think. The first problem we have now is where to live," he said.

"What do you mean, Dad? Can't we just go home?"

Steve turned to his daughter. "You saw all those people outside our gates, Lex—the news stations, the reporters. I don't want those people bothering us, at least not until we figure this thing out."

"But what about my friends? What about school?"

"I don't know, Lex. Give me some room here, okay? I'm just as frustrated as you are."

Gina intervened. "Alexis, I'll figure out something for you. Maybe you can stay with the Halls for a while." Hailey Hall was her best friend at school. When you saw one of them, you usually saw the other.

Thank God for his wife and her wisdom. The situation was instantly defused. "Really? You think I could?" Alexis pleaded.

"I'm sure it will work out. Just give us some time, okay?"

"Okay, Mom."

"Now, about Taylor," Gina began.

"He can stay here with us," Dr. Jacobs said. "And I can arrange a university faculty apartment for you, as well. This could spin out of control in a hurry."

Steve and Gina exchanged a look, and Steve knew the decision had already been made. "We accept," Steve said. "I'll go back to the house late tonight and pick up some things."

"No, we'll go back together after the kids are settled. You don't know where to find anything anyway," Gina chided.

"Okay, that's decided. Let's get you guys an apartment." Lara picked up her phone to make the arrangements.

While Dr. Jacobs placed her call, Gina called Dina, her best friend and the mother of Hailey. Dina was excited to hear from her. "Have you seen what's going on at your house?" she said.

"I'm afraid so. We had to leave the house in a hurry."

"Where are you?"

"I can't say right now, Dina. We're a little scared about all of this." Gina continued. "That's why I called. Can Alexis stay with you for a little while until this blows over?"

"I'd take her in a second. You know that. But, Gina, you need to realize what's going on here in the neighborhood. There are cops, reporters, news vans, and strangers all over the town looking for you. It's really not safe for any of you to be here."

"Oh no," Gina said.

"Oh yes," her friend said. "You would not believe what's going on. I've certainly never seen anything like it."

"Dina, thanks. I gotta go. I'll call you later." She wasn't sure how to tell Alexis she wouldn't be staying with the Halls.

Chapter 22

Steve and Gina stayed until Taylor and Alexis were safely ensconced in their new living quarters. The apartment was situated in a secure area of the campus where visiting faculty took up residence during semester-long assignments. The University Police had been summoned, and the family was introduced as participants in a new study that required the utmost discretion as to their identity and existence on campus. The chief of police assured them he would personally see to their privacy and security.

Before the children were put to bed, Alexis was impressed with strict instructions not to contact any of her friends until she received permission. "Honey, do not use your phone for any reason other than to call your mother or me. It's important to keep Taylor safe until we get back."

"Why?"

"Because, by now, every reporter in the state is trying to locate us," Steve admonished her. "Your phone can be monitored for your location, whether you realize it or not. Please do as I ask. It's important to keep Taylor safe. Will you do that for me?"

"Yes," she managed. Steve knew she wanted to share her newfound excitement with her friends like any typical teenager. "I'll explain when we get back."

He hugged his daughter, hoping the hug would convey his regret. Then Gina and Steve left for home. When they arrived, it was after midnight and the street outside their home was empty. Steve discovered several business cards, with notes attached requesting an interview, taped to his gates. He gathered them all and deposited them in the car console without reading them. They parked in the garage and found several more notes and cards taped to the kitchen and front doors, indicating several reporters had trespassed on their property. These went into the trash. If they would not respect Steve's rights as a property owner, they would not respect such a complicated family situation. The process of culling out the undesirables had begun.

They turned on a minimum of lights and began to pack. "I don't know where to start," Steve said as he surveyed the family room.

"Medications, clothes, schoolbooks, snacks for Taylor, his Boston Red Sox cap, phones, laptops, toys, Disney tapes, for starters. I'll think of the rest as we pack," Gina said.

"We'll need both cars," Steve said.

"You're right." Gina stopped for a moment. "What is it you're not telling me?"

"What?"

"You heard me. You can't even keep a straight face. What is it?" Steve had never been able to get anything past his wife. She read him as easily as she read the children.

Now the subject he'd been hoping to avoid was at the forefront. Gina would not give this up. He knew her too well.

"Let's sit down," Steve said.

They sat on the couch in the quiet of the night and held hands. "When I touch an autistic child, I feel a chill first. When I hug them, I experience pain."

"Pain ... what do you mean by pain?"

"Hold on, Gina. Let me get this out. It's just a feeling. It's nothing to be upset about. It goes away immediately. It's nothing more than a pinprick. Relax."

"Then what aren't you telling me? Come on, Steve. We're all affected by this, not just you. I have to know, for the kid's sake if not yours."

Gina made a compelling argument, and Steve recognized the truth in her plea. He relented. "Okay, but this stays between you and me, no one else—not the kids at all and not Lara just yet. It's just a feeling now."

"Stop stalling."

"Okay, okay. When I feel the pain, I think something is seeping out of me."

"What? What are you saying?" She was frantic. "Tell me right now. Tell me exactly what you're feeling. No more BS."

"It feels like I'm losing some vitality, like some part of me leaves. I'm exhausted afterward. That's what Janet was referring to when she said I broke something. She felt it, too."

"My God, Steve, what are you telling me?"

"I don't know, honey. It's just a feeling."

"Like your other feelings? Your accurate feelings?"

"Look, I'm trying to tell you something I'm not sure about. I became concerned when the little girl asked if it hurt me. It was like she felt it, too."

"I don't believe this is happening." Gina collapsed into a ball on the couch, a balloon deflating, and hugged her knees to her chest. "Please tell me this isn't happening."

He wanted to reach out to her, comfort her somehow. He felt helpless, despondent. He held his head in his hands and closed his eyes.

A sharp rap on the windowpane startled him out of his reverie. He snapped his head around at the sound and bristled. If that was a reporter … He lunged from the sofa and ran to the window where a dim face pressed against the glass, shielded by an open palm on each side, so the person could see inside the dimly lit room. Steve was angry at the intrusion, more than angry. He vaguely heard Gina's voice warning him, "Steve, Steve, stop. Don't do anything you'll regret. Stop!"

The figure recoiled at his charge, hands held up in submission. He heard a man's voice say, "I'm sorry. I'm sorry. I have to speak to you. I have to. Please!"

Gina took control by grabbing Steve forcefully by the arm and pulling him away from the window. "Stop it, right now! Let me handle this."

Steve stepped back, still fuming. Gina opened the window a crack and asked, "Who are you and what are you doing here?"

"I'm a police officer. I live nearby …"

"Show me some identification," she said. Steve turned on the outside porch light.

The man reached into his back pocket and produced an ID wallet. He slipped it through the crack. They both examined the badge for the number, committing it to memory, and compared the photograph to the man standing outside under the porch light. He was six feet two, weighed 210 pounds, and was completely bald. Gina handed his wallet back. He was a cop.

"What do you want?"

"Just to talk."

Steve butted in. "Let me guess, you have an autistic child."

The man dropped his eyes to the ground. It was so sad to witness. Gina turned to her husband. "You stop it right now, Steve. This is just the beginning."

She pushed up the window. "Edward, what are you doing here in the middle of the night?"

"I thought … I mean, I thought—"

Gina finished his sentence. "That you could convince us to see your child?"

"My son, yes. He's only five years old and he's so out of control, we may lose him."

"What do you mean 'lose him'?"

"He bites; he scratches anyone who comes near him. My wife is the only one who can even touch him. I haven't held him since he was three. Social Services recommended he be institutionalized for his own good in a lockdown facility." The man was almost in tears. "I can't lose him. I can't."

"I understand, Edward. Where is your son?"

"He's at home. I could have him here in thirty minutes. I won't tell anyone. I promise." He was pleading now, begging for his son.

Gina was the epitome of patience. "What's his name?"

"Teddy," he answered.

"Edward, you call this number tomorrow after eight o'clock and ask for Dr. Jacobs's office. Tell her we asked you to call for an appointment for Teddy. We will meet you there. No guarantees and you tell no one. If you do, all bets are off. Do you understand?"

The man was near tears of joy. "Yes, I understand. And you won't regret this. I already stopped two people from breaking into your house. I'll pay you back somehow. I will."

"Wait, wait, what did you say? People tried to get into this house?" Steve asked.

"Yes, I identified myself as a police officer, took their information, and sent them on their way. They won't come back. I put the fear of God in them."

"And you think that will keep them away?"

The man stopped to consider the question. Steve pressed him. "Would it stop you?"

"No, I guess not." Edward turned to leave.

"Wait a minute," Steve said. "I'll be right out." He turned to Gina. "You stay here. We don't know this guy."

Steve locked the door behind him and met Edward on the porch. The man offered his hand. "Please call me Ed."

Steve shook his hand and said, "Steve."

"How can I thank you, Steve?"

"Don't thank me yet. I need to ask you something. Do you have any cop friends who have autistic kids?"

"Two that I can think of, off the bat," he answered.

"How well do you know them?"

"Pretty well. It's a tight community among cops. We talk to one another. No one else would understand."

"Do they know about this yet, about me?"

"I haven't spoken to them, but this is all over the news. You're famous."

In their haste to meet Dr. Jacobs, they had all but forgotten to watch the local news. The enormity of their situation was becoming clear.

"Can you call them? Could you arrange for them to come with you tomorrow and bring their children with them?"

"Are you serious?"

"Yes, but I'm going to ask all of you for a favor afterward."

"Anything," he said. "We'll do anything."

"Be careful what you promise. I'm going to ask you to provide security for my family. This could get complicated."

"We'll do whatever is needed." Ed hesitated and then asked, "Are you sure this will work?"

"I'm sure."

Gina, listening through the open window, interrupted him. "Don't tell him that unless you're positive." She knew the heartbreak of their own past failures.

Steve turned to his wife. "I'm positive."

He turned back to Ed. "Now go home and get some sleep."

Ed said, "If it's all right with you, I'll stay until daylight and then get some friends over here tomorrow."

Steve smiled. "That would be great, Ed. Thanks."

Chapter 23

They met with Dr. Jacobs at eight o'clock and informed her of the impending visit of three police officers and their children. "What are you talking about? I'm trying to develop a valid protocol and you invited three subjects that I haven't even met. Steve, I can't let you do that."

"Lara, you have no idea what is about to happen to us, or your program. You didn't see all the news vans scattered in front of our home. You didn't see the mob trying to get through the gates. Last night Gina and I met a police officer who had prevented several intruders from invading our home. There were written messages left for us that would break your heart. This morning, on the news, I got to see how bad it's getting. All these parents outside our home were holding up signs: Help my Autistic Son! We Need Your Help! Please Grant Us a Miracle! Mercy! Reporters are calling our phone every two seconds. My daughter can't even use her phone. It's been inundated, too. It's only going to get worse."

"How did this happen so fast?" Lara groaned.

"I don't know," Steve said. "But Gina and I can't handle this alone. We're scared for our kids. We need help. These cops can help us."

"No, Steve. I have to set up the protocol first. Can't it wait?"

"No, Lara, it can't. My family's safety comes first. If you don't agree to this, I'm walking. Either we treat these kids today, or there are no trials."

"Fine," she relented. "They go first. But you must let me put two of my own subjects into the trial to preserve some validity to the study. Get your guys here at ten o'clock sharp."

They asked Alexis to watch over Taylor, and Dr. Jacobs arranged for a teaching assistant to ensure their safety. Alexis complained a bit until Gina stepped in and explained the need for privacy and what had happened at the house. To her credit, Lex absorbed the information readily and realized she needed to be there for her brother. Her friends could wait.

Steve and Gina arrived at one o'clock to find a waiting room full of people: five couples and five children—four boys and a teenage girl, ranging in age from five to sixteen. Hearing the commotion, Dr. Jacobs appeared and quickly ushered Steve and Gina into her office before any exchange could take place. She explained how the process would work. Steve would not know the extent of any of the children's autistic tendencies, and the results would be verified by an army of graduate assistants who had evaluated the subjects earlier that morning. "Are you ready?" she asked.

"Yes." If he was nervous, Gina couldn't detect it. "Please let Teddy go first."

"I already figured that one out." Lara smiled. "He's first. Come on." She escorted Steve to the now familiar room with the one-way glass. He looked at the mirrored wall and wondered how many people were watching.

Lara picked up on the vibe. "It will be just Gina, me, Teddy's parents, and three graduate assistants," she said. "I thought it best to keep the other parents out until we see the results. It might be too emotional," and then she added, "for all of us."

The first little boy, Teddy, was pushed into the room by his mother, who then turned and left the room without looking at Steve. He knew what she was feeling, how emotional this was for her. The little boy ignored Steve and banged on the locked door in a frenzy. He was not happy. He kicked it several times before turning his rage on Steve. Steve felt the familiar chill course through him. Teddy ran at him, screaming unintelligibly, with his little arms wind milling in a blur, a little ball of aggression.

Steve was ready for him. Taylor had gone through this same period in his short life. He caught Teddy in stride under the armpits and used his forward momentum to arrest him in a hug. He held him fiercely while the little guy sunk his teeth into the left side of his neck.

"Aaaah," Steve let out a yelp of pain. But he held on.

Inside the viewing room, Gina bolted for the door. Dr. Jacobs had anticipated her reaction and barred her entry. "Wait, please wait," she said. "You can't help him yet."

Gina spun around when she heard a woman cry out, "Oh my God! Oh my God!"

It was Teddy's mother. She was glued to the glass, tears coursing down her face. Ed, the big police officer, stood next to her, crying just as hard.

Gina looked through the glass. The little boy was sitting on the carpet next to Steve. He was obviously speaking to him. He was trying to help him up. Lara turned up the speaker volume. "Are you okay, mister? I'm sorry. I'm sorry. I didn't mean it. I'm sorry."

Steve struggled to a sitting position, clearly an effort. "I'm okay, Teddy. I just need a minute to get up. You didn't do anything wrong. Here, sit down with me for a minute."

The boy complied, holding on to Steve's big hand with his two little ones while he recuperated. He stared at Steve like he was seeing him for the first time. "That felt great," he said. "Can I hug you again?"

Steve pulled him into his arms and gently hugged the little guy. "I have a better idea; why don't you go hug your mom and dad? I think they've been waiting long enough."

Gina, Lara, Ed, and his wife, Marge, filed in. Teddy ran into his mother's arms. "Don't cry, Mom. I feel great!" The poor woman sobbed hysterically, holding on to her precious little man. Ed held them both. Then Teddy turned to his father. "Hi, Dad," he said, bringing fresh tears to his father's eyes.

"Hey, Teddy, I need a hug, too." His son hugged him for the first time. The big man melted.

Steve remained on the floor. He put up his hand to quiet Gina from speaking. Let them enjoy this moment. She sat down next to him and examined his neck where he'd been bitten—nothing, not a mark.

Dr. Jacobs tried to usher the couple out of the room with their son, but Ed was not so easily removed. "Wait, I want to see Steve," he protested.

"Ed, please, I need a moment. I'll be there in a minute. Please," Steve repeated.

Ed nodded his acquiescence through his tears and followed his family out of the room.

After they left, Lara asked, "How do you feel?"

"Better now," he said. "How's my neck?"

"There's nothing there," Gina said. "How does it feel?"

"Fine now, but it hurt when he did it."

"Can you get up?"

"Yeah, I'm good." He stood up and took a seat in the chair. "I felt the same chill, the same pinprick, maybe a little sharper this time, but it's gone away just like last time."

"Do you need to rest?" Gina asked.

Steve looked at Lara. "No, I'm fine. Let's do another one." Gina noticed he directed his answer to Lara, not her. Her lips compressed into a thin line. She walked out of the room.

Lara looked askance at Steve. He said, "She'll get over it. She's just a little worried."

Chapter 24

The next child sent into the room was the sixteen-year-old female. Steve sat quietly in his chair, purposely left ignorant of her peculiarities so the protocol would be preserved. The girl kept her focus away from Steve, much like he expected, and she walked on her tiptoes like a younger version of his son used to walk. He waited until he thought she was unafraid, and then he approached.

"Would you like a hug?" he asked.

She didn't respond or even look at him, but she stood her ground. Steve closed the distance between them in much the same way you would approach a strange dog—no sudden movements—and reached out slowly to envelop her in his arms. When she didn't flinch or protest in any way, he hugged her. She hugged him back politely.

He knew immediately what was going on. He turned to the mirror and said, "Okay, I know what you're doing, Lara. Let's move on."

The teenager gave herself away when she looked at the mirror, too. Lara opened the door. "You can tell the difference that quickly?"

"Instantly," Steve said. "There's no feeling, and besides, I've been living with an authentic version for the last thirteen years."

The girl mumbled, "Sorry," and left the room.

"Can we continue now?" Steve asked.

"Coming right up," Lara said. "Go sit down."

The next little boy was about ten years old and was comfortable, almost aloof. He stood by the door and looked at Steve as if he was a piece of the furniture. Steve had also been through that stage with Taylor, so he felt no misgivings about walking over to him. He put his arms out and asked for a hug. The boy reciprocated by gently resting his arms on Steve's shoulders in a limp embrace, and then he shuddered and grabbed hold of him for real. Steve felt the chill and then a stab of pain in his back like the last one. He hugged the boy back and then reeled with a sensation of vertigo. He almost fell but held on through sheer force of will.

"Thanks, mister, that was great," the boy said. He leaned back in Steve's arms and inspected his face. "Are you okay?"

"I'm fine, son. I just need to sit down. How are you?" Steve released the boy and sat heavily in the chair. This feeling of exhaustion was getting monotonous.

The boy dismissed the question. "I know I hurt you, mister. I could feel it."

"What did you feel?" Steve asked.

"Like a pinch, a hard one."

"Where?" Steve pressed him.

"In your back, in the middle," he said.

"You're right, son. That was a great answer. But you don't feel it anymore, do you?"

"No sir."

"See, I'm all better now. It's fine."

The boy's parents entered with Lara. Gina was conspicuously absent. The man, Gene, was one of the other cops. His son was consoling his mother as Gene approached Steve, a look of concern on his face. "Are you alright?" he asked.

"I'm fine," Steve said. "This just tuckers me out a little is all."

"You sure? You don't look so good."

"I'm fine. Go see your son."

Gene went to his family, tears in his eyes. The young boy hugged his father, his face buried in his chest. Steve heard him say, "I love you, Dad." And that did it. He was crying, too.

Steve guessed the next little boy was about seven years old. He was shy, standing just inside the closed doorway. Steve was confident, now that he'd been through this twice in one day. He approached slowly, noting the boy turning his back to him as though that simple act would isolate him from Steve. He gently placed his hands on the boy's shoulders and felt the familiar chill seep over him. He turned him around and embraced the child.

The boy stood immobile, and in an instant, he pulled Steve into a fierce embrace, his little arms wrapped around his waist. "Thank you. Oh, thank you, mister." The boy was crying. "I wanted out so bad. Thank you. Thank you."

Steve ignored the sharp pain in his back. "Out? Out of where?"

"The dark place … where I was," the boy said.

Steve held on as best he could, and when he couldn't stand any longer, he collapsed in the chair. No one entered the room this time. "Are you okay, mister? I felt that."

"What did you feel?"

"I hurt you."

"You didn't hurt me, son. I just get tired after a good hug," Steve explained.

"But I felt it. I'm not lying."

"I know. I know you're telling the truth. But it goes right away. I promise." He lifted the boy's face to his. "Look at me, son. I'm fine. It's nothing."

"You're better now?"

"Perfect, now let's get your parents in here."

Lara entered with the parents in tow. She went directly to Steve this time. "We heard the exchange. We need to talk."

"I know. Is Gina still here?"

"No, she went back to your apartment."

They watched as the parents wept in joy, holding their son in a mutual embrace. They were all crying, even the boy, which made it even harder to bear. The parents broke away and came to Steve. "Are you okay?" It was the other cop.

"I'm fine, just a little tired from all this excitement. I'm very happy for you," Steve said.

"You have no idea," the man replied. "You have no idea." He was the other friend Ed had contacted for the experiment.

"No more talking, guys," Lara said. "There are protocols to observe. There will be plenty of time to discuss this later. Sir, I need you to take your son and follow the assistant out."

The cop took one last, long look at Steve and left with his wife and son. He knew something wasn't kosher, a cop's instincts.

After they were gone, Lara said, "Are you up for one last time?"

He almost said no. He was tired, very tired. "One more and that's it for today."

"Are you sure?"

"Yes, let's get it done. I need to see my family."

Lara left and another little boy, this one about eleven or twelve, entered. He walked slowly across the room and stood in front of Steve, still in his chair. He looked over Steve's shoulder as though he were studying a painting behind him. Steve took his hands in his. "You can come in now, Lara. It's not going to work this time either."

Lara entered and the boy said, "What did I do wrong?"

"Nothing, Eric," she said. "He can tell. He can feel something. You helped us to confirm that. You were a big help. Now go to your mother. I appreciate all your efforts."

She asked Steve, "Is it that obvious to you?"

"Yes," he said, "immediately obvious."

"Can you stay and talk for a while?"

"I'd rather not. I need to lie down. Let's talk tomorrow." He rose from the chair and left without another word. He was not looking forward to seeing his wife.

Chapter 25

Steve walked into the university apartment to discover the kids were absent. Gina was waiting for him at the small kitchen table. "It's time to talk, Steve. You need to tell me everything if you expect me to go along with this."

"I know, honey. I know." He surveyed the room. "Where are the kids?"

"I sent them to the store with Patricia." Patricia was a long-term nanny they'd hired many years before as an occupational therapist. She'd transitioned into Taylor's caregiver to help keep an eye on him during his wandering stage, and she'd become an integral part of the family ever since. The truth was she couldn't bear to leave Taylor.

"Okay, then let's talk."

"I need to know what you're feeling when you do this. I saw you in pain. It appeared to get worse each time you did it."

Steve sat down next to his wife and considered how to put what he felt into words. "Gina, it felt like a pinprick the first time and pretty much the same every time after that. It was the intensity that changed. It was a little sharper each time, not appreciably so, but enough for me to notice. It doesn't hurt for long; just a few seconds and then it goes completely away. The short-lived pain is a small price to pay for the result. Don't you agree?"

"I'm not sure I do. If this pain is getting sharper, or more intense, we need to consider what the long-term ramifications might be. You didn't see what it did to you. I did."

"What do you mean?"

"You were hurt, Steve, in real pain. I can't watch that, and I don't want the kids to see it. You're their father. They won't take it well. You have to realize that."

"Honey, you saw those families. I can't very well say no."

"I'm talking about our family, Steve, not theirs. I know this new ability you've acquired is something none of us understand, but I won't allow this to continue unless you agree to monthly medical checkups, or more often if I think you need it."

"Gina, you have to realize we can't simply deny this is happening, as hard to believe as it is. Maybe there's a cure we're not seeing yet. Maybe this is the start of something that could impact the whole autistic community. We can't just stop. Dr. Jacobs is working diligently to discover how this all works. We have to give her that chance."

"I know that. I just don't want you hurt in the process. I want us to be more careful until we know how this is affecting you." She asked, "What is this chill you feel before the act, and why are you exhausted after it's over?"

"I don't know. I wanted to get back here to see you, so I put off the exit interview until tomorrow."

"I have one demand if you expect me to watch this go on and support you through the process."

"What is it?"

"You are to be monitored medically, wear some sort of monitor when you perform. I need to know more about how this is affecting your health."

"That's reasonable. I'll talk to Lara about it."

"No, we'll talk to Lara together."

"Okay, okay," Steve relented. "One good thing happened to us today, though."

"What's that?"

"I doubt we'll be getting any traffic tickets in the foreseeable future." He chuckled. "Those were some happy cops who left that room today."

"It is wonderful to witness the immediate impact it has on people; I have to admit." She paused. "You know I want Taylor to benefit, too;

which brings up another question. Why can't you try this on Taylor? Explain it to me again."

"I still don't understand it myself. It's just a feeling; no, it's more than that. I know for a certainty if I hug Taylor, he will emerge the same way the others have. But I will have lost the ability to affect any other children."

"How do you know that without trying it? What makes you so sure?"

"I can't honestly answer that. I think it's the same way I was sure something changed in me when I was struck in the mountains. I woke up that way, and I was certain of the change. Whatever message was planted in me was planted deep. I can't explain it any other way. I just know it."

"Have you shared more of this with Lara? It has to be the obvious next step for a father."

"Yes, we discussed it. You were there. I wanted to speak to you before discussing it further. Now that I have, I'll bring it up again tomorrow along with my medical tests. I promise."

"Okay, now give me a hug. I need one," Gina teased. "The kids aren't home."

"It might provoke a reaction." He laughed.

"I'm counting on it."

Chapter 26

The next morning, Steve and Gina met with Dr. Lara Jacobs. She laughed. "I was just about to insist on a medical evaluation before we continue and you solved that issue for me. Or should I say Gina solved it for us?"

It was Steve's turn to laugh. "Yes, Gina solved your problem. Are you two going to make a habit of ganging up on me?"

"Probably," Gina said.

They decided on a medical protocol for Steve going forward. He would be attached to several monitors to assess any physical impacts on his body while he performed. Medical personnel would also observe him during the process. He would undergo a physical examination after each encounter, and any changes would be noted and studied. They would also limit the trials to one child per day, or less often if warranted. Gina was mollified. Steve was pleased. He could continue with his best friend in his corner.

The next subject Steve had promised to discuss with Lara was Taylor. "I'm glad you brought this up, Steve," she said. "I was wondering all night why he was not your primary objective when you discovered this new ability."

"During my first encounter at the school with the little boy, I learned more. I knew I couldn't touch Taylor for fear of losing the ability to reach these kids. I don't know how, but I knew it for a certainty. I knew it that instant. I told Gina. I thought you would think I was coming unhinged if I told you this, but there's no other choice now. I know it deep down in a way I cannot put into words. I seem to acquire more knowledge each time I perform."

"Have you had any other revelations you haven't shared with me yet?" Steve hesitated. "I'm not sure."

Gina interrupted. "The pain is increasing. Each time he hugged a child the pain intensified and lasted a little longer. Tell her, Steve."

"It's too early to tell, Gina. I think the pain increased, but I haven't done this enough to tell if that's accurate or not. Maybe the fact that I did three in one day accounts for that."

Lara appeared concerned. "Steve, you need to be more upfront and transparent if you want me to continue working with you."

"He will," Gina answered for him. "We've already extracted that promise from him."

Lara smiled at her reply. "Now that I know who the boss is in your house, I have something to share with you."

"What?"

"Ed is in the next room. I'll let him tell you."

The big police officer entered the room on cue. He greeted them all with a hug, on the verge of tears again. "Ed, we have to get past the emotional response if we're going to be friends," Steve said with a smile.

Ed sat down, a little sheepish at his lack of emotional control. He wiped the moisture from his eyes and said, "I recruited a dozen police officers to guard your home twenty-four seven. Each of the families you helped yesterday reached out to their brotherhood on the force, and we all agreed to post an obvious police presence at your home until this issue blows over."

"Ed, I appreciate it, but that's really not necessary," Steve said.

"Yes, it is. Last night, it took four of us to prevent over a dozen attempts to invade your home. This thing has taken on a life of its own. If they find you here, the same thing is going to happen. You need to heed my advice. Your home is off limits for a while."

Steve and Gina exchanged a look of concern. They both thought of Alexis and her anticipated reaction to this news. They didn't need to compare notes to know what the other was thinking. This was getting complicated.

"Steve, listen to me. Your life, as you knew it, is over. There are news vans from all over the world camped out on your street and hundreds of parents with their autistic children in tow. They're referring to you as a miracle worker. The volunteer cops have been offered money or other favors if we tell them how to find you. They're desperate. It's only a matter of time before someone discovers your whereabouts, and then it'll start all over again. You're going to need professional help to manage this. You, too, Dr. Jacobs."

"I know, Ed. My phone has been ringing off the hook. Somehow the word got out. We tried to impress everyone with the need for discretion, but it leaked anyway. Fifteen minutes of fame is difficult to resist. There are other siblings, relatives, school officials, and God knows who else already aware of this new phenomenon. It's no longer possible to contain. It has to be managed."

"How?"

"We have a public relations department here that is quite good. I suggest we let them handle the dissemination of information at scheduled news conferences and keep ourselves isolated from that responsibility. If we get involved, all our time will be spent answering questions. This is too big, too complex for us to handle on our own."

Ed interrupted. "Dr. Jacobs, this is not a public relations issue. Now that the world knows Steve cured three autistic children here at this university, they will descend on this campus in droves. They will identify this department, if they haven't already, surround it, and wait for Steve to appear. You must understand that their children's health is their prime motivation and nothing we do will be sufficient to dissuade them from seeking a cure. I would bet there are parents and news teams on campus at this very moment. I'm concerned about getting you out of here today in one piece."

"Does anyone know we're living here on campus?" Gina asked.

"Not yet," Lara said. "But we need to prepare for that eventuality. Reporters are not dumb people. They'll figure it out soon enough."

"I'm worried about my children's safety," Gina said.

"Good," Ed commented. "That will make what I have to say easier. Now, your apartment here, and your kids, are being guarded by volunteer cops, friends of mine, and the fathers of the other two boys you cured. The chief of Campus Police has agreed to allow a few off-duty officers on campus to protect your family, but we need to be more proactive. Soon this will become an official security risk that will require a larger guard detail. If your location leaks, the results will be overwhelming for a small force. I am going to suggest we move your family today to an undisclosed location that we can defend."

"Defend?" Gina asked.

Ed took on a conciliatory tone. "Gina, your children could easily become bargaining chips. Some of these people are desperate. The might do anything. You are in the same position. I know how they feel. I've felt the same things—a cure. Think about it. Would I gladly go to prison to free my son from his? The answer is yes. And I'm a cop. You, more than anyone, know how they feel. That's all they have on their mind."

"Then I want them moved. I will not put them at risk," Steve said. "You, too, Gina. You cannot stay and put yourself at risk either."

"The hell I can't," she fired back. "Don't even start with that, Steve. We are a family. We will stay a family. If this spirals out of control, you cure our son and then the world will know you have no more superpowers. I can only take so much. You will not put our children at risk."

"Wait a minute," Ed said. "Are you saying you can't cure your own son?"

Lara answered for him. "He suspects that his ability will disappear if he hugs his own son. We were just discussing that, but I felt your message was more important at this point."

"Tell him the rest of it," Gina said.

"We think Steve is experiencing an increasing degree of pain each time he performs," Lara said. "We are going to bring in the medical department to monitor him each time before we proceed any further with our study."

"Is this for real?" Ed was incredulous.

Steve only nodded. He was afraid to speak.

"Does anyone else know this?"

"Just the people in this room," Lara said.

"You'd better hope it stays that way," Ed said.

"Why?" Steve asked.

"If the world gets wind of that one fact, your son is in grave danger of being kidnapped, or worse. You can't cure him and lose this ability if he disappears."

"Oh Lord," Steve moaned. The impact of Ed's observation hit him full force. "What are we going to do?"

"I'd like to suggest something," Ed said. "We should remove your family, all of you, to a secure location that only we know about. We need to do it now before this evening's news cycle. After this location hits the airwaves, the campus will be deluged with hopeful parents and their children. I'm worried about getting you out of this building already."

"Why?"

"Your picture was on the news last night."

Gina said, "I agree. Let's get moving and we'll discuss these other issues later. I want the kids to be safe."

"Steve, you stay here. No one outside this room knows you're here. I'll take Gina to the kids. They're already off campus with two of my men. I'll be back in twenty minutes and pick you up out back, where the trash disposal trucks are," Ed said. "It's safer if you two are moved separately. No one knows what Gina looks like. If she's seen with you, they'll connect the dots."

"You already had a plan when you walked in here?" Steve asked.

"Yes, I owe you that, that and much more. I have my son back. Nothing is going to happen to yours if I can prevent it." He rose from his seat. "Come on, Gina. We need to move quickly. I'm parked in back."

"No," Gina said. "We stay together. Put Steve in the trunk. I'll ride up front with you." Everyone was smart enough not to argue with her.

Ed and Gina exited through the rear of the building and scanned the surrounding area. There was no one in sight. They signaled Steve forward. Ed opened the trunk and Steve folded his frame into the space. Gina closed the trunk, and she and Ed got into his car without interruption. He pulled away from the structure and drove only a quarter mile across campus before they were forced to stop. The entrance and adjoining visitor's parking lot were flooded with vehicles. There were news vans, private cars, and overwhelmed campus police vehicles scattered all over the pavement. Ed could see the San Diego Police on the street, directing additional cars away from the entrance. He held his badge out the window and one of the officers forced a break in traffic so they could drive through. No one paid them the slightest attention.

"Thank goodness we got him out of there," Gina said. She craned her neck around to watch the growing crowd. "Damn!"

Ed drove south on the freeway for three exits before he ascended an exit ramp and parked on a side street. He opened the trunk. Steve hurried into the rear passenger compartment and they drove off.

Chapter 27

Ed drove them to his home, where they were reunited with their children and Patricia. Gina turned on the television to catch the news at noon. To her horror, the competition for the public's attention, and the advertising revenue that would accompany it, was in full bloom. Every channel started the news cycle with shots of the campus where the Wilsons were supposedly in residence. There were overhead shots of their home in San Diegueno, where several police cruisers blocked off public access to their street. Neighbors they had known for years were visibly upset at the onslaught of visitors, and Steve could only watch helplessly as people he'd joked with only days before expressed their frustration in being caught up in a situation, not of their making, on the local news feeds.

If there was one bright spot to all this coverage, it was its impact on Alexis. No one needed to explain to her how their life had irrevocably changed. It was right there on the screen. They were now little more than fugitives from their father's newfound notoriety. He was called a miracle worker, a saint sent from heaven, a harbinger of change, and several other sobriquets, all with tongue firmly planted in cheek. It seemed the anchors and field reporters were having a bit of fun at Steve's expense. They even suggested he had perpetrated some sort of hoax to attract attention to the "scourge of autism." Further developments would be forthcoming.

The scene at the university was even worse. Parking lots overflowed, and cars were parked on lawns or abandoned on the street, contributing to the gridlock. There was no place on campus where the students could park their cars or walk unmolested by news teams or the hundreds of parents with children in tow, asking where they could find Dr. Jacobs. Classes were canceled until further notice. The police department was out in full force, attempting to gain control of the burgeoning crowd. Lara was in hiding. Her department was shuttered. Her regular clients and their children would have to forgo their regular treatment until they were notified. News helicopters were now broadcasting live pictures of the chaos below.

Gina turned off the television. "What on earth has gotten into these people? Someone is going to get seriously hurt!"

"It's going to get worse," Ed commented. "Wait until this goes national and then international. This is nothing."

"Ed, you're not helping," Marge, his wife, said. She came into the living room, where the Wilsons had gathered. "Is this your son?"

"Yes, his name is Taylor," Gina said.

"Hi, Taylor," Marge said.

Taylor ignored her until Steve directed him to reply. "Hi," he said and pointed to her.

"He wants to know your name," Steve said. He pointed to Marge and said, "Marge."

"Hi, Marge," Taylor managed. Then he retrieved his iPod and resumed playing his favorite game, Bejeweled. His duty was done. Marge was forgotten.

Marge looked puzzled at the obvious. Taylor was still profoundly autistic, and her son was not. Ed said, "Marge, not now. I'll explain later."

Marge kept her silence. Teddy, her seven-year-old son, entered the room. He went directly to Steve and said, "Hi, Mr. Wilson."

Steve smiled down at him, then kneeled to put him at eye level and said, "Hi, Teddy. How are you?"

"Fine," he replied. "Can I have another hug?"

"Of course." Steve took the little guy in his arms and unexpectedly burst into tears. Ed and his wife followed suit, guilty in the knowledge of the anguish Steve was experiencing. They couldn't imagine the inner strength required to refrain from hugging his son and ending their own torment. Teddy held on to Steve and patted him on the back. "It's okay, Mr. Wilson," the little boy said. "It's okay."

Gina and Alexis came to his rescue. "I know, Dad, I know," Alexis said. "It's going to be fine. Teddy said so."

Steve contorted his face into a smile for his daughter and hugged her. He wiped his eyes. "Thank you, little one. Thank you." He hugged Gina and apologized to Ed and Marge. "Sorry, that happened before I knew it."

"Don't you ever apologize to us," Marge admonished. She hugged him fiercely. "We could never thank you enough. Thank you for the gift of our son. You are forever a part of this family. Never forget that."

"In that case, where's the bathroom?" Steve joked. He was clearly embarrassed by his unexpected reaction to Teddy. He wanted a moment alone to recover.

"Right this way," Ed said. He directed him to the adjoining hallway.

The Wilsons settled in for the evening. There was only one spare bedroom, so they made pallets on the floor for Alexis and Taylor to sleep on. The parents took the double bed. Ed went out to retrieve their meager belongings from the university and brought home some food to share. He reported the university was now under control after the San Diego Police Department assured the trespassers that Steve had fled the campus and then evicted them. Disappointed parents, with their special children in hand, were displayed on the midday broadcast, weeping at this recent development. No one knew where the Wilson family was.

Steve called in to his medical supply business. The call went straight to voice mail. He called Cecile's cell. She said, "I was wondering when you were going to call."

"What's going on there?" Steve asked, brushing by the formalities.

"I sent everyone home this morning. I'm going to set something up to service the customers remotely until this is over, Steve. Don't worry. Everyone here understands. We'll take care of things on this end. You take care of your family."

Cecile explained that several news teams had descended on the industrial development that housed his business and created total chaos for all the residents. Several employees had been followed home. The police had to respond to the avalanche of business park complaints caused by the intrusion of the press, which also attracted a curious public. The Wilsons' entire life had been turned upside-down; their home, their business, and the children's school had all been invaded and were now inaccessible. They were fugitives in their own town. Steve hung up, thoroughly depressed.

The evening news cycle was worse, far worse. Word had spread across the entire country in a matter of hours. International news services had accepted the baton and were openly questioning the validity of the information emanating from a small town in Southern California. "Only in America" was used as the banner headline in more than a few teaser ads. The disdain from the world's medical community was on full display. Steve was being painted as a charlatan and an impostor, and those were some of the milder terms used.

Later that evening, an enterprising reporter introduced the religious community to the new miracle worker from San Diego. The outrage from the men and women of God who ruled the airwaves, begging for money, was palpable. They railed against the false prophet who claimed to heal the sick and asked for increased donations to combat the evil designs of this latest affront to Christianity. The commentary was decidedly un-Christian. One national channel trotted out a renowned professor in religious studies who commented, "I think I'll reserve judgment until this gentleman raises the dead."

"Or maybe cures cancer?"

"Why not?"

Ed turned off the television, disgusted, and the adults hustled the children to bed. Afterward they watched the late news together, still dominated by the Wilsons' story.

They sat down at the dining room table to talk. "This has gone off the rails," Steve said. "I can't allow you to put your family in danger this way, Ed. We should find a more secure place to hide. If anyone connects Teddy's radical change to me, your family will be inundated by the press in a matter of hours."

"I know," he said. "This is only a temporary solution. We have to get you someplace safe so you can hold a secure news conference and put a stop to this madness."

"And start a riot? I'm not going to address anyone. We need a professional for that. I've already put too many people I love in the crosshairs. An appearance by me will only fan the flames."

"Steve, it's only a matter of time before the authorities and politicians get involved."

"This is none of their business," Gina said.

"It will be when they invoke public safety, the greater good. We need to get out in front of that," Ed said.

The table went silent. They were all thinking the same thing: Taylor. "I can't." Steve gave voice to his quandary. "If I do that, hug him, think of all the autistic children I might have helped and didn't. Ed, how would you feel if I had refused to help Teddy but knew I could have? I can't live with that. I can't. There has to be another way."

"How do you know that for sure?" Ed asked.

Marge stayed silent. She still wasn't clear about the reason Steve was reluctant to heal his son.

"Ed, when I hugged that first kid at the school, something powerful went through me. The certain knowledge that I was not to cure my own son, or that this ability would cease if I chose to do so, was real. That knowledge coursed through me at the exact same time the healing took place, as though I always knew this was the price I would have to pay. I pulled off the road three times to go through with it, regardless of the ramifications, but something held me back. I couldn't, at least not until I saw Gina. I had to talk to my wife first. Then, when I hugged the three kids yesterday, the feeling of foreboding grew stronger. I am certain. I know it the same way I know my heart is beating. It just is."

A shroud of silence descended on the four adults. They all knew the awful truth of his predicament, especially Ed and Marge. They had their son back. How could they deny that same opportunity to others? There had to be way.

Gina broke the silence. "Tell them the rest of it."

"What?" Marge asked.

"He gets a sharp pain whenever he heals a child. And he thinks it's getting worse. He also gets exhausted each time. He has to lie down to recuperate. You saw it, Ed. I saw it, too."

"Gina, we're not sure of that yet. I said I thought it was sharper the second time. I'm not sure," Steve protested.

"Of course not," Gina said. "You're sure you can't heal our son, but you're not sure the pain is increasing. Is that what you want me to believe?"

"I've agreed to be monitored, honey. There's not much else I can do at this point."

"Then let's go to bed," Gina replied. "We'll come up with a solution tomorrow when we're thinking more clearly."

That ended the discussion. They retired to their respective rooms, but no one slept.

Chapter 28

More trouble appeared before daylight. A news van was staked out in front of Ed's house, waiting for the sun to rise. When the first streaks of orange appeared in the east, a reporter, with a microphone in hand, rang the doorbell. Ed peeked through the eyehole and whispered to Steve, "It's happening. We've got to get out of here."

"I'll get the kids," he said.

The house phone rang. Ed ignored it, allowing it to go to voice mail. Then his cell phone buzzed. The caller ID showed the call coming from Gene, the other cop whose child participated in the first study. Ed picked up.

Gene said, "I got a news vans outside my house."

"Me, too."

"Frank called to wake me up. He has the same issue at his house."

"That was quick," Ed replied.

The doorbell rang again. Ed ignored it. "We need to get the Wilsons out of here," Ed said. "We need to call some guys in."

"Ed, listen to me. I'll get some guys over there right away, but this is not going to end here for you, me, or Frank. We're going to have to face the press at some point. The brass downtown is going to get wind of this soon, if they haven't already."

"You're right. Okay, let's get the Wilsons settled somewhere first, and then we'll talk to the captain. Let's try for a noon meeting."

"Okay, I'm on it."

Ed answered the door in a tank top and shorts. At six feet two and over two hundred pounds, he was an imposing figure. "Who are you?" he asked.

"I'm Ron Johnson of Channel Nine. We'd like to speak to you about your son."

Ed went on the offensive. "Do you know what time it is?" He invaded the hapless reporter's personal space. "Get off my porch ... now!"

The man and his videographer backed off the porch, but he did not relent. "We just want to ask a few questions, sir. Are you the father of a little autistic boy? Were you at the university yesterday?"

Ed fought for control when all he wanted to do was see how far he could pitch this cretin across his front lawn. "You've got the wrong house. I don't know what you're talking about. If you don't leave these premises right now, I will have you arrested, and I promise you won't enjoy the process. Is that clear?" He closed the door. The two men retreated to the boundary of the property, but the van remained on the street.

It took all of Gina's patience to get Taylor fed and dressed. He was fast asleep when she had to rouse him, and he was notorious for dawdling in the mornings. Any attempt to rush him would result in more sullen recalcitrance or even provoke an outburst. When the San Diego wildfires devastated their neighborhood, a reverse 911 call ordered them to evacuate. The Wilsons had to waste precious time finishing a jigsaw puzzle before Taylor would allow himself to be moved. He had to complete his task. It was one of his compulsions. They all pitched in and finished the puzzle in record time. The family remembered the predicament with a mixture of amusement and embarrassment. Gina prayed this would not be a repeat performance. Finally, after ninety minutes, she had Taylor ready to leave.

Alexis was uncharacteristically quiet throughout. Gina sensed her need to talk privately. "After we get settled, you and I will sit down and talk," she told her daughter.

Alexis nodded her acquiescence. She was already a veteran of second place.

Ed led them into the rear yard and through their neighbor's adjoining property, and they emerged on the street behind their house. A large

SUV waited at the curb. Ed introduced the family to the two off-duty cops, Joe and Tom, and they drove off.

"We booked a cottage suite at a resort in Warner Hot Springs in my name. The room is paid up for a week or until we can find a permanent location for you," Tom explained. "It will be safe for the time being. We're both on leave for the week, and we'll be staying right next door." The family endured the two-hour drive in silence.

The resort, situated in the high desert east of San Diego, was developed as a series of early California cottages spread out under massive oak trees, with parking slots next to each structure. They had a large, screened-in porch to relax on, a kitchen, dining room, and three comfortable bedrooms. There was a restaurant and a lounge on the grounds if they chose to go out for the evening. There were two gigantic swimming pools, one of which was fed from the hot springs underground that kept it at a comfortable one hundred degrees year-round. There was a golf course across the highway, tennis courts, basketball courts, horseshoe pits, and a small airport that offered glider rides or flying lessons. There was a bowling alley, a billiards room, and a video-game room dedicated to the youngsters. It was in the middle of nowhere, far from any major city, which suited the Wilsons fine. Their privacy was at a premium.

The family unpacked the clothing retrieved from the university by the cops; each child was assigned to his or her own room, and Gina and Steve settled in the master suite, complete with fireplace, minibar, and a wide-screen television. Just as Gina finished hanging up her meager collection of clothes, Alexis came into their room crying. She was carrying her laptop.

"What's the matter, Lex?" she asked.

"My laptop blew up."

"What do you mean by 'blew up'?"

Lex spun the device around so Gina could view it. "Dad, kids my age don't use e-mail anymore," she explained. "I don't use it. Now look at my e-mail. It goes on for pages. There must be hundreds, maybe thousands, of e-mails on here. How did they get my account?"

"Let me see," he said.

He scanned the e-mails and said, "Let me see your cell."

Lex handed over her phone. Steve powered it up, and it immediately began vibrating with incoming texts and calls. He scrolled through her social networking accounts. "Your e-mail address shows up on your social networks. It's been in plain sight for anyone to see. And your Facebook and Instagram accounts are flooded with messages. You haven't called or texted anyone on this, have you?"

"No, Mom told me not to."

"Good, don't contact any of your friends unless Mom or I say it's okay," he said. "Gina, please check our laptops and social networks." In all the confusion, neither parent had a spare moment to access their computers or phones and had even neglected to recharge their cells while Alexis lived on hers. Both parents' phones were plugged into the wall socket now.

"I don't have to check. Mine is on there, too." Gina opened her laptop and powered it up. "Uh-oh," she muttered. Her e-mail accounts went on for pages and pages of unopened messages from strangers. She opened Steve's private e-mail. "Yours is pretty clean compared to mine."

"I don't use social networks, except for work, and that one crashed already. I use my work e-mail almost exclusively," Steve said. "No one has my personal address."

"They do now," Gina said, looking up from her phone.

"Did you check your work addresses?" Lex asked.

"Oh, no," Steve said. "I have to contact Cecile again. This is getting out of hand." He typed a quick e-mail to his business manager and received an immediate "not in service" reply. "The system has already crashed, too late. I'll have to call her." Steve pulled both cells from the electric wall socket. He powered them up. "We have the same problem, Gina. All our inboxes are full. This is insane."

"Can we use the landline here?" Gina asked.

"Not if we want to remain anonymous. If anyone traces this number, the press will be at our doorstep within a few hours."

"How about using Joe or Tom's cell?" Lex suggested.

"Brilliant. Let's ask them."

Steve went next door and explained their predicament. He'd only gotten halfway through his tale of woe when Tom handed him a paper bag with three burner phones in it. Steve examined the cells and said, "How'd you know?"

"We're cops. Ed told us his cell was full of messages from strangers. We figured yours would be worse," Tom said.

"Thank goodness someone is thinking," Steve said. "We haven't had time to catch a breath, let alone anticipate our needs."

"No worries," Joe said. "That's why we're here. Take these to your girls. I'll bet Alexis will be glad to have her right arm back," he joked.

"You're not kidding; she'll be ecstatic. Gina, too. Thanks, guys."

Steve handed over the electronic lifelines to the delight of both women. "Remember to thank the guys next door," he said. "Their cell numbers are preprogrammed. So is Ed's."

"That will be our first call," Gina said.

"Or text," Lex added with a smirk. She was back to being a teenager, a good sign.

"I'll call Cecile for an update," Steve said. "Where's Taylor?"

"Playing Bejeweled on his iPod," Lex said. "He's fine."

Steve said, "Thanks, honey," but she was already gone.

Chapter 29

The Wilsons spent the next three days swimming, playing games together, and enjoying their anonymity. No one at the resort paid them any attention. They bought groceries with cash, and Gina provided some semblance of normalcy for Taylor by cooking his favorite meals. They played a toned-down version of tennis and basketball with Taylor, and Steve even played a round of golf using rental clubs. It was almost a vacation.

The e-mail situation continued to be a nightmare. As soon as they cleared the inbox, it filled up again. There was no use trying to use any of their accounts. The world had found them electronically. They communicated with Cecile, and concerned friends and relatives received updates through her via another private e-mail account she set up for that purpose. Steve and Cecile set up a new e-mail account that they shared. Any messages Steve needed to send to her were put in "drafts" and never sent. The recipient only had to open the drafts box to read the message and then reply in another draft. They retained their privacy that way and opened a line of communication for Lara and others to use without exposing their location to hackers hired by news organizations or private citizens with an agenda.

Steve and Gina read through hundreds of e-mail messages to gauge the measure of public interest in their whereabouts and were amazed to discover the level of desperation contained within them. "Look at this one," Gina said. "This man is offering one hundred million dollars if you'll treat his son. There are requests for interviews from all the major networks. I even have the private cell numbers of all the famous anchors, not to mention parents of autistic children who are athletes, movie stars, and famous writers."

"Does Lara have these, too?" Steve asked. "Maybe she can put these offers to good use."

"She has them all," Gina said. "I gave her access."

There were offers for books, movies, interviews, and various offers of compensation, including the one from a wealthy foreigner if only Steve would consent to see his son. There were also threats from nonbelievers, parents of autistic children, and Christian organizations, excoriating Steve for raising false hopes and promoting a hoax on Christians everywhere. After reading one e-mail that said, "You are the spawn of the devil. Go back to hell," they shut down the laptop in a state of depression. The depth of human despair and the lack of empathetic humanity were on full display together. As soon as they sent the e-mails to the trash, the box filled up again.

They watched the news on television and read about themselves on the web. To their credit, the San Diego Police Department Public Relations Office had taken the responsibility for a press conference to protect their own. None of the affected police officers appeared. A firm but polite female officer explained that three autistic children had shown remarkable progress after receiving treatments by Dr. Lara Jacobs of San Diego University. She explained the jury was still out on any lasting impact on the children and asked the public to give the families some privacy until they had concrete evidence of permanent recovery. No credit was given to the theory that a California man was responsible for their recovery. That unnamed gentleman had an autistic son who, in fact, had not shown any improvement. Interest increased exponentially as a result, the opposite of what they'd intended. It seemed the world was playing its own version of Where's Waldo; each newscast theorized a new location where the Wilson family was hiding. The most popular destination choices were outside the United States, ranging from the South Pacific to the Arctic. Steve and Gina were not amused. All of this had happened so fast. Their children were suffering the unintended consequences of Steve's newfound notoriety.

They settled the kids in bed and went to the resort lounge to talk in private. Tom stayed outside their bungalow to watch over the kids, and Joe accompanied them. He took up position at a nearby table, out of earshot. After their drinks were served, Steve said, "We can't continue living like this, honey."

"I know."

"I think I have a solution. I want your opinion."

"Go ahead."

"Since I served in the Air Force, it occurred to me that one of the most secure places on the planet is a military base. What if we could convince the federal authorities to allow us to live on base until a more permanent solution can be found?"

"Like Camp Pendleton?" she said.

"Exactly," Steve said. "They have secure transports, helicopters and jets; schools and activities for the kids; chow halls; medical facilities. It's like a self-contained little town."

"Maybe Lara could conduct her trials there, too," Gina suggested. "It could work."

"I could offer to include any military dependents with autism in the study. I would rather put these skills to use for our military men and women than anyone else, anyway."

"You could include the wealthy foreigner," Gina said. "One hundred million dollars would go a long way to fund research on autism."

They fed off each other's enthusiasm; each new suggestion was more outrageous than the previous one. Steve ordered more drinks. They were experiencing a euphoria they hadn't enjoyed in a long time. Joe was smiling at their antics—talking with their hands, laughing a little too loud. Although he couldn't hear their conversation, he didn't need to. Their body language made their upbeat mood obvious.

When they ran out of steam, Gina switched to a more serious subject. "Do you remember when you promised me one Christmas that Taylor would learn his name?"

"Yes."

"It took you over eighteen months, eighteen months of saying his name repeatedly, ten times a day, fifty times a day, a hundred times a day until I was sick of it. Every time I heard you call his name, my heart sank. What if he never learned it? What if he never came around?"

"But, he did," Steve interrupted.

"Don't talk, Steve. Let me get this out."

"Sorry."

"It was the longest eighteen months of my life. I thought you were a fool. I thought you were the supreme egotist who would never accept Taylor's autism. You had to fix it. I accepted that it was unfixable. You didn't, and I resented you for it. I couldn't stand the sound of his name coming from your lips, day after day. You wouldn't quit. You believed in him when no one else would. And when he climbed down from that playhouse and stood in front of you in response to his name, I cried. You cried, too, tears of joy for something so simple. You never stopped believing. Now it's my turn to believe in something larger than us, a spiritual connection that exists in the world we cannot see, something we can tap into. I've come around, honey. This is a wonderful adventure we're on. We'll see this through together."

"I remember something else I taught him." Steve touched his index finger to his eye, flattened his palm against his heart, and then pointed to his wife. It was the first bit of pretend sign language he taught his son, the last ritual they performed each night when Steve put him to bed. It meant "I love you."

Gina kissed him. They were one again. They had a plan. "I need one more promise from you, Steve."

"What's that?"

"You'll hug Taylor for me one day."

"I'll hug him for all of us. I promise."

"Let's head back. I want to check on the kids," Gina said.

Steve paid the tab and they left. They held hands as they strolled through the darkness. A state of euphoria had descended over them, fueled by the drinks and the hope for a solution. Tom trailed a short distance behind to allow them a measure of privacy. It was fortunate he did.

A man stepped out of the bushes next to an unoccupied cottage. "Stop right there. I have a gun. No one needs to get hurt."

Steve and Gina froze in terror. A man wearing a watch cap pulled down over his face advanced on them, a gun in his hand. Steve felt his stomach turn over in sheer terror. He stepped between his wife and the hooded assailant.

"You're coming with me," the man said. "Get moving." He gestured toward the bushes he'd appeared from.

Before he could utter another word, he felt the cold steel of a gun barrel being pressed into his neck. They heard Tom say, "Police. One move, anything at all, and you're dead."

He reached around and removed the weapon from the man. He pulled the watch cap off his head and ordered the man to kneel on the ground. He quickly cuffed his hands behind his back and searched him for any weapons. He removed his wallet and put it in his back pocket.

"It's not loaded," the man squeaked.

"Shut up," Tom ordered. He pulled him up to a standing position and steered him away from the Wilsons. He called Joe on his cell and told them what happened. Joe stayed with the children while Tom escorted his prisoner to his partner. "Go to your kids," Tom said. "I've got this."

The Wilsons hurried back to their cabin, desperate to make sure their kids were unharmed. To their relief, they found both fast asleep in their beds. The unused adrenalin evaporated, and the air went out of the balloon. Now that the immediate danger was over, Gina began to shake with fear. Steve shook, too, with rage. He wanted to hurt something, strike out at the affront to his family. He went to the door. Gina said, "No, don't leave us. Don't go!"

Steve turned. He recognized the desperation in her voice and went to her. He held her until the shaking subsided. Then she began crying softly, aware the children were asleep in the next room. Steve felt helpless, unable to defend his own family. They just stood there, holding on to one another for a long time.

An hour later, Tom knocked on the cabin door. Steve opened the door after checking to ensure it was him. Tom said, "I'm sorry that happened. We thought we were secure."

"Who is he?" Gina asked.

"A desperate father," Tom answered. "He has a ten-year-old locked down in a secure facility in Oceanside. He was going to kidnap you, Steve, and take you there to treat his son."

"Oh my God," Gina blurted. "This is insane. What are you going to do with him?"

"The sheriff is on his way. He'll be taken into custody and charged with a felony. What he did is serious."

"Do you have to?" Gina asked.

"I'm afraid so," Tom said. "It's out of my hands."

"Damn," Gina said. "Damn."

Steve said, "How did he find us?"

"He's a computer scientist. He tracked your cell phone."

"A citizen can do that?"

"He did."

"Was the gun unloaded?"

"Yes, he told the truth about that."

"Steve, tell him about Pendleton," Gina said.

Steve relayed their previous discussion regarding his plan to approach the military to protect them on base, and Tom responded with an enthusiastic endorsement. "That would be optimum," he commented. "When are you going to call?"

"First thing in the morning," he replied. "As soon as this evening's event gets out, we're no longer safe here."

As Tom turned to leave, Gina said, "And we won't be pressing charges."

Tom didn't respond to her statement. The wry look on his face said it all. He closed the door. "I'll be just outside."

Neither parent slept.

Chapter 30

Steve called the Camp Pendleton base commander's office and identified himself. He was put through to Commander Henry Brown. After pleasantries were exchanged, Commander Brown asked, "Are you the gentleman everyone's been hearing about on the news?"

"I'm afraid so," Steve answered. "And I have a very large favor to ask of you, sir. I have no one else to turn to." He explained what he needed and offered to treat as many military dependents as Dr. Jacobs would allow. He offered payment for his quarters and assured the officer his family would be on their best behavior. He promised anything. He begged him to consider all the children he would be assisting. The commander hung up with a promise to run his idea up the chain of command and have an answer by noon the following day. Steve was to call him then.

He called Lara Jacobs and told her of their plan. "Perfect, Steve. I'll call him today and add my weight to the request. You might call your congressman and ask him, too. Take advantage of your notoriety," she said.

"I'll do that. What a great suggestion!"

To his surprise, he was put through to the man immediately. After a few minutes of polite conversation, Steve related his request to the senator. He was completely supportive and promised to provide any assistance he might need. "Would you mind placing a call to the base commander?" Steve asked.

"I would be very happy to call for you," he said. "After you're settled, perhaps we could get together on the base."

"Absolutely," Steve agreed. "We would be honored."

He called Cecile to get an update on the business situation. She'd already put every one of his suggestions in place to keep the business running smoothly. All employees were using their personal cells and laptops for business, and working from home. The building was closed until further notice except for the shipping crew, who agreed to work from 11:00 p.m. until 7:00 a.m. to ship the orders. "Stay as long as you need to, Steve. We've got this covered."

He called Ed last on his new burner phone. His cell number was indeed preprogrammed into the burner cell. When he answered, Steve asked about little Teddy and was informed of his progress over the past few days. They discussed the events of the previous night, and Steve relayed his plans about moving to the base. "I can't thank you enough," Steve said. "I don't know what would have happened without Joe and Tom protecting us."

"Don't thank me, Steve. You gave us a gift we can never repay." They ended the call with a promise to get together once things fell into place.

Steve spent a nervous night praying the commander would agree to his unusual request and grant them a secure base of operations. At noon, he dialed the number. Henry answered in a tone of voice that gave him away. "We would be delighted to host you and your family for as long as it takes," he announced. "We will provide as many support personnel as required, and security will be handled by the Marines. Your family would be treated with the utmost care."

Steve almost lost it then. He hadn't realized how much stress he was under until a solution presented itself. "I can't thank you enough, sir. This is more than I could have hoped for."

"Just do the best you can for my men," he replied. "That's all I ask."

Steve hung up with the promise to arrive by 0800 the following morning. He was overwhelmed with relief when he ended the call.

By 5:00 a.m. they were on the road back to San Diego. They drove west on Highway 78 and then north on Highway 5 to the Camp Pendleton gate. The vehicle was inspected per regulations and then passed through with directions to the commander's office. Alexis was rubbernecking at each new group of soldiers they encountered. She'd never been exposed to any sort of military personnel, and now she was inundated by soldiers everywhere she looked. Taylor was playing his ubiquitous Bejeweled game, oblivious to everything outside.

Joe parked in front of the commander's office and Steve got out, accompanied by his wife, and asked Alexis to keep an eye on Taylor until he and Gina met with the commander. They entered the office and were received by a junior officer who asked them to sit while he informed his commander they had arrived.

The commander came into the waiting area to greet them. He was a tall, fit man with short, buzzed gray hair. He wore a tan office uniform, without the coat, but his tie, every button, and every crease, even his belt buckle, was perfectly aligned. The man, at almost sixty years old, was a walking advertisement for fitness, efficiency, and authority. He approached Steve and Gina with his hand outstretched. "Good morning, sir. My name is Commander Henry Brown. Good morning, ma'am."

They shook hands all around, and then Henry escorted them into his office. It was just as neat and buttoned down as the man himself. "Please take a seat," he said. Gina and Steve settled into side chairs arranged before a massive walnut desk. The American, California, and Marine Corps flags stood proudly behind the desk.

When they were comfortable, Henry said, "We are so pleased to have you as our guests on base here. This seems to be a highly unusual situation we find ourselves in. I had a lengthy discussion with the senator, who is an old friend and a military veteran. I understand you served as well, Mr. Wilson."

"Yes sir, in the Air Force, in the seventies."

"May I ask why the Air Force?"

"Two reasons, sir," Steve said, "air conditioning and wall-to-wall carpeting." It was an old joke Steve trotted out for those who experienced the horror of the battlefield. He didn't feel his service was the equal of those who put their lives on the line for their country.

"I've been in the Corps for decades, and that's the first time I've heard that one," he said, laughing. "Every man did their part back then. Were you an officer?"

"No sir, I was an airman. I used my military benefits to pay for college when I mustered out. It was more than a fair trade for someone who couldn't afford a higher education."

"Then it worked well for both parties," he said. They bantered back and forth until they had exhausted the pleasantries and then drilled down to the details of their stay. A three-bedroom home in the officers' on-base neighborhood awaited their occupancy, and a separate wing in the new base hospital had been reserved for Dr. Jacobs and her staff. Patients would be registered at the gate before they were allowed on base and escorted by a marine to each appointment. The base military police would handle security for the Wilson family. No one without a prior appointment and approval for base entry would be allowed near the family. He fully understood the desperation Steve's notoriety had produced. He'd seen far too many children stricken with the specter of autism in military families. He would offer any assistance they needed to treat as many patients as possible for as long as required.

As they were leaving the office to get settled in their new quarters, the commander shook Steve's hand and said, "I'm so pleased to learn of your willingness to treat so many military dependents, Mr. Wilson. You have my personal gratitude."

"Sir, it's the least we can do. I know from experience that it takes approximately ninety thousand dollars per year, multiplied by approximately eighty-five years of life, to treat and house autistic children into adulthood. That's $7,650,000. Not many people can afford that kind of care. We can't, and I own my own business. And if they run into additional medical challenges, the expense escalates. Unfortunately, immediate family members cannot understand how expensive and pervasive autism really is, or are unable to pitch in and help. And in some rare cases, they attempt to steal from those who cannot defend themselves. It's heartbreaking for parents to witness the selfishness and greed of relatives who are willing to take advantage of these kids, when they should be helping them instead. I will stand for them. If you would have any potential children put on a list for Dr. Jacobs, she can assess them and schedule them accordingly. There will also be some other patients entering the base, selected by the doctor, to fulfill her protocols, but your military families take precedence."

"Thank you, Mr. Wilson. I understand. The base is at your disposal. Please contact my office should you need anything."

"Thank you, sir. And please call me Steve."

"And I am Henry to you … in private, of course."

"Of course," Steve said. "One more question, please."

"Yes, Steve?"

"I expected the senator to be here. I agreed to meet with him."

"As I mentioned, he is a personal friend. He is also very smart. If this experiment goes well, he'll arrive afterward and take the credit. If it goes awry, he winds up with egg on his face. He asked me to convey his regrets and postponed your meeting to a more 'convenient' time." The commander's inflection made his opinion of political expediency obvious.

"Thank you, again, Commander."

"You're quite welcome."

Chapter 31

The home they were assigned was fully furnished, with three bedrooms, a kitchen, a dining room, a living room, and a small office. Gina arranged to have their personal items retrieved from home and brought to the base. Their cars were still parked at the university, so Lara had two students drive them to the Wilson home and put them in the garage. The Wilsons were supplied a military driver, whose son would also be one of the first subjects to be treated, and the base facilities, from groceries to recreation, were available to them. Gina arranged for Alexis to have visiting privileges for her friends when approved by one of the parents. Alexis would attend school on base. Lara's staff would tutor Taylor. He was happy wherever his family was. The concept of home ownership, or any sort of ownership, would never occur to him. The family was effectively trapped by their own celebrity.

Two days after their arrival, Steve and Gina met Lara at her offices in the base hospital. "This was a great idea, Steve," she said. They hugged like old pals. The shared experiences they'd undergone had melded them into a unit. Gina and Lara already had been on a hugging basis before his incident in the mountains. They shared a familiar embrace.

"When do you want to get started?" Gina asked.

"In a few days," Lara said. "We've decided on an every-other-day clinical trial until we are certain of the effects the event has on Steve. And I need a medical examination done on him to establish a baseline and fit him for any monitors we find appropriate. Then we will assess any potential candidates. Let's set Monday as our goal for the first trial."

"Where is the physical going to take place?" Gina asked.

"The physician is waiting next door. He is a military internal medicine specialist, and he has access to any other specialists we might need. Steve will be in the best of hands, Gina. I knew that was a priority for you. When we finish up here, Steve will go next door."

Gina smiled. "And I'll be going with him."

"Somehow I knew you were going to say that."

Steve remained silent. He knew when he was outnumbered. His wife could accomplish that feat without any assistance.

"We need to discuss how to handle the mountain of requests for interviews, treatments, and appearances. My office has been overwhelmed. We've had to switch over to a different computer network since mine crashed. My website and e-mail account are trash."

"I'm sorry, Lara. My business is in the same shape. We've had to make alternative arrangements to operate. Fortunately, I have a manager who can run the business in my absence. I'm a figurehead now. As to the interview and appearance requests, the answer is no. If it's okay with you, your office can field any requests for medical information, and the public relations office here on base has agreed to handle the news organizations."

"You don't want to do any publicity, Steve?"

"No, this is something I don't understand yet, and the stuff I've been reading about the 'miracle worker' and 'talking to God' makes me very uncomfortable. I'm not ready to address that sort of thing yet. I don't know if I ever will be."

"You could probably raise public awareness to a degree I've only dreamed of," Lara said. "It could do a lot of good."

"Tell her about the wealthy foreigner," Gina said. "He offered one hundred million dollars if Steve would 'cure' his son."

"We received that e-mail, too. I also have a list of famous athletes, Hollywood celebrities, politicians, pastors, talk show hosts, heads of state, and foreign governments who have requested a meeting with you. The list is endless. I would expect the White House will stick their nose in, just as soon as they determine you're not a crackpot who will embarrass them when you're exposed as a fraud."

"Can I avoid that? I'm not a political animal."

"You are living on a federal military facility. How do you think that happened so fast?"

That took the wind out of their sails. So far, their home life, their business, their children's education, and every aspect of their social life had been destroyed. Now the specter of a political invasion of privacy loomed over the family. Steve already knew what his wife was thinking: hug Taylor and this will be over.

They concluded their meeting, and Steve and Gina entered the examination room next door. Steve was subjected to the most rigorous physical examination he'd ever undergone. Data on every bodily function was recorded. Questions on family medical history that he could never anticipate were asked of him. Gina took care of that area. The physical invasion of his personal privacy had just begun. The psychological invasion had yet to appear, but it was just over the horizon.

Their driver, David, was waiting at the curb for them. They entered the rear compartment, silent, each lost in the complexities of their new life. Steve wanted to talk to his brother, Tim, and Mark. They were there when it happened. They would understand. They believed him. First, he needed something else. He asked their driver, "Is there a church on base?"

"Yes sir, several of them," he said. "Which denomination do you prefer?"

"The quietest one," Steve said.

"I know just the place."

They pulled up in front of a small chapel constructed of white stucco, with a mottled orange, Spanish, barrel-tiled roof. A bell tower stood sentinel over the arched front entrance. It was tiny and, best of all, deserted this afternoon.

"Will this do, sir?"

"Perfect," he said. "Honey, do you mind if I do this alone? I just need some time."

"Not at all," Gina answered. "I'll be at home with the kids."

"Thank you."

Steve entered the dark, cool interior and sat in a wooden pew in the rear of the small structure. He still said the formulaic prayers he'd learned as a child, but this visit was an attempt at his favorite spiritual game, a perfect prayer, a conversation with that perfect entity responsible for human existence. He, or she, or it didn't have a name or a description. Those were constructs designed by men for reasons Steve could only imagine. He didn't need an interpreter to speak to that higher power, nor an intermediary to confess to. He didn't need someone who claimed to speak to God to relay his message or to explain the wonders of that spiritual entity. He simply needed time alone to contemplate recent events and use his private time to express his gratitude for every aspect of his existence, even the current mess he found himself in. The focus on gratitude was the key to the "perfect prayer." He was certain of that. A perfect expression of gratitude was what he sought. He knew he would never accomplish his goal. He also knew the attempt was the goal. It was only then he felt truly at peace.

He prayed for grace. He prayed for strength. He prayed for wisdom. He prayed for his family's safety and welfare. He was scared, and he didn't want anyone to know it.

As he prepared to leave, a petite, middle-aged woman with short, curly brown hair and a great big smile appeared. She had a mop and pail with wheels attached to the bottom, and she was pushing her tools through the door. Steve turned at the noise and couldn't help smiling back at her. Her upbeat mood was infectious even at first glance.

"Oh, forgive me; I didn't know anyone was in here," she said.

"Not at all," Steve said. "I was just leaving."

"Take your time. I can come back later."

For some reason Steve could not fathom, he asked, "Who are you?"

"I'm Sister Annette, pleased to meet you."

"I'm Steve Wilson."

"I know who you are," she said. The big smile erupted again. "By now everyone knows who you are."

"You find that amusing?"

"Most things are if you let them be."

Steve found himself smiling at the odd woman. "Do you clean this chapel every day?"

"Not every day, two or three times per week. Someone has to."

"You're not paid to clean it?"

She smiled again. "No, I do it out of love, and for my peace of mind."

"You find peace while you mop?"

"I find peace in serving others. The mop is just a tool of service."

The more she talked, the more intrigued Steve became. "You found peace?"

"It found me. It will find you, too, in time."

"How could you possibly know that?"

"Because you are in service to others," she said.

"And that's the secret to peace?"

"Yes."

"That sounds so simple," Steve said.

"Most truths are," Sister Annette said.

"I wish I was as sure as you are."

Sister Annette stopped next to his pew. "Tell me something, Steve. When you pray for your own rewards, how do you feel?"

He thought for several seconds. "I'm not sure ... not really at peace, though."

"A little empty?"

He thought again. "Maybe," he ventured.

"And when you pray for others, even those you don't love, how do you feel?"

Now he took even more time. Finally, he said, "Good ... lighter inside."

"At peace is another way to say that," she commented.

Now it was Steve's turn to smile. "Sister Annette, I am pleased to make your acquaintance."

"Just Annette, if you please. If we're going to be friends, we need to stop being so formal."

"Annette, thank you. I hope we meet again."

"I'm sure we will. Have a nice day, Steve." She began to mop the tile floor.

"You, too."

Chapter 32

Steve left the chapel in a much better frame of mind. He was afraid of the future when he entered. Now he contemplated the coming days and weeks with a sense of anticipation, excitement even. He discovered he was happy. He remembered his grandmother, who was a very religious Irish Catholic, and who lived to the ripe old age of ninety-six. She always produced a smile for Steve whenever they met, and she always filled the young man's mind with the possibilities the world held for him before they parted. Now he thought he knew why he always felt good whenever they talked. He suspected his maternal grandmother was in service to him as a little boy, raising his aspirations along with his mood. He smiled even more. He didn't call David, his new driver. He walked home.

When he entered the house, it was as if the mood inspired by his new friend entered with him. Gina met him with a smile and a kiss, Alexis gave him a big hug, and Taylor looked up from his iPod and smiled. Everyone seemed excited to be settled on base. The chaos of the past several days melted away. They were a family, no matter how bizarre the circumstances. He liked the feeling.

"David told me how excited he is to have his son be part of the trials," Gina said. "He couldn't stop asking questions."

"What did you tell him?"

"That I didn't know any more than he did," she answered.

"Good, I want him to be surprised when I tell him his son is first."

"He is?"

"He is now."

Gina stared at the man she knew so well. "What happened at the chapel? Did you have another episode?" she joked.

"No, but I made a new friend, Sister Annette. She was mopping the place. We had a very simple conversation that got me thinking—thinking of you and other people in my life who have been absolute gifts. I just didn't realize it."

Gina was infected with a smile. "Well, thank you, kind sir. I was wondering when you were going to figure out how wonderful I am."

"Oh, I figured that out long ago," he said. He took her in his arms. "I should tell you that more often."

"Gross," Alexis said, coming up behind them. "Get a room."

Steve laughed and said, "You're not too old to spank, you know."

Alexis laughed back at him. "You've never spanked a child in your life. I doubt you know how."

"Game, set, and match to Alexis," Gina said. "Quit while you're still standing, Steve."

"Okay, okay, I give." He held up his hands in mock surrender. "I'm going to my office for a while. Call me if you need anything." He held his palm up to Taylor when he passed, and his son pressed his hand against his father's; they both expanded their palms until just their fingertips were touching. Taylor flexed his fingers once and then released. It was an old silly habit between them, but it somehow had far more meaning now.

As he left the room, Gina called after him, "Hey, I want to meet your new friend."

"I want you to meet her, too. You have a lot in common."

Chapter 33

Steve underwent more physical testing over the next two days while Dr. Jacobs was busy assessing each potential candidate. The commander had flown in thirty military dependents and their parents, and assigned them to temporary duty at Camp Pendleton. The military was taking care of its extended family, and Steve wholeheartedly approved. Lara fought to include several other candidates she was familiar with into the rotation to validate her prior research, and Steve suggested she include the wealthy foreigner and put the money to good use for research and intervention for those children whose parents could not afford it. She agreed to be custodian of any monies received because of treatment.

Monday arrived and Steve found himself once again in a sterile room furnished with a one-way mirror, two chairs, and a couch. Twenty-two electrodes were attached to his body and scalp where the candidates could not see them. The wires led out from behind the couch into an adjoining room behind him, where they were attached to different monitors.

He pressed Lara to make David's son, Dennis, the first candidate as a personal favor, and she agreed. Other than Dennis, Steve would not be furnished with the identity of any other candidates. Lara wanted to remove as much emotional stimuli as possible. This would be his last favor.

Steve sat on the couch and watched the little boy enter. He appeared to be about six or seven years old and sported a wild blond mop of hair and freckles. He looked at Steve, examined his surroundings, found nothing of interest, and approached. Steve remained seated and silent as Lara requested. Dennis climbed up on the leather couch and began jumping up and down as if he were on a trampoline. He ignored Steve. He'd found something that interested him far more than another human being.

He bounced for a couple of minutes until he landed on Steve's lap. Steve grabbed him under each armpit to put him back on his feet, and something came over Dennis. He stared directly into Steve's eyes and reached out for him. Steve pulled him close, and Dennis's tiny arms surrounded his neck.

No one entered the room. Steve could feel the little guy sobbing into his shoulder. He gently patted him on the back and shushed him. He ignored the pain in his back and the wave of cold that washed over him. This was too important. Steve suspected he knew the cause of his emotional outburst. He said, "It's all right, Dennis. It doesn't hurt anymore. Did that scare you?"

Dennis pulled back to peer at Steve. "Yes. Are you all right, mister?"

"I'm fine, Dennis. You can't feel it anymore, can you?"

"No."

"See, it doesn't hurt at all. I'm fine."

"That scared me," Dennis said.

Steve manufactured a laugh. "Me, too," he said. "But I'm better now. Let's call your parents in here. I'll bet they want to talk to you, too."

Lara entered the room with David and his wife, Sharon, trailing her. Little Dennis ran to his parents and was swept up into David's arms. Both parents were sobbing, and their son was holding each of them in turn to soothe them. It was a compelling scene to absorb without losing it as well. Lara ushered them out and returned to Steve.

"How are you feeling, Steve?"

"Okay, tired," he admitted.

"Did the pain increase?"

Steve hesitated, unsure of how he wanted to respond.

"This is a clinical trial, with obvious severe limitations and clouded by doubts that are emanating within the psychological community, deservedly so. I'm trying to establish a baseline here. Don't make this more difficult for me. I need the absolute truth from you," she admonished him. "You made a commitment to me. I expect you to honor it."

"The answer is yes. It was more intense. I think it lasted a little longer, too. At least it felt like it. The chill was the same as before."

"We'll have that answer once we analyze the data we collect. I wish we'd hooked you up before. I simply could not anticipate your physical response to the trials. We'll have better measurements as we continue. Then I can compare your responses to the actual data. Hopefully, this will give us a basis to predict future impacts."

"Can you unhook me?" Steve said. "I'd like to rest for a few minutes before I answer your questions."

"Of course," Lara said.

"Where's Gina?"

"She elected to stay away from the trials until we get a better handle on its impact on you."

"Did you ask her to stay away?"

"Yes," Lara replied. "I think it's best for the trials, and I think it's best for your family."

"Lara, with all due respect, you don't have the right to make decisions for my family without my input. If you want a commitment from me, I have the right to ask the same of you."

"Fair enough," she said. "It won't happen again."

Chapter 34

It took two more hours for Steve to escape the confines of the hospital lab trials. He elected to walk home because he knew David and his family needed the time to adjust to their new dynamic. He looked forward to the day he and Gina would have the same opportunity. He took a small detour to pass by the chapel, hoping his new friend might be there. He also felt the need to commune with that higher power after the episode at the hospital. He hoped it would calm his nerves and give him a respite from the incessant attention he received each time he participated in the study.

He entered the chapel and sat in the same pew. The silence enveloped him, gave him a sense of peace. The cool, dim interior relaxed him. He closed his eyes and gave in to the feeling of regeneration.

After a few minutes, he heard the front door open. He turned to the sound, and there was Sister Annette, pushing her mop and bucket inside. She wore her ever-present smile.

"How are you, Steve?"

"Fine, Sister," he said.

"Annette," she reminded him.

"Annette, how are you?"

"Fine, thank you. What did you do today?"

"I participated in a clinical trial to cure autism."

"And how did that go?"

"Great, a little boy was cured."

"Cured?" she said.

"Well, he seemed to be acting like a typical seven-year-old when I left."

"What an incredible gift!"

"Yes," Steve replied sheepishly. "The parents were gushing."

"No, I meant the gift given to you, not them. The feeling of serving others at that magnitude must be so rewarding for you. How fortunate you are!"

His confusion must have been apparent. She said, "Don't you gain an incredible feeling of gratitude each time you perform? Isn't that why you're here—to give thanks?"

Now he was embarrassed. He wanted to deflect the question, avoid the honest answer on his lips. He could not. "Annette, I didn't think of it as a gift. I guess I thought it was more of a curse."

"For heaven's sake, why?"

"All the attention has turned my life upside down. My family is in turmoil. My kids have been removed from their schools, their friends, and their home."

"And how are they handling that?"

"Remarkably well," he said. "We're as close as ever."

"So, what else is bothering you that shouldn't?"

"My business has been forced to close, and all my employees have been forced to work from their homes."

"Has your business suffered?"

"No, there's been a significant uptick in orders since this began."

"Are your employees happy?"

"Yes. Cecile, our manager, told me they're really enjoying the notoriety … and the increased commission checks."

"So that's not an issue either?"

"I guess not."

"What's the real issue then?"

He hesitated for a few moments and then admitted, "I'm scared."

"Of what?"

"I don't understand what's happening to me. I hurt each time I do this. It's getting worse. I have a strange feeling it's affecting me, shortening my life somehow."

147

"I'm sorry about the pain, but we all experience pain of one sort or another. Think of all the people afflicted with Parkinson's or Lou Gehrig's disease, the pain they endure. As to your life, each day shortens it already. That's a natural progression. And you're not guaranteed one more day, let alone a long life. And now you have a choice as to how short it becomes, don't you?"

"What do you mean?"

"If you don't perform this service, your life reverts to its original span, does it not?"

"I don't know. I guess."

"How many people do you think get that choice?"

"Not many," he said.

"None," she countered. "Steve, these issues can easily be viewed as additional gifts. Your family is closer. Your business is flourishing. From my point of view, you are blessed. You have a free will. Being happy is a choice, a conscious decision to enjoy your lot in life, no matter the circumstance."

Steve could feel his burden begin to lighten. This strange woman had that effect on him. "There is one more issue I'd like to share with you," he said.

"What is it?"

"I have this feeling … no, not a feeling. I'm certain that if I cure my own son, this ability to help others will disappear. And if I continue to perform, I'm afraid I'll become so weak that I won't have the strength to help him, too. It's a palpable, deep-down dread I can't escape. It never leaves me."

"So, you somehow have been imbued with this incredible gift to cure others, yet you don't have the faith to believe your son will benefit as well?"

"Maybe that's the price I have to pay."

"And would that be so bad? You can impact so many others with your gift, yet you pay attention to the worst thing that might happen in some indefinable future. You waste precious time worrying about an event that may never happen. Perhaps you should focus on enjoying the present instead of worrying about the future. I suspect you are choosing to be unhappy."

"Why would I do that?"

"Only you can answer that. But I can tell you that if I were to receive such a gift, I would do as much good as possible in the time allowed and enjoy every second of the process."

"You really believe you can turn off worry like a faucet?"

"I know you can. There are so many examples to choose from. There is a famous African-American woman on television who grew up through horrible violence and assault done to her person, and yet, she is wealthy, successful, and quite generous to others. She faced down her demons and continues to flourish by serving others. She even inspires others to lose weight, have their own shows, or be their own bosses. It is her service that brings happiness, not another dollar in the coffer. "There are many wealthy people all over the world who give most of their money away to others, to supply clean water to strangers in other countries, provide education for the disadvantaged, build medical wings of hospitals; the list goes on and on. Ordinary people donate body parts to help strangers to live, serve in soup kitchens, tutor young people with learning disabilities, and build homes for the poor. There are musicians and actors, athletes and doctors who donate their time and special talents to help others. All these generous individuals did not grow up in a bubble of safety and privilege. They knew pain. They knew sacrifice. And yet, here they are, giving back despite their less than ideal past.

"There are people who have given their very lives for others. Think of Father Damian and the leper colony on Molokai and Mother Teresa in India, or the grade school principal who jumped in front of a bus to save two toddlers, or a man who jumps into a lake to save a child only to drown in the attempt. You are not as special as you may think. Those others are special. Your test is yet to come. Will you serve others, or will you serve yourself?"

Steve darted his eyes to Annette at the harshness of her question and found her smiling. She radiated serenity. His challenge evaporated. He asked, "So you think all of those people didn't worry?"

"Of course, they did. But they also learned that it is a waste of precious time, your time. They learned to control it, not let it hold them prisoner. You also have that choice. We all do." Her voice became gentler. "Steve, I know you worry about Taylor—if you will have enough money to take care of him long after you're gone, if people will abuse him in your absence, if he will ever contract an illness you can't make him understand. That's only natural for a father. So, let's consider a father of an autistic child who is poor and has no resources, let alone your gift. You know he worries. And his worries probably carry more weight, are more serious than yours. Think of a homeless family with an autistic child, or one who should be institutionalized because he is a danger to himself and others. And, Steve, there are many other disabilities apart from autism that are just as debilitating to families. I don't have to list them, do I?"

Steve was feeling ashamed. He recognized the truth even when he didn't like it. "No, you don't. I guess I've been a little selfish, Annette. I'm sorry."

"And don't waste any time feeling sorry. Choose to be happy. Life is for the living. Go home and see your family. Enjoy your gifts, all of them. You'll do the right thing. I'm sure of it. Now get along with you. I have work to do here."

Steve left the chapel feeling much lighter.

Chapter 35

On Wednesday, Steve received a diminutive, twelve-year-old female, who was severely autistic. She had no speech, receptive or expressive. She acted out with frequent outbursts of violent screaming and physical attacks on her siblings. There was little doubt she would require institutionalization in a lockdown facility when she matured. When she entered the room, she avoided eye contact with Steve and immediately went to a corner and buried her nose in the juncture of the walls. Steve rose from the couch to find himself comically attached by wire to several monitors. He laughed at his dilemma and then made a funny face to the mirror by sticking his thumbs in his ears and wiggling his fingers at the onlookers. He stuck out his tongue. Then he pulled the monitors loose and approached the young girl. He spun her around and clasped her to his chest. She screamed in his ear and raked his face with jagged nails to free herself. Steve held on. The child shuddered and then pulled him close. She was sobbing. Steve held her tenderly as though she were his child. He patted her back. He soothed her with gentle whispers. "You're fine now, young lady. You're fine. Relax. It's all right."

"Are you hurt?" she asked in a barely audible voice.

"No, I'm fine. We just had to get past your fear." He didn't have any idea why he said it, why he knew it to be true.

"There are no marks on your face." She was peering at him as though she were a dermatologist searching for blemishes.

"See, you didn't hurt me at all."

"But I felt it."

"You felt yourself taking away my pain. That's all," he replied. "Thank you."

"You don't feel pain?"

"Not a bit," he lied. "Now why don't you go see your family?"

She hugged him this time. "Thank you for releasing me."

"What do you mean by 'releasing' you?"

"It's scary being stuck inside your mind. There was so much I wanted to tell my mom and dad, and I didn't know how to say it. Now I can." The young girl was positively beaming. "Thank you, mister. This is the best thing that's ever happened to me."

"You're welcome. Now go." Steve was having trouble maintaining any semblance of dignity. He could feel the tears forming.

As soon as she left the room, Steve collapsed on the floor. Lara rushed in, along with a military physician, Dr. Barnes. They helped him to the couch. Barnes took his pulse and, detecting no immediate danger, began quickly reattaching the monitors in hopes of capturing any residual data.

Lara asked, "How do you feel?"

"Great," Steve said, "great. That one was worth it." He wiped his eyes with the back of his hands.

Lara stared at him curiously. "You know what I mean, Steve. Quit screwing around. You took off the monitors. We have no data to examine."

"I won't lie. That one hurt more than the others."

"How? In what way?" Dr. Barnes asked.

"Like the difference between being punched by a five-year-old and a thirty-year-old. Yeah, that's a perfect analogy." Steve was quite satisfied with his answer, almost proud.

"I wished we'd captured that data," Dr. Barnes said.

"You got nothing?" Lara asked.

"Nothing," he confirmed, "a complete blank."

"Steve, you cannot remove those monitors for any reason," Lara said. "The data may save others in the future."

"Do you mean when I'm no longer around?"

"What? What did you say? Why would you say that?"

"I don't know. It just came out."

"I wouldn't repeat that in front of Gina. She'll cancel this whole study."

"Nah," he said. "She knows I have to do this."

"Why did you say you had to get past her fear?"

"Did I say that?"

"Yes."

"Then I must have felt it. She was violent, wasn't she?"

"How could you possibly know that?"

"I don't know. I just do."

"Think about it, Steve. It's important."

"I sensed she lashed out at others out of an unreasonable fear, not aggression. I knew it the same way I would know it if it were me."

The two doctors exchanged a glance. "There's some sort of transference occurring here," Lara said. "Something I don't understand."

"Welcome to my world," Steve teased.

"You're not funny, Steve."

"Yes, I am, Lara. Admit it."

"Why are you so happy? You just collapsed on the floor."

"Because I choose to be." He laughed.

It took two more hours of physical examinations before Dr. Barnes released him. Steve walked home and stopped by the chapel. He stayed for an hour. He contemplated his gift and the happiness it brought to others. He was content. Sister Annette did not appear.

When he walked in the door of their base home, Gina asked, "Are you going to walk home each time, or are you going to have David drive you?"

"I like to walk. I like to stop by the chapel on the way home, and I don't want him to have to wait for me. Besides, I'll bet he's going through a major adjustment at home."

She smiled at her husband. "We can get another driver, you know. I'm sure Commander Brown would authorize it."

"No, I like walking. Where's Alexis?"

"At the bowling alley with two of her friends," Gina said. "I arranged a playdate with Lindsey and Alyssa."

"They're on base?"

"Yeah, it seems Alexis is famous among her friends. There's no shortage of requests to visit."

"Good, I want her to enjoy this experience," he said. "Where's Taylor?"

"At the playground with Patricia," she answered.

"We're all alone?"

"Yes," she said.

"Good, let's enjoy the experience," Steve wiggled his eyebrows to imitate a lecher.

"Come here, you fool."

Chapter 36

Three months later, Gina informed Steve they would be visiting Lara and Dr. Barnes together. She drove him to the base hospital, and they were received in Lara's office. No one else was present.

"What's the big mystery?" Steve asked.

Lara fielded the question. "We thought it would be prudent to have a sit-down with both of you before we continue our studies."

"Why?"

Lara said, "Have you noticed you've been losing weight?"

"Yes, a little. My pants are a bit looser. But I've been walking every day. I should hope to lose some weight."

"Fifteen pounds in three months, Steve?" Gina said. "You can remove your trousers without unbuttoning them. I've seen you."

"Well, we increased the frequency to every day this month. Maybe that's the cause," Steve said.

Dr. Barnes said, "Your EKG shows the intensity and duration of pain to be increasing as well. The graph looks like the Dow Jones on its most volatile day. They didn't peak that precipitously last month. I think we should dial back the trials until we have some clarity as to how this affects you."

"That's not necessary."

Now it was Gina's turn. "It's not just your decision, Steve. This affects the whole family. Even Alexis, a myopic teenager, asked if you were all right."

"And I'm a doctor. I took an oath to do no harm. I may refuse to continue," Dr. Barnes said. "You've returned fifty-seven children to normalcy so far, and we're no closer to understanding this enigma than we were before we started."

"Maybe we're not supposed to," Steve said.

"You need a break, Steve. I'm not going to stand by and let you do this," Gina said. "Please stop for at least a week. Then we'll see how things are going."

"I could use a break, too," Lara added. "Two weeks."

"Me, too," Dr. Barnes said.

Steve scanned the room. "You decided this before you called this meeting."

"That's right, honey. And that's exactly what we're going to do," Gina said.

"What am I supposed to do for two weeks?" Steve complained. "I can't go anywhere without causing a commotion. I haven't left the base in three months."

"Get some rest, recuperate, gain some weight back," Lara suggested.

Steve surveyed the room. "Is there any way we could travel, leave the base for a vacation?" He knew he couldn't just exist within the confines of the military base, even if it had all the distractions of a small city.

"There is still a great deal of attention being paid to your situation. We receive daily requests from affected parents, developmental specialists, news organizations, religious affiliations, and assorted fringe groups," Lara explained. "We sequester each family you've affected and explain the need for discretion, but you have to understand that each of these children have relatives, friends, and siblings involved. There is no way to hide the results. Once people begin to talk, news organizations get wind of their involvement and then you have another news cycle to reinvigorate the discussion. If you're discovered off base or recognized, the results could be scary, dangerous even."

"Maybe I should start listening to the news again," Steve said. "Gina and I decided it would be better for the kids if we eliminated any television news until we can leave here."

Gina and Lara exchanged a look of bemusement. Steve caught it. "What?" he asked.

"Do you really think Alexis is not aware of your notoriety, that she doesn't have access to the web? Really, Steve, do you live in an alternative universe?"

"I thought we restricted access to her computer and her social media."

"First," Gina began, "Alexis, and most kids her age, don't use computers anymore. Her cell is her computer for all intents and purposes. Her laptop is useless as soon as anyone acquires her address. Her phone has to be exchanged every week or so, since reporters have managed to acquire her numbers as fast as we change them. Her Facebook and Instagram accounts have been trolled. She's slowly being isolated from her world by your fame, even her electronic world. And some of the posts left on her social media are disgusting."

"What do you mean? Why didn't you tell me?"

"And what good would that do? You're even more isolated than she is, or me. Outsiders have approached many of the soldiers on this base and offered money or less savory rewards to bring them on base. They had to announce a Commander's Call to address the situation. No one on base is to acknowledge your presence, ever."

"Tell me about the posts on Alexis's social media."

"You can read them for yourself if you like, but I wouldn't recommend it. They refer to you as everything from a 'miracle worker' to the 'antichrist.' There are people calling for your arrest as a charlatan, others who want to become members of your new church, and still more who want to go to your Las Vegas premiere show. You have requests for interviews from politicians, celebrities, movie producers, news organizations, ordinary people, and, oh yeah, your new fan club." Gina was exasperated.

"My fan club? I thought we agreed you and I would not listen to this crap," Steve said.

"We have children, Steve. Do you really think it's a good idea to pretend Alexis is not aware of all this, that I shouldn't monitor what is happening to her? She gets requests for intervention on someone's behalf every day. And I haven't even mentioned the offers I've received if I could convince you to grant an audience. You'd love those."

Lara broke into the familial discussion. "Look, we're coming up on the holidays. I need to take two weeks off to correlate this data into something usable. I have several grad students who have been involved since the inception of these trials. I need to spend some time with them, too. Dr. Barnes has other responsibilities as well. He's been working double time since he came on board to perform his regular duties and help us out. Your family needs some down time, too. Give us all a break, Steve. This isn't just about you."

Gina said, "If we give it some thought, I bet we can come up with a creative solution to our isolation—use a disguise, private air travel, something to keep us from going stir crazy."

Steve perked up at the suggestion. "Okay, honey, I get it. I apologize to all of you. I just haven't been thinking clearly."

"I can't imagine why." Dr. Barnes laughed.

"Let's figure out a way to have a little vacation, Gina, get away for a while like we did at Warner Hot Springs," Steve suggested.

"I doubt Warner Hot Springs will welcome us back. They've had our former room booked for the foreseeable future, and vacationers from all over the world have it booked up for years to come. They think it's a religious shrine or something. The locals are not at all pleased with the congestion."

Steve shook his head ruefully.

Gina said, "Don't worry, honey. We'll figure it out."

"Okay, two weeks it is," Steve said. "Gina, do you mind if I walk home from here?"

"No, of course not," she said." Take your time."

"Thanks, guys," Steve said. "See you in two weeks." He walked out without a backward glance.

Chapter 37

Steve walked to the chapel. He needed some time to think about all this. He hadn't seen Sister Annette in over two months, and he wondered where she had gone. He'd visited the chapel on a regular basis, three or four times a week, but she hadn't returned in all that time. He had no idea where she lived, if it was on base or off. In fact, he didn't know much about her at all.

He entered the chapel and took his customary seat in the rear of the small enclave. He knelt and rested his butt on the bench behind him, and dropped his head on his hands to rest on the pew in front of him—a classic Catholic pose. He was mentally and emotionally exhausted. He hadn't told Gina how tired he really was for fear she would put a stop to his daily treatments of the children. And now she had, despite his dissembling tactics.

The sound of the door opening broke his reverie. Then the familiar squeak and bump of the bucket wheels being pushed over the Mexican tile caused him to pop his head up and turn. Sister Annette flashed her brilliant smile at him once more. The twinkle in her eyes conveyed pleasure at finding him there before she uttered a word. Strangely, he felt refreshed.

"Hello, Steve. How are you?" she asked.

"Fine, Sister, I mean Annette." He paused. "And, how are you?"

"I'm feeling great." She pushed her bucket with the mop handle down the aisle until she was abreast of Steve. She stared at him. "But you seem to be a little off kilter. Have you lost some weight?"

"A little," he said.

"Are you still worrying? Is that the cause of the weight loss?"

"No, Annette, not at all. You helped me to be more aware when I fall into that trap. It's the trials that take a little out of me each time," he explained.

"So, your suspicions about the treatment's impact on you are real?" Annette asked.

"You remembered."

"Of course, Steve," she replied. "Has the pain increased, too?"

This was the only person he could be completely honest with. She had no agenda. "Yes, it has. It's sharper now, lasts longer each time, and is moving around my body. It seems to have moved into the front of my torso as well. It's more generalized like it hurts all over instead of just in one location. It's deeper, too."

"Is it bearable?"

"Yes, it just takes more time to recover now." He hesitated for a beat and then said, "Annette, I need to talk to someone in the strictest confidence."

"Then go ahead and talk," she said. "No one will ever hear of this conversation."

Steve took a moment to consider the import of what he was about to say. "Each time I perform this service, my life is being shortened. I know it now. I feel it the same way I've felt everything else that's happened to me."

"So, what you suspected is indeed true? And this worries you even more about curing Taylor, the timing of it?"

"Exactly," he said. She knew! She understood! He continued, "There's more, Annette. When I hug these kids, I feel what happened to them, how they were treated. I experience it myself."

"What do you mean?"

"Of the fifty-seven children I've met, most have been treated well. Some have not. I feel their pain when they were spanked, pinched, or even slapped. I feel the blow just as they did. Some have been put through much worse—abuse of the worst kind, things I can't repeat, dark things." He was very near tears.

Annette laid a hand on his shoulder. She said nothing. Her touch spoke volumes. He was not alone. His spirit began to rise again. She had that amazing effect on him.

After a minute passed, she said, "You've received an incredible gift. With it has come a price. Will you accept all of it or just the good part? Did you accept your son but not his disability? You don't get to choose which parts of life you accept and which you don't. You don't have that power. You accept life. You deal with it, all of it. There are many people in this world dealing with a terminal illness. You're not special. How you handle it may be special one day. That's up to you. What will you choose?"

Steve ignored the comment. "I don't think my wife is going to accept much more of this. They canceled the trials for two weeks. They're concerned about my weight loss. We're trying to figure out how to go on some sort of vacation without anyone discovering our whereabouts."

"That's an easy fix," Annette said.

"How?"

"Contact the base commander. There are military bases all over the world. Pick one. Hawaii is an obvious one. Spend Christmas there."

"That's a great idea!" Steve said.

"Of course, it is." Annette laughed. "Why else would I suggest it?"

"You're too much, Annette. You really lift my spirits."

"All part of the service," she said.

Steve hesitated. He had some questions he wanted to ask Annette but didn't feel he had the right to invade her privacy. He said, "Annette, can I ask you a personal question?"

"I can't see why not."

"Why did you become a nun?"

"That's easy, to serve others," she said.

"Why are you a Catholic nun? How did you choose?"

"I suspect, like you, because I was raised as a Catholic. And I'm a woman, so the next step was obvious. Why do you ask?"

"It's an area of my life—faith, I mean—that I have the most trouble with," Steve said. "The rituals of the Church don't do much for me anymore. I've had misgivings ever since my incident. I haven't attended Mass in a very long time. It doesn't feel authentic to me anymore."

"You're having a crisis of faith?"

"Yes."

"Good, you should question any religion."

"Really? Why?"

"Religions are formed by men for control and power. They are strictly paternal organizations. I'm a woman and, as such, treated unequally within my church by doctrine, simply because I'm a woman. I have a crisis of faith every day."

"And yet, here you are," Steve said. "Why?"

"I believe I was put on this earth to serve others. It pleases me. It gives me peace. The Catholic Church, for me, is a tool I use to serve others. My church is not perfect. I simply accept the bad with the good. I move forward."

"You don't believe the Catholic Church is the only way to heaven?"

"Steve, do you mind if I sit down? This is going to be a long discussion."

"Please do," he said. Steve slid over in the pew to accommodate her.

"I believe the Catholic Church is one avenue to heaven, if you believe in heaven as a physical space. And so are many other faiths. The only requirement in my mind, at least, is that you serve others in some capacity and treat your fellow man the same way you wish to be treated. All religions are based on redemption. They promise the salvation of your immortal soul, a place in the afterlife. If you do as they instruct, you will be saved. Over the centuries, religions have enforced their constructs by torture, murder, rape, and war. I doubt the higher power that each of these religions prays to would condone these heinous acts perpetrated upon innocents. The Catholic Church tortured nonbelievers into submission during the Inquisition, excluded women from positions of power, and committed egregious acts upon innocent children. Protestants burned women at the stake as witches or heretics in the name of their God. Christian ministers tell old widows to place their hand on their television and pray with them and their illnesses will be healed—and then send the last of their Social Security check to them as recompense. Purported purveyors of Islam claim that bombing innocent people, torture, rape, enslavement, sexual abuse of children, beheadings, crucifixion, and burning captives alive are rightful exercises of their religion."

Steve noticed she was not smiling anymore.

"None of these acts are true expressions of God's will or that higher spirit we claim to worship. The largest gatherings of hypocrites in the world can be found in houses of worship on their holy days. And if a true god were to approve of these unspeakable acts as methods to enforce his validation, I would give up now. He, or she, or it does not. I am certain of that. In fact, I believe there is a special place in hell for those who prey on the helpless in the name of God."

Annette took a moment to impress her next statement. "I believe all religions, or disciplines, can contribute to the creation of wonderful, giving, caring human beings, but they are not a prerequisite. The act of prayer is very like meditation, or serious, honest introspection. It should be deeply personal. The act does not bring God closer to us; it brings us closer to God. It improves us. We get connected to something greater than ourselves. We are not the center of the universe in that moment; our God is."

"I'm glad you said that," Steve commented.

"Why?"

"Because the two greatest Christians I've ever met were Buddhists."

"Hmmm ... who were they?" Annette asked.

"One was my father-in-law. The other was a teacher."

"Point taken," she said.

"And why do you question heaven as a place?" Steve asked.

"You told me about your 'incident' in the mountains. You told me how safe, serene, comfortable, and peaceful you felt in that moment. I couldn't imagine a better feeling. Perhaps heaven is a feeling, a state of being, and not a place. Perhaps when you're connected to your true purpose in life, you're already in heaven. I'm not smart enough to prove these things. I simply have faith in my own beliefs, not those of others. The journey to salvation is a personal one. You have the right to your own beliefs. Trust them. They were a gift you were given."

"I wish I had your confidence," Steve said.

"I'm not that confident, Steve. I question my faith every day," she admitted. "Now let me ask you a question. How do you feel after you've treated an autistic child?"

"Incredibly happy," he said. "When I see that veil of confusion lift from the children, I get a high I can't describe. When I see the tears of grown men and women flow without shame, I am so thrilled inside, I can't explain it." He was smiling as he talked.

"And how do you feel when you think of your son, Taylor, the child you can't help?"

"Terribly depressed, angry—so angry I can't dwell on it. I want to break something. I want to fix him so badly."

"But he's given you so many gifts just as he is."

"What do you mean?"

"I'm sure it takes a great deal of humility to admit you produced an imperfect child or to remain calm when others are not tolerant of his behaviors. I'll bet it takes an inhuman amount of patience to wait for seconds or minutes for him to answer a simple question, such as 'How are you?' over so many years, or to wait while he attempts to ask for something. It must be humbling to wipe his bum, or brush his teeth, or help him bathe, when he's practically an adult. It must take a great deal of restraint to refrain from retaliating when he bites, kicks, or pinches you, or screams in your face. I can't imagine the endurance required of you and Gina over the last thirteen years to wait for him to go to sleep so you can finally rest, or to teach him simple acts like buttoning his shirt, zipping his pants, or tying his shoelaces."

"That one only took seven years, but he's so proud of himself when he ties his pajama strings; he still shows it to me every night." Steve smiled at the thought.

"And how does that make you feel?"

"Very happy," Steve admitted. "I'm just as proud as the father whose boy scored the winning touchdown. The obvious sense of pride and achievement on his face is priceless."

"So, these things make you happy?"

"Of course," he said.

"Then Taylor has made you a better person?"

"I guess."

"You guess?" Annette gave him a look. "If you brought the most famous person in the world to meet Taylor, what would he do?"

"Nothing, fame means nothing to him. Money, fame, notoriety have no meaning in his world."

"Then he would ignore them?"

"Most likely," Steve admitted.

"And yet he responds to you when you walk into the room," Annette continued.

"I'm his father."

"Yes, but you represent so much more to him," she countered. "You represent love, kindness, safety. Don't you get it? Taylor will respond only to the best attributes human beings have to offer, not the false promise of fame or wealth."

Steve felt shame burning his face crimson. He looked directly at Annette. "I should have said I know, not I guess."

"Yes, you should have. Now go home and enjoy the gift of Taylor, your only son. I've work to do."

Steve wanted to reach out and embrace this wonderful woman, but he knew he shouldn't. When he was at his lowest, she turned him around with little effort. He rose and smiled at her, then left her sitting there. He turned as he opened the door. "To be honest with you, Annette, Gina does all the heavy lifting."

"I already knew that. She's a woman."

Chapter 38

Commander Brown summoned Steve to his office the following morning. Steve was concerned the other shoe had dropped, and he would be required to have an audience with some politician to compensate for the use of the base as a sanctuary. He was admitted to the office, where he found two other officers sitting before the commander's desk. An empty chair was beside them.

The commander shook his hand, introduced him to the other two officers, Dale and Richard, and then asked him to be seated. "These gentlemen are pilots, the very best in the world, Steve. They have friends whose children you've treated. They are flying from Miramar Naval Air Base to Barber's Point Naval Air Station on Oahu tomorrow at oh-eight-hundred. Their plane, a military version of a civilian Gulfstream, is empty. They have requested your family accompany them to Hawaii."

Steve blurted, "You're kidding!"

"No sir, I'm not."

"I was just talking about this with a friend, and now it's being offered out of nowhere. Did someone else suggest this to you?" Steve asked.

"These two gentlemen here suggested it, and I endorse it wholeheartedly," Commander Brown said.

"What an odd coincidence," Steve replied. "This could not have come at a better time. My family is at the end of their rope." He was not about to challenge the commander's reply. He would keep his suspicions to himself.

"Good, I've already arranged quarters for you and your family on base in Oahu. You have an oceanfront bungalow waiting for you over the holiday. Enjoy your Christmas. Several of my soldiers are having their first Christmas unencumbered by autism because of you. This is our way of saying thank you."

"Thank you, sir. Gentlemen, thank you. This is an incredible gift." He stood and shook hands with each of them.

"You're welcome, Steve," Commander Brown said. "Now go tell your family to pack their bathing suits."

Steve practically ran home. He knew Annette had something to do with this sudden windfall. He'd thank her when he returned.

The flight from San Diego to Oahu took five hours and ten minutes. The military plane was luxurious, outfitted for dignitaries and senior government officials. A steward prepared breakfast for them. There were video games on a flat screen for Taylor, and his favorite snacks were already on board. There was a selection of teen fashion magazines and DVDs and a laptop for Alexis to use during the flight. Everything they could possibly want had been anticipated and stowed for their use. Steve and Gina suspected Dr. Jacobs had some input as to Taylor's needs. They held hands as they deplaned in Hawaii.

A senior officer greeted them at the bottom of the retractable stairs. "Welcome to Hawaii, sir," he said. "Your luggage and personal effects will be taken to your bungalow and stowed for you. Please follow me." The family was driven in a sedan to their quarters across the base. It was a comfortable three-bedroom bungalow situated directly on the west-facing beach. Taylor ran out of the little house as soon as he spied the water. Steve ran after him, laughing. Gina and Alexis trailed behind. They were laughing, too.

"I remember when you had to put him on your shoulders for twenty minutes before he calmed down and wasn't afraid of the noise the surf makes," Alexis said. "Now you can't keep him out of the water."

"Yeah, he used to block his ears with his thumbs to make the sound disappear. Now it's a siren call to the sea." He hugged his daughter.

Gina chimed in. "And every time he ran into the ocean, we had to run after him to stop him from swimming out beyond the surf."

"Until we realized he swam better than any of us. He would just float out on the receding waves and let the swell bring him back. I remember seeing half the kids on the beach in Maui trying to imitate him." Steve laughed at the memory. Taylor would relax in the water off Kaanapali Beach and let the currents maneuver his inert body, as though it was a raft, out from the sand and back again. It took Steve a week before he trusted his son to his own devices. The joke was that if he washed out to sea, he wouldn't drown. He didn't know how. They'd probably find him on Lanai somewhere.

The officer approached the giddy family. He was smiling, too. "Here are your keys. Your bags are stowed, and there's food in the pantry." He handed Gina his card. "Please call me if you need anything we haven't thought of. There are maps of the base in the kitchen and a car in the garage. The base is yours." He left them on the beach and drove away.

The Wilsons celebrated Christmas on Oahu in perfect seventy-eight-degree weather. They attended Christmas Eve Mass with Steve at five o'clock and then enjoyed a superb meal at a beachside officers' mess afterward. They swam every day, snorkeled, went paddle boarding, and even surfed the small break in front of their temporary home. They acted as a family unit again, without the complications they experienced on the mainland. No one knew who they were or why they were on base. They were tanned, rested, and ready to resume their former duties in San Diego when New Year's Eve rolled around. Alexis volunteered to watch over Taylor while Steve and Gina went out for dinner.

Once again, they were seated at the perfect table, centered on the oceanfront, as the sun put on a spectacular display just for them. Beams of light pierced the billowing clouds, illuminating them in shades of peach, orange, and yellow. Soon the colors morphed into reds and purples and finally deep grays, outlined in fading blue. The stars insinuated their distant, lantern-like presence into the tableau by gradually piercing the growing darkness and producing a magical ambience the couple could practically feel.

They were sharing their first sip of wine when Gina joked, "Hey, we're having dinner in Hawaii and you don't have to get up and walk Taylor around while Lex and I finish our meal alone."

That inspired Steve to tell a story of his own. "Do you remember Dr. Newton and his son, Kelly, the tall skinny African-American kid?"

"I remember when we met Kelly and him," Gina said. "You were staring at his son in Baskin-Robbins, and when you saw the father staring at you, you got a little nervous."

"You got that right. When a six-foot-nine, 250-pound man gives you the evil eye, you should get nervous."

"Well, he melted when you went over and told him we had the same model at home."

"And you invited him and Dr. McCormack to bring their families over for Christmas drinks, and we told our most embarrassing stories to one another. That was a brilliant move," Steve said.

"Yeah, I remember laughing and crying at the same time. It made me realize we weren't alone. Other families were dealing with the same issues, some more serious than ours."

"And Kelly and Taylor spent the next several years in school together. It's a shame about the divorce."

"It can happen to the best of couples. That's a lot of stress," Gina said. "Why bring that up now?"

"It reminded me of something special: you. Did I tell you I love you today?"

"Hey, that's your line for Alexis. You're not allowed to use it on me."

"Then here's a different one." Steve lifted his glass. "Here's to the best mother a child could hope for and the best wife and partner a man could hope for. I just don't know how you do it day after day, week after week, year after year. You really are an incredible human being. I probably won't trade you in for a newer model for a few more years yet."

"You think?"

"I think."

Chapter 39

The return trip to San Diego was just as delightful as the flight out. They landed at Miramar on January 2 and were driven by van to Camp Pendleton. Gina got everyone situated in their home again, and Steve went to the chapel in hopes of finding Sister Annette to thank her. He knelt in his regular pew and said a prayer of gratitude. While in Oahu, he discovered a book by Wayne Dyer in the bungalow. On the back cover was a prayer attributed to Saint Francis of Assisi. He wanted to share his discovery with Sister Annette. He thought she would appreciate his find because it related so well to their prior discussions. He closed his eyes and recited,

Lord, let me be an instrument of Thy peace.

Where there is hatred, let me sow love;

Where there is injury, pardon;

Where there is doubt, faith;

Where there is despair, light;

Where there is sadness; joy;

O Divine Master, grant that I may not so much seek

To be consoled as to console;

To be understood as to understand;

To be loved as to love;

For it is in giving that we receive;

It is in pardoning that we are pardoned;

It is in dying to self that we are born to eternal life.

He stayed there for an hour, but Sister Annette did not appear. He was disappointed but hopeful he would be able to share his find with her soon. He returned home.

When Steve came through the door, Gina said, "Lara called. She wants to meet with us tomorrow at eight a.m."

"Good, I want to get started again."

"This is just a meeting before we restart the program. You'll go through another physical, and then she wants to sit down with us and Dr. Barnes first."

"Okay, I suppose that's best."

The following morning, Steve and Gina reported to the hospital and Steve was put through his physical. That lasted the entire morning, so Gina and he had lunch in the hospital cafeteria and then returned to Lara's office. Lara and Dr. Barnes were already seated at a conference table when they entered.

"How did I do?" Steve asked.

"Pretty good for a sixty-year-old man," Dr. Barnes said.

"Ha-ha," Steve replied. "I'm nowhere near sixty."

"The results of your tests say you are."

"What are you talking about?" Steve said.

"Your blood panels, urinary panels, liver, kidney, lung, and heart functions all correlate with a man much older than your present forty-three years. Your weight is twenty pounds lighter than when we began these trials, and your recovery times from your stress tests have increased substantially. I think that about covers it," he said.

"And what does all that mean?" Steve said.

"It means you're aging at a greater rate than anything I've ever witnessed. Our theory is that, if you continue, you're writing your own death certificate."

"What? That's not possible. Is it?"

Lara insinuated herself into the conversation. "Steve, you've known this all along, haven't you? The children you've treated all have conveyed to us they felt you being injured during their treatment. You said yourself that you felt the pain increasing along with the duration. You know exactly what I'm talking about. Don't deny it."

"That doesn't mean I'm dying," Steve protested. "It doesn't prove anything."

"Steve, if you love me, I'm asking you to stop. The children need their father, and I need my husband back. You can experiment on Taylor and then it's over," Gina said.

"Honey, I love you. You know I do. Please don't ask me to quit this yet. There are so many more children I can help. If I hug Taylor, I won't be able to help anyone else. I know it."

"You can't possibly know that. And you've already helped five dozen kids. It's Taylor's turn. And look at you. Your hair is gray, you don't hear so well anymore, and you move slower. Quit pretending. It's not working."

Steve covered his face with his hands. He rubbed them back and forth as if the movement would stop this madness. After a few moments, he looked at each of them in turn. "I can't promise you I'll stop. I need to think about this for a while, honey. Just give me a little time, okay?"

Gina relented. "Okay, Steve, one week. Then we move forward, one way or another."

"What does that mean?"

"Do you think I'm going to sit by and watch you kill yourself? Do you think I'm going to allow our children to watch that go on? No, I won't, Steve. I will not." Gina got up and exited the room, slamming the door so hard the wall rattled behind her.

Steve said, "Sorry about that."

"Don't apologize to us," Lara said. "We agree with her."

Lara and Dr. Barnes got up and left the room together without another word.

Steve was alone.

Chapter 40

Steve left Lara's office and began walking home. He knew they were right. He was tired, more tired than he'd ever felt. And his hair had turned gray—not too much, just some streaks around the temples, a little on top. Gina was right. He could take off his pants without unbuttoning them. He was now at his high school weight, probably not good either. He trudged ahead.

He thought of the prayer he'd read in Oahu. It was a service prayer, intended for him. He thought it was a reminder of his duty to all those children he could help. And that last line about "dying to self" seemed especially appropriate. Without conscious thought, he headed to the little chapel in hopes of finding Sister Annette. She always elicited the correct solution from him as though she had a special lens that enabled her to see him clearly.

He spent an hour sitting alone in the dim interior. It seemed especially dark this time, as if the tiny building sensed his forlorn mood and responded accordingly. Annette did not appear, pushing her bucket and mop, nor did the confines of the chapel lift his spirits. He finally gave up and left. He didn't want to go home and face his wife. He walked down to the beach. It was deserted on this weekday. The kids were in school, and the adults were working or tending to other duties.

Too tired to continue walking, Steve sat on the sand with his back resting against a warm, mounded dune. He stared out over the Pacific Ocean and fell asleep in the waning sunlight. He dreamed. He dreamed Taylor and he were walking along the sand in Maui, Kaanapali Beach, where they'd spent so much time together. He dreamed of walking along the cement path that fronted the beach with Taylor on his shoulders, teaching him the names of the bronze statues in front of the hotel next door—the turtle, the dragon, the mean man, the dolphin, the anchor—patiently waiting while his son struggled to find the motility to form the words, mangling them, but oh so proud of his attempts.

He thought of the kayak ride out beyond the surf when Taylor was older but still incapable of using a paddle, forcing Steve into strenuous exertion that left him breathless after fighting the tides and forcing the small plastic craft back to shore. He remembered the whale sightseeing tour when the gargantuan creature wallowed in buoyant comfort alongside the boat, delighting his son for reasons he would never comprehend.

Taylor was like that; the simplest things gave him indescribable pleasure, causing paroxysms of laughter. The water slide next door to the hotel, a man-made waterfall spilling thousands of gallons per minute into the pool below, the swinging bridge over another pool, burying his sister in the sand, popsicles full of grit, eating dinner on a beach blanket at sunset—these were all wonders to him. All those images flashed by his closed eyes in a kaleidoscope of their past.

He remembered the elderly woman at the outdoor ice rink in Sun Valley, Idaho, who stood up alone in the grandstands and clapped her hands at Steve's futile efforts to teach his young son to ice skate. He'd fallen for the umpteenth time to avoid crashing down on Taylor, and he'd scowled at the pain as he got back up. He felt ashamed when he heard that applause and saw her standing; he was at the end of his patience that day. She somehow sensed it, and her applause brought him back. He remembered a stranger in a restaurant who asked to shake his hand after witnessing Steve attending to his son on a difficult evening. The man complimented Steve on his patience and care of Taylor, causing him to walk away, fighting back tears. They were angels sent when he needed them most.

He remembered a woman in their neighborhood who arranged a meeting at Children's Hospital for Gina and him with the head of the hospital, the head of the new autism department, and a leading researcher into its causes. They thought they were attending a lecture to a roomful of hundreds of parents, only to find this wonderful woman had used her influence to grant them a private audience. And then she graciously disappeared with the excuse of picking up her daughter from school, allowing them the privacy to ask potentially embarrassing questions. Another angel.

He remembered another neighbor who brought her young son every Wednesday after school to play with Taylor, spending each afternoon for six months patiently cajoling her boy to play alongside him. Taylor never responded appropriately to the young boy's overtures, but she continued to bring her son despite the lack of social intercourse. She simply showed up, unannounced, exuberant at the opportunity to spend another hour or two being ignored by a unresponsive child. Another angel.

He remembered all the friends and relatives who included Taylor in their invitations, offered to babysit so he and Gina could take a break, or bought toys they thought might facilitate his development. He thought of the dozens of graduate students, therapists, doctors, dentists, caregivers, and teachers who had gone far beyond their duties in caring for his son.

Then his dream flung him into the future. They were back in Maui, walking along the beach. This time Taylor was talking with him—real sentences, real questions, a real conversation between father and son. He was asking Steve about love, girls, marriage, his career, having his own children, buying a home—all the conversations every father would love to participate in with a son. They played catch, shot baskets, and tossed a football back and forth. They went fly-fishing in swift-flowing streams, hunted in the Rocky Mountains, surfed the break on the beach in Maui, and skied the powder in Utah together. He taught his son how to be responsible in his relationships with women and male friends, respect the elderly, and drive a car. In his slumber, Steve had all the conversations with Taylor he would never have and did all the things together they would never do.

When he awoke, it was late. The sun was low over the water, creating a shimmering yellow bridge to the west. He was ready to talk with Gina. He'd come to a decision.

Chapter 41

Steve entered the house and called out for his wife. She came out of the bedroom, her eyes red and swollen from crying. He opened his arms and Gina slipped into them. "Don't say anything, Steve; just hold me."

They stood like that for minutes, enjoying the contact, until Steve broke the mood by asking, "Where are the kids?"

"Patricia took them to dinner. I thought it best they were out of the house before you returned. I know we need to talk."

Steve issued a huge sigh. "You know what I'm going to say, don't you?"

"Yes, I do. You're going to tell me you are going to continue, even if Lara won't. You'll do it anyway, with or without the study."

"Gina, I was at the beach. I thought of all the conversations Taylor and I will never have, all the things we'll never do together. I thought of all those other fathers who are in the same situation, or worse. I know it's selfish to think in those terms, but I'm a dad; I can only think like one. I can't imagine what goes on in your head. Honey, there's no way I can stop doing this yet. I need to do it until I've reached every possible child, exhausted every opportunity. This is a precious gift I've been given. It's intertwined in my DNA. I cannot waste it. Do you understand?"

She looked resigned. "I do, Steve. And I promised I was onboard, that I would love you in sickness and in health, that I would honor your belief in a greater power. I'm not sure those vows were meant to cover this situation, but nevertheless, it was a vow. I don't agree with it. I don't like it. But I will stay for as long as you're healthy. Just don't take this too far. I never agreed to watch you die. Promise me again, Steve. You will hug Taylor … soon."

"I promise I will hug Taylor. Nothing will prevent that."

Gina hugged him harder.

Steve said, "I need to contact Lara, tell her I want to continue."

"I already did that," Gina said. "You're not nearly as complex as you think. The trials will resume on the day after tomorrow."

"And Dr. Barnes?"

"That's a problem. He won't continue. He was very frank with me. He said he wouldn't participate in your suicide."

"Can we get a replacement?"

"We'll try. But it's not that simple, Steve. Any doctor we find is going to speak with Dr. Barnes first. There's also a question of liability, not to mention ethics. I'm not optimistic."

"Let me talk to him first."

"Go ahead. He's in his office right now."

"I'll be back in a little while." He called for an appointment and was told he could come over right away.

Dr. Barnes was waiting for him in his office, seated behind his desk, which indicated to Steve this would be a strictly professional discussion. He'd never been so formal in their relationship thus far, so Steve recognized the change and adjusted his approach to fit the new dynamic in their previously personal exchanges.

"You look like you're going to lecture me," Steve said.

"How prescient of you," he replied.

"Let me lay out something for you before you take my head off, figuratively, of course."

"Go ahead, Steve, but you're wasting both of our time."

"I'm a father, like you."

"Please don't play that card with me."

"Dr. Barnes, I know you think I'm crazy. You may be right. You also know I'm going to continue the trials, with or without you. That's a given. This will go on. I also understand why you refuse to continue. And I respect you for your stance. Let me, at least, expand your view of my position.

"What no one seems to understand is that I can't just stop." Steve held up his hand to stop a response. "I need to get this out. You, as a medical

178

professional, are the perfect candidate to understand my position." Dr. Barnes settled back in his chair, silent.

"When all of this began, I was understandably scared. I couldn't process this phenomenon. I had no point of reference. You know all the names the press has called me—the snide comments, the pointed innuendo. Your office has been largely left alone because no one knows of your involvement. If the public knew you were my doctor, your life and that of your family would be quite different; I promise you. When I realized the enormity of this situation I put my family in—the families of my brother and four sisters, Gina's two brothers and two sisters, her mother—I knew I had to deal with it for their sakes, as well as mine. Look what's happened to Dr. Jacobs. Her professional life is over. Her peers consider her a charlatan and a prima donna. Her university life is done. Her practice is now located on a secure military facility. She didn't sign up for this.

"My brother and four sisters can't even visit us because of all the attention it would attract. The base entrance has been staked out. Gina hasn't seen her mother or siblings in five months. All of them have had inappropriate attention paid to them by the press, and their children have been harassed on their way to school. They've all had to call the police to protect them from unwanted visitors. Their lives have been disrupted and put in jeopardy. Our families are virtual prisoners of my notoriety. Their lives have been destroyed. And it will not stop.

"Dr. Barnes, there is only one possible end to this nightmare. I have not shared this with anyone, not even my wife, so I expect what I must say to you will stay in this room. I'm invoking doctor-patient privilege. My life has irrevocably changed. There is no place for us to go where we'll be welcome. We can never return to our small town or my children's schools. They've been inundated by an invasion of so many news organizations, they can't physically accommodate them. The roads are clogged; the grocery store has been staked out. My neighbors can't even go to their mailbox without suffering through another interview. We can never go home or hope to have a normal life. My front gate is decorated in religious symbols and healing requests. Now, my vacant home has to be guarded by volunteer policemen. How long can that go on?

"We can't live on a military base for the rest of our lives. So far, the politicians have kept their distance for fear of being publicly humiliated by an impostor. That's the only upside, but how long will that continue? As soon as the trials are finished, they will descend on us like rain. The evangelical community is calling for my head. There is no safe place for my family. I live in constant fear someone will harm my children or my wife. I can't tolerate this danger to my loved ones much longer."

"You can treat your own son and put an end to this if what you feel about treating your son is true," Dr. Barnes said. "I'll assist you through that."

"And then where do we go? I will have nothing to offer in exchange for our security. The protection offered on this military base will evaporate. The families I've helped will forget in time and move on. And it won't stop other parents from seeking me out. It won't stop them from pursuing my family. And do you know why I'm sure of that? Because I would do the same for my son. I know firsthand how desperate they are. They're not going to believe it anyway. Parents of autistic children are going to haunt my family forever. Dr. Barnes, I feel I must continue for as long as you dictate I'm not in danger of irreversibly damaging myself. Then I'm going to treat Taylor and try to figure out how to live with it. We have to move forward, at least for a little while longer."

"You've given this a great deal of thought."

"That's all I've done. My first obligation, as a father, is to protect my children. I know now that I can no longer do that. They will be in perpetual danger until we can find a logical explanation for this. The only way to accomplish that is to continue the trials in the hopes we find the cause. You know that's the truth. I've no choice. I live with it every moment."

"I don't envy you. I did once. I don't anymore."

"Dr. Barnes, do you believe in God?"

"I'm a scientist, not a creationist. I was initially interested in your case because I was intrigued. I was convinced there would be a logical reason behind all this, something science could explain. And if I found it, so many others could be cured or even prevented from developing autism to begin with. But I'm just as baffled as you are. I admit I have no explanation."

"But you do believe these children have been cured?" Steve asked.

"They've all exhibited typical behavior after their experience with you. Steve, if I'm reading you correctly, you're insinuating that because I can't explain how these children were cured, I'm supposed to believe in a Catholic miracle. Am I correct?"

"No, I'm not asking you to believe in any religion. Those are parameters imposed by man. I am asking you to believe—in yourself, in the wonders of the human experience, in something greater than yourself. Religion, which is nothing better than competition for followers and their assets, has caused more death and destruction than any other force on this earth. This is something that transcends mere religion. This is about all of us, how we connect, how we love one another."

"Now you're venturing into New Age crap," Dr. Barnes said. "That's even more offensive."

"That's not what I mean at all," Steve protested.

"Then tell me what you think has happened. Why are these children being cured, and why are you being systematically debilitated?"

"Lara said it best. There is some transference going on between us. I can sense their fear. I can feel their frustration in not being understood, their acute desire to communicate, and the resultant anger when they can't. I think it's the result of my closeness to Taylor. I understand him, his needs, and his desires because he is me. He is of my flesh, my intellect, and my thought patterns. You should see Gina with him. She knows what he wants simply by observation—his posture, the type of temper tantrum, the severity of his moods. She knows! She knows what he wants before he even asks for it. If you want to see a 'miracle,' watch a mother with an autistic child. They are connected. They are one.

"There's more. Taylor exhibits my personality traits, likes and dislikes, even hobbies. He loves to draw. So, do I. He loves to do puzzles. So, do I. He spells better than anyone I know. I enjoy that same challenge. He loves the water. So, do I. I could go on and on. He exemplifies his mother the same way. She's quiet. He's quiet. She's kind. He's kind. He even loves the same foods she likes. He doesn't have the facility to learn these things on his own. He has no language. There's no traditional way for us to teach him anything. He is a direct copy of us. We are connected in a way no one could possibly understand. My hypothesis is that we are all connected on some level. That's not New Agey crap. That's the human condition.

"And these children have much to teach us. Taylor does not understand wealth, fame, pride, envy, greed, or even ownership. In Maui, he would step on other people's blankets on the beach because the sand was too hot on his feet. It's not their blanket. It's just a blanket. Try explaining that to a pissed-off beachgoer. Taylor doesn't care what kind of car I drive or how big our home is. He doesn't need the newest sneaker or jeans. He doesn't even care if his clothes match. He's never been spanked. He doesn't know what violence is. He doesn't want to be a tough guy. He just wants love, kindness, a connection with others. He is a perfect victim of everything we detest. He would give you anything he had. All you need to do is ask. He would accompany anyone who asked him to. He would give assistance to anyone who asked for it as a matter of course, not for a reward. He doesn't know what a reward is. If humankind acted the way my son does, the world would become a far better place.

"You have a young son," Steve continued. "I saw him walking with you not too long ago. He walks exactly like you. He stands like you. He smiles like you. You didn't have to teach him that. Look around you; observe other children. They learn by osmosis. Lara calls it transference. I call it a connection. I am connected to these kids. I know it. I feel it, the same way I'm connected to Taylor."

"And the chill, the pain, the debilitation?" Dr. Barnes asked. "How do you explain that?"

"I don't know the clinical way to explain it, but I feel the same sensation coming from them, the same connection. First, I feel the cold, the isolation, the imprisonment. Some of them have been hurt, beaten, or worse. Some of them have been abused, starved, or left alone in dark, cold places—a closet maybe, or a cellar. They've been punished in one form or another. That's what I feel. One child thanked me for 'letting her out' of a dark place. Another thanked me for taking the pain away; another felt a hard pinch. One just cried in relief, one was terrified of other people and lashed out at them, and another little girl thanked me for releasing her. She was stuck in her own mind. I know what they feel. I know the horrible things that were done to them. I absorb it. I feel it. And it hurts me just like it hurts them."

"I had no idea you felt all of that," Dr. Barnes said.

"Let me tell you something really sad," Steve said. "I not only know about the abuse but I also experience it. That little girl who thanked me for getting her out of that dark place, well, that dark place was a closet that a babysitter would lock her in while the parents were at work. No light, no heat, no nothing. I could feel what she felt—the fear, the abandonment—and there was no way to tell her parents what was happening to her. And she knew it would happen each time her parents left for work. She knew it was coming. It pissed me off in a way I've never experienced. I want to release every child I can, Dr. Barnes. I have to."

"You actually experience it? You feel it as they did?"

"Even worse things, things I can't talk about," he said.

Steve stared off into space for a few moments to gather his thoughts without breaking down. "Every parent of an autistic child feels it somehow, their pain, their frustration, and the parents of any child with other disabilities can, too. They are connected to their children in a way that defies logic or science. It just is."

Steve pressed on. "Dr. Barnes, I can't quit yet. If you felt the same things these children experienced, you wouldn't quit either. No one would. Would you please help me help them?"

"I was under the impression you were intent on becoming some sort of martyr. Are you saying you're not going to continue until that inevitability occurs?"

"No, of course not," Steve said. "I want to treat Taylor. That means I'm not planning to die. I just want to treat as many children as I can before I quit."

"That is not the impression everyone is under. You've made it sound like you would give your life for these children."

"How did I do that?"

"You made a comment about Lara finding a cure after you were gone."

"I did?"

"Yes, I was there. I heard you. That's what prompted me to resign from the trials."

"No, I'm not going to kill myself, and no, I'm not going to leave my own son out of the protocol."

Dr. Barnes formed a steeple of his fingers under his chin. He didn't reply for almost a full minute. "I will talk to Lara in the morning. This will come as a relief for her. I want to put you through another thorough physical examination and then I will calculate a timeline to end these trials, now that I know we're on the same page. I didn't like the results of your last physical. Barring that, you must agree to stop when I tell you. If I agree to continue after conferring with her, I will impose some severe restrictions on your diet, your activity levels, even your sleep routine. You will listen to me, or I will quit.

"My professional opinion is that you should treat Taylor now, and then we can assess whether you've lost the ability to treat these children. If your prediction that you will lose this ability is true, that result will become another new phenomenon we need to study.

"And you are to supply me with a full release of liability. I don't like to ask you that, but that's the reality of the world the medical community lives in."

Steve smiled. He knew he had him. "Was it Shakespeare who said, 'First, kill all the lawyers'?"

"No comment."

Chapter 42

Steve was subjected to another rigorous physical, and the trials resumed two days later. Gina surprised Steve with his next patient. When the clinic door opened, Kelly Newton, Taylor's childhood friend, walked in. He was six feet three at only fourteen years old, slender, and handsome, with café-au-lait skin and dark eyes. The skin was flawless, but the eyes were vacant like windows with the shades drawn. Steve called him over to the couch. "Kelly, hi. Do you remember me? I'm Taylor's father. Do you remember?"

Kelly advanced to Steve but held back, just out of reach. "Come closer, son. Don't be afraid. You and I are going to have a wonderful experience together." Steve thought of another tactic to bring him closer. He didn't want to risk angering Dr. Barnes by removing the leads to the monitors again. "Kelly, shake my hand." He extended his hand to the young man. "Kelly, remember how to shake?"

Kelly reached out a tentative hand, and Steve grasped it in his. He felt the chill seep into his body, and then Kelly melted into him. He sat next to him and wrapped his arms around Steve. Then he hugged him for real. He held on and sobbed into his shoulder, his slender body shaking with the effort. "Mr. Wilson, Mr. Wilson, is this real? Are you hurt? Did I hurt you?" He pulled back and stared at Steve, exhibiting the first direct eye contact Steve had ever witnessed from him.

Steve hugged him again for good measure. "It's real, Kelly. It truly is. And I'm not hurt. Being able to help you has been a real pleasure."

"But I felt a bruise in your chest, a deep pain."

"That was my heart singing, son. That was my heart feeling happy. There's no pain any more, just happiness. How do you feel?"

"Like you took a big weight off my chest. I can breathe now. I can talk. I can separate sounds. I don't feel afraid anymore." He took a deep breath. "I want to see my dad now, Mr. Wilson. Can I see my dad? I want to show him I can talk."

"Of course, you can, Kelly. He'll be right outside, waiting for you. Can I ask you something first?"

"Yes, Mr. Wilson?"

"When you couldn't talk before, what did it feel like to try to speak?"

Kelly answered without hesitation. "It felt like what I wanted to say wouldn't come out because other thoughts got in the way."

"Can you explain what that means?"

"I thought of what I was going to say, but it couldn't get from my brain to my mouth because what I was going to say went someplace else."

"So, your brain stopped you from talking?"

"It would forget what I wanted to say, and it would think of something else."

"Was that frustrating for you? Did it make you angry?"

"Yes; I wanted to say something to my dad, but it went someplace else. Can I go see my dad now?"

"Yes, Kelly, and thank you," Steve said. "It makes me very happy to hear you talk."

Kelly bounced off the couch and ran to the door. Before he left, he stunned Steve. "Taylor wants to talk to you, too," he said.

Lara pulled the door open and stood aside. Steve got a glimpse of his father, all six feet nine of him, blubbering like a baby and holding his son in his arms. The door closed. Steve slumped in the couch. That one hurt, but it was a good hurt. Now he understood why Lara had avoided any emotional involvements in the study. It was too painful to watch someone he knew receive what he could not give his son. He closed his eyes to staunch the tears and waited for the exit interview.

Lara entered, trailed by Dr. Barnes. She was visibly excited. "That was perfect, Steve. That was more than perfect!" She totally missed his reaction to Kelly's parting shot. Dr. Barnes said nothing. He removed the leads from the monitors attached to Steve and went into the next room to examine the data.

"What do you mean, Lara?"

"There are several researchers who believe the autistic brain lacks the neural pathway insulation that keeps thoughts on track so they can move from the brain to an action center, such as the mouth."

"How about saying that in layman's terms?"

"Think of the brain as a computer that transfers messages from the central processing unit to the monitor, or the brain to the mouth. In an autistic individual's case, the brain processes a thought for the mouth to translate, but the transmission wires lack insulation, and the message spreads like a virus, occupies all the neural pathways simultaneously, and freezes the computer. Instead of following along its intended path to action, it dissipates by spreading throughout all the circuits at once, effectively short-circuiting the intended path and losing the data. We see it as an autistic individual experiencing confusion, the blank stare, the inability to form words, but the call to action is being lost in the brain somewhere. His brain is buffering like a computer, stuck in a loop. Does that make sense?"

"Yes, it does," Steve said. "It makes sense."

"It's only a theory, but it explains so much. Kelly said it in a way that makes me think we're on to something. Have you ever asked Taylor a question he couldn't respond to, and then he blurts out the answer a couple minutes later?"

"Yes, sometimes I would ask him what he did that day and he would struggle to find the appropriate words, get frustrated, and shut down. Then, two or three minutes later, he would come up to me and say in his halting vernacular, "I went to the zoo. I saw a giraffe." He would be very proud he could recall and respond. He didn't realize the appropriate length of time to respond had expired."

"Think of it this way. You know those smart homes that you can control remotely with an iPhone?"

"Yes."

"Well, imagine you send a message to turn the thermostat up to seventy degrees, but the same message is sent to the refrigerator, the oven, the washer and dryer, and the light switches, all at the same time. It doesn't make any sense to those appliances the message was not intended for. It confuses the message and delays the response, or produces the wrong response. Taylor struggles through the same maze to find the appropriate receiver for a posed question. It goes to all his senses at once. That's why he blocks his ears to outside interference. His brain can't filter the extraneous messages."

"I wish you'd told me this a long time ago. It explains a lot."

"It's just a theory at this point, Steve. We need proof. That's why these trials are so important to me. If we can identify the neural malfunction, we may be able to fix it. Consider people who struggle with dyslexia. They learn to slow down and recognize which elements they are seeing incorrectly and then reinterpret them appropriately. Perhaps it takes them longer to read and comprehend written material, but they can eventually make sense of the content. And they go on to lead very productive lives. There are many famous inventors, actors, musicians, and founders of the largest companies in the world who are dyslexic: Leonardo da Vinci, Alexander Graham Bell, Thomas Edison, Albert Einstein, Richard Branson, John Lennon, Ansel Adams, F. Scott Fitzgerald, Jennifer Aniston, Orlando Bloom, Andrew Jackson, to name only a few."

"That's quite an accomplished group," Steve said.

"The best of the best," Lara said. "The focus of my research is to find the key that will unlock the potential of everyone on the autism spectrum to the best of their abilities."

"I knew I liked you for some reason."

"You're still not funny, Steve."

"Yes, I am. You just can't recognize the message."

Chapter 43

Steve left the clinic and walked deliberately to the chapel. The trial had taken more out of him than he'd anticipated, and his pace was markedly slower. He knew each trial required more time for him to recover, but this one was especially taxing. When he arrived at the tiny structure, he collapsed in the pew and closed his eyes. He was too tired to kneel and say a prayer for his son just yet. He would rest a bit first.

Steve slept through the sound of the door opening and the squeak of the bucket wheels. He woke to a touch on his shoulder, a gentle massage. His eyes fluttered open to find Sister Annette perched on the edge of the pew next to him. He smiled.

"How are you doing, Steve?"

"Good, Annette, really good," he said. "How are you?"

"Oh, I'm fine, Steve. But you look tired."

"Yeah," he replied, a bit sheepishly. "I didn't mean to fall asleep in here. It seems a little disrespectful." He looked up at the ceiling. "No cracks in the ceiling, though," he joked.

"I think it's the lightning bolts you have to look out for," Annette responded. "Why are you so tired?"

"The trials seem to be taking a little longer to recover from, this one especially."

"Why this one?"

"It was a young man I've known since he was a little boy. He went to school with Taylor all through elementary school."

"I would think that would be even more rewarding than treating a stranger, rather than more tiring," she commented.

He let out a sigh. "It is, Annette. It's just a little close to home, though."

"Oh, I get it. It made you think of treating Taylor."

"Exactly," Steve admitted. "But Kelly also told me Taylor wanted to talk to me. That one went straight to the heart."

"I'll bet," she said. She waited for Steve to speak. She knew he had more to say.

"I haven't seen you in a long time, Annette. What have you been up to?"

She knew he was deflecting the questions about him. She replied, "I've been busy. This isn't the only place I serve, Steve."

"Do you clean other churches?"

"In a manner of speaking, yes."

"What's that supposed to mean?"

"Other parishes, other people need help, too. The sisters in my order branch out to many people."

"Where do you live? Is it a convent?"

"Nearby, off base," she said.

"In Oceanside?"

"I'd prefer not to answer that, Steve. The order is very circumspect about our service. We don't advertise. We advocate."

"That's a polite way of saying none of my business."

"Yes, it is," Annette said. "Now let's get back to you. You seem very worried when you should be very happy."

"I am worried a little," he said. "I know I'm slowing down. I can feel it. I worry that I won't be able to time this out properly, fix Taylor when it's time, when I still have enough vitality to be a proper father to him afterward. There will be a lot to do to bring him up to speed."

"And talking to Kelly brought this on?"

"Yes."

"Well, that's understandable. What I don't understand is your lack of faith. We've talked about this before. You've had this incredible experience, gained the ability to not only understand what an autistic child is experiencing but to feel it as well. And you don't have the faith to believe you will heal your own son at the proper time?"

190

Steve smiled. "When you put it that way, I guess it seems a bit ridiculous."

"Because it is," she said. "You've come this far on your faith in your son, your family, and other people who are important to you. You trusted them to believe the unbelievable. And yet, you don't trust yourself? Come on, Steve. Worrying about the future never changes it. It just makes you feel bad for no reason."

"So, I'm worrying needlessly?"

"Yes."

"How can you be so sure?"

"Because I have faith in you."

"Why?"

She ignored the question. "This young man who told you Taylor wanted to talk to you brought all this worry on, didn't he?"

"Yes."

"But you already knew that in your heart, didn't you?"

"Yes."

"So, it wasn't much of a revelation, really, was it?"

"No, I guess not," Steve said.

"And I've never seen you act so selfishly," she said.

Steve felt like he'd been slapped. "What does that mean?" It came out harsher than he intended.

"Have you ever stopped to think about Gina? You think you're worried? You have some modicum of control here. She has nothing but her faith in you to sustain her. You ought to start acting as though you deserve it. And your daughter, Alexis, how do you think she feels?"

"Oh God, I wasn't thinking."

"No, you were too busy worrying about your own little world."

"I better get moving. I need to address this."

"Good idea," Annette teased.

Steve stood, reenergized. "Annette, do you ever worry?"

"All the time." She laughed. "How do you think I became an expert in it?"

Steve remained standing, looking at his friend. "You really do help me to see things more clearly, Annette. I very much appreciate having you for a friend."

"Thank you for telling me that, Steve. I appreciate having you as a friend, too."

When he got to the door, he heard Annette say, "Steve? Don't worry anymore about Taylor. You're going to heal him. I have faith in you."

"You promise?"

"I promise."

As he walked home, he recalled Gina asking him for a promise. Now he'd done the same thing.

Chapter 44

When Steve arrived home, Taylor looked up from his iPod and smiled. Steve went to him and asked, "What level are you on?" He'd seen his son playing on level fifty-seven in the past and he'd never gotten past level twenty-four when he tried the game. Taylor was proud to answer in his halting voice, "Level … thirty-seven." Steve gave him a high five and went to look for Gina.

He found her in the laundry, emptying the dryer. He kissed the back of her head and said, "How's my girl?"

"Great," she said and blew a strand of hair off her forehead. "How are you?"

"I'm good. Bringing in Kelly was special. Thank you."

"I hoped you'd like that."

"I did. Can we take Taylor down to the beach for a walk?"

"Sure, let me fold these clothes while you get him ready. He needs to use the bathroom and get his wallet, watch, and Boston Red Sox ball cap." It was a weekday. The New York Yankees hat was for the weekends only. Steve never understood the logic behind the switch, but that was Taylor's decision.

"I'll meet you in front," Steve said. "Where's Lex?"

"At the bowling alley. She and her new friend, Sarah, like to show off for the soldiers."

"Is that wise?"

"Under the circumstances, yes," Gina said. "She's a good kid. She'll be fine."

Ten minutes later, they were walking along the sand. Taylor held

Steve's hand as always. Since Taylor was already as tall as his father, they looked a little odd holding hands, a middle-aged man and a young teenager. Some observers surmised they were a gay couple and acted standoffish; other people got it right away. Steve had some amusing stories to tell as a result; others were not so amusing. Gina tucked her arm in his other arm, and they walked along.

"What's up, Steve?"

"I want to know how Lex is handling all of this. You, too."

"I'm fine. You know my feelings on this, and you know I will stand behind your decision. Alexis is another matter. You're her father, the only one she will ever have. I was wondering when you were going to wake up. You need to talk with her. She's floundering."

"In what way?"

"All her friends are back home. They don't visit as often as before when this was a novelty. She attends school here on base now, so she's developing a new set of friends. That's not so simple for a teenager, Steve. I remember you telling me you resented your parents moving you to California in your junior year of high school. You might give that some thought."

"I will. How much does she know?"

"Just that these trials have weakened you," Gina said. "Our discussions haven't gone any further than that, yet."

"Do you want me to tell her privately?"

"No no no," she emphasized. "We'll do that together."

"Okay, should we do that soon?"

"Why?" She looked concerned. "Are you planning to treat Taylor soon?"

"No, not just yet," he said. "There are plenty of others I can help before I do that. But it takes longer for me to recover. I'm weaker. My weight is down over twenty pounds so far. I would feel better if we let her know our plans. I don't want her to worry about me."

"It's a little late for that. She's aware of your weight loss and the gray hair."

"Then let's explain everything to her now."

"Okay." Gina compressed her lips. "Let's do that. And while you're at it, explain that you took years, maybe decades, off your life to do this for strangers. I'm sure she'll understand."

"Come on, Gina," he said.

"No, you come on. I said I would stand behind you. I do understand why you're doing this, why you can't turn your back on the other children. I would probably do the same. But don't expect me to like it. You're choosing to become an old man. That's the bottom line. I will be living with an invalid if this continues, and so will our children."

Taylor could sense the friction between his parents. He squeezed his father's hand and then held it in both of his. It was his way of communicating discomfort, nervousness. Steve patted his hands and said, "It's okay, buddy. Mom and Dad are just talking. It's okay."

He began walking again. "Let's table this discussion until after the kids are in bed."

"Sure," Gina said. She wouldn't look at him.

After the kids were asleep, Steve turned to his wife. "It's a nice night out. Let's go sit outside and finish our talk."

"Okay."

They sat outside on the patio. Steve brought out two glasses of wine and handed one to his wife. "Cheers," he said.

"What are we toasting?"

"Common sense," Steve said.

"Do you want to let me in on it?"

"Yes, of course. I'm not going to do this until I'm an old man. That's what you were thinking, isn't it?"

"That's what you led me to believe. That's what you implied on the beach," she said.

"I realize that now. Listen to me. I'm sorry. That was a terrible thing to leave hanging. I'm trying to tell you I want to do this for as long as possible and then treat Taylor. Then we'll see if I'm right about losing the ability to connect with these children. I'm not going to do this forever."

Gina sipped her wine. "Well, that's a relief." Sarcasm was in full bloom. "You want to let me in on how long this will continue?"

"Not much longer. Honey, I'm sorry. I get so wound up in treating these kids that I sometimes forget the impact I'm having on you and our kids. I'm truly sorry. I'll talk with Alexis and let her know this is not going to go on indefinitely."

"Let's do it tomorrow. I can tell she's worried. And we need to have another discussion with Dr. Barnes. I want to see this new timeline he drew up."

"You're going to set a definite date, aren't you?" Steve knew he was being cornered.

"You bet."

"Okay, okay, now give me a hug."

"That won't stop me from being angry with you."

"You never know until you try." He laughed.

"Come here, you idiot."

Chapter 45

Steve and Gina met with Dr. Barnes and Lara. When Steve explained they wanted to estimate the appropriate time to treat Taylor and set the date to do that, based on his current rate of deterioration, Dr. Barnes was visibly relieved. "I was going to suggest exactly that myself," he said. "I told you when we talked before that would be a requirement for me to continue."

"And I agree," Lara added. "It will also be quite interesting to see if you lose this ability after treating Taylor. We'll have to test some others after him, you know."

"I hadn't thought of that. I don't need proof, but you do."

"The trials require it, to put it more correctly," she said.

Gina jumped in. "Regardless of whether Steve loses this ability or not, I will not allow him to treat any more children once Dr. Barnes calls a halt to these procedures. Are we all agreed?"

Lara said, "Gina, we need to test at least three children after Taylor to be certain. Then we'll halt the trials. If Steve loses the ability, as he says he will, it will be a moot point. If he does not lose the ability, we will stop to preserve his health. Either way, we stop. But give this some thought: If he retains the ability, your life is going to become very complicated. The public, and I will include politicians in that group, is going to descend on you like locusts, Taylor especially."

Before anyone could comment further, Steve said, "Don't worry. I'm sure Taylor is the last one. I know it in here." Steve touched his chest. "Believe me, he will be the last one."

"Even if we assume that to be the case, your family is still going to be inundated after these trials are completed," Lara said. "You need to make plans for that eventuality. The best possible outcome will be that you lose the ability. Then, eventually—and even then, it's a maybe—the public will lose interest and leave you alone someday. The other possibility is too grim to consider."

"Can't you report he lost the ability in either case?" Gina asked. "That way, we have some chance of a normal life."

"That would invalidate the entire study and violate everything I stand for in the academic and mental health community," Lara replied. "The study would be called into question in its entirety, as if we'd perpetrated an elaborate hoax."

"Why don't we worry about that after we know the outcome? We're getting way off track here," Dr. Barnes said. "And I have some more tests I want to run on Steve first. I'll set them up for the first of the week."

"Is there a problem?" Gina asked.

"No, I just want to be thorough."

"Okay, let us know when it's set up," Steve said. He and Gina left feeling a lot better about their future.

After the couple left his office, Lara asked, "Why the additional tests?"

"I saw something in his blood panels that disturbs me. It's probably unrelated to the study, and I don't want to alarm them until I'm certain," Dr. Barnes said. "I'm going to schedule a brain scan for Monday."

Chapter 46

That evening, after school let out, Steve called Alexis into his office and asked her to sit down. "Am I in trouble?" she asked.

"No, should you be?"

"No, but you look all serious. What's up?"

"I wanted to talk to you about what's been going on in your life, honey. I know things have been difficult for you. Your mother will be here in a minute. She wanted to be in on this conversation." Gina walked in on cue.

"Hey, you were supposed to wait for me," she said.

"We did. We haven't started yet," Steve said.

"Then go ahead. I haven't got all day," she teased.

"Lex, I want to explain what's been going on, so you don't worry too much." Alexis remained mute but attentive. "You know what happened to me in the mountains and the treatments we've given to autistic children."

"Yes?"

"I think you've also noticed the physical effect it has on me."

"Yes."

"I want to apologize for not discussing this more thoroughly with you all this time. I just got wrapped up in what I was doing instead of paying attention to the people who mean the most to me, especially you."

"That's okay, Dad. I understand."

"No, it's not okay. I should have kept you and your mother more informed as things developed. And for that, I apologize." He turned to Gina and asked, "How am I doing so far?"

"You're getting warm. Please continue. I'm enjoying this." Steve knew

Gina was using humor to display the authenticity of their relationship in front of their daughter, and he loved her for it. The difficult times were when she really knew how to handle her family.

"Well, we've come to a decision to stop the trials. They've had an obvious deleterious effect on me, and your mother and I, along with Dr. Jacobs and Dr. Barnes, felt it would be best to stop after I've treated Taylor. We wanted to share this decision with you before anyone else."

"Yesss!" Alexis almost shouted it. She jumped up and hugged her father.

"Well, I'm glad that made you happy," Steve said. "But it will still be a while before things get back to normal. We don't know how Taylor will respond and what that will do to our family dynamic, but I think we all agree it will be a welcome change, if not a challenge."

"I don't care, Dad. I'm excited for Taylor, for all of us. This is great!"

Her obvious enthusiasm made Steve more aware of how little attention he'd paid to his eldest, how deeply he'd impacted her life. "I'm so sorry, Lex. I should have talked to you a long time ago."

"No worries. I'm just glad I'll be able to go to a college that's not on a military base. I thought I was going to have to enlist to get away from you," she joked. "And you still may walk me down the aisle one day without a wheelchair. And my brother can stand up for me, too! This is great!"

"I have a suggestion," Gina said. "Let's all go out to dinner at the Officer's Club and celebrate. This will be one last dinner to share before we transform Taylor and our entire family. We need a camera—"

"Phone, Mom, duh!"

The mood in the tiny office was euphoric. A bright new future had opened for them all at once. They were giddy with the possibilities. Steve and Gina hugged their daughter in turn, and then Gina went to make reservations.

That evening they were ushered to a table overlooking the Pacific Ocean. They barely noticed the sunset because they were so excited about Steve's decision to treat Taylor. They got him settled down with his iPod so he could play Bejeweled while the adults talked. Steve ordered a bottle of wine to mark the occasion, and once the waiter poured the glasses, he said, "Well, guys, it won't be long before Taylor is joining us in these conversations." They clinked glasses. Taylor looked up and added his water glass to the festivities.

"That will be a welcome change from the past," Gina said. "Do you remember when we lost him on Del Mar Beach at night? I wish he would have talked then."

"Yeah, I must have run past him a dozen times calling his name, and he never answered me. I was worried he decided to take a swim in the ocean."

"And then my friend, Holly, found him playing in a hole someone dug during the day. He must have wanted to play in it all day, and when he got the chance to escape, he went straight there."

That started the family trading humorous stories about Taylor. "Do you remember when he used to push over the floor lamps to watch the bulbs explode when they crashed?" Gina asked.

"Yeah, I had to duct-tape them to his furniture so he couldn't push them over. I wonder how many times he tried to shake them loose."

"How about the time he stood up in the theater and jumped up and down facing the projector lights?" Alexis added. "And facing all the people in the show, too. I wonder what they thought of that one."

"How about when he ran up to the screen and jumped up and down, flapping his hands? I'll bet the crowd appreciated that!" Steve said. "Down in front; sit down," he pantomimed.

"Or the time he flushed all my hair bows and clips down the toilet," Alexis said.

"If I recall correctly, he flushed everything in your bathroom down the toilet," Gina said. "Not to mention flooding the house as a result."

"And he ripped up my art project the night before it was due because it had a corner sticking out." Alexis laughed. "My teacher said she'd heard the one about the dog eating my homework, but not a little brother destroying it."

"Well, it did have an imperfection. He was only trying to fix it," Steve said.

Gina said, "I remember you taught him to take off his wet bathing suit before he came into the house so he wouldn't drip all over. Then he took off his suit in front of two hundred people at a pool party because he thought that what was he was supposed to do."

"The rule of unintended consequences," Steve said. "I never thought about what he would do elsewhere."

They all laughed at the memory. "Soon those occurrences will be a thing of the past," Steve said.

"Are you sure, Dad?"

"Positive, honey; it works every time. I'll bet Taylor will be able to explain what it felt like to be autistic afterward, too. I'm really eager to hear that."

"I can't wait, Dad."

"Me neither," he replied.

"Amen," Gina added.

Taylor, on cue, looked up and smiled. Steve wondered how much he understood when they weren't paying attention to him. He'd find out soon enough.

Chapter 47

Steve heard the imaging machine shut off and silence overtake the room. The mechanical device that controlled the bed he was on retracted out of the magnetic resonance imaging tube. He'd been subjected to a full body scan and then another more focused scan of his brain. Dr. Barnes explained it was necessary to compare his physical changes to his original baseline so they could understand how he had been impacted during the trials. Steve didn't pay much attention. His mind was on the future.

The date had been set for two weeks from today. He would treat three more children each week: one Monday, one Wednesday, and one Friday for a total of six. Taylor would be the seventh, on the following day. The whole family would be present for that special moment.

He donated more blood and urine samples and then met with Dr. Barnes. "That's it for today, Steve," he said. "I'll get a look at your results over the weekend and call you later." They shook hands, and Steve left the hospital feeling better than he had in weeks. Once the final decision had been made, everything else fell into place. They were on the road to recovery as a family and on their way to an exciting future. Steve let his imagination run wild as he fantasized about talking to his son and laughing with the whole family. They had a lot of catching up to do.

He entered the tiny chapel in hopes of finding Sister Annette to share his news. He spent an hour in deep reflection, mindful of the intense gratitude he felt to that higher power. He'd experienced such deep joy in treating these children and absorbed the depths of their despair in the process. The acute difference in those emotions was a rare experience for another human being to be blessed with. He was so grateful that mere words failed him. Eventually, that warm contentment he felt when he approached a perfect prayer spread over him like an electric blanket in winter.

Annette didn't appear, but he walked home in a wonderful frame of mind. The sky was bluer, the birds sang in perfect harmony, the wind off the Pacific was gentle, and the sun bathed him in warmth. Life had blessed him with the extraordinary.

When he arrived home, the kids were out of the house. He greeted Gina with a kiss and sat down on the couch next to her. He said, "Honey, in all these years, I rarely saw you get down, and never in front of the kids. You never stopped caring for Taylor, even when he was at his worst. You kept Alexis on an even keel through every challenge. And you put up with my antics, too. How on earth do you do it?"

Gina smiled at him, a secret smile, one that conveyed a hidden knowledge only she was aware of. "I'm a mom. We don't get to choose how our children turn out, or our husband for that matter. What good would it do to complain? It changes nothing. I still have to get up the next day and care for my children."

"But Taylor is not a typical child."

"No, but he could have turned out to be even worse—an ax murderer or the most despicable human being on earth, a Hitler, a terrorist. He could have had a terminal cancer or another affliction that was even worse. His autism is a challenge, I grant you that, but how many autistic children have we met who were more severe? A lot," she said. "You never really know."

"I guess not, but how do you just accept it?"

"Steve, our son is a happy child. He doesn't worry like you do. He doesn't fret about the future. He accepts things for what they are. You pray to the Christian God for relief. I accept my life as it is. To me, acceptance is the key to happiness. I don't want to waste any precious time trying to change the past. No amount of praying is going to change it. I'm perfectly happy with Taylor just as he is. That's why I have a hard time understanding what you're doing."

Steve wanted to explain what he felt when he treated these children, what he learned in the process. He almost did, but Dr. Barnes interrupted their conversation by cell.

"Could you and Gina come to see me tomorrow morning at nine a.m.?" he asked.

"Was there an issue?" Steve inquired.

"No, nothing to worry about. I just want to discuss some of my findings before we continue."

"On a Saturday?" Steve asked.

"I have no patients on Saturday. It's perfect."

"Okay, see you tomorrow."

The next morning, they arrived at nine o'clock, as requested, and found Dr. Barnes and Lara in deep discussion in his office. There was no receptionist to greet them, so Steve advanced through the reception area and knocked on the open doorjamb. Barnes looked up and said, "Come in, come in. Have a seat."

Steve felt his stomach do a little flip at finding Lara in attendance. Gina picked up on it, too, but remained silent. They took a seat. A serious atmosphere permeated the room. They skipped their normal greeting. "What's going on?" Steve asked.

"I neglected to get a series of questions answered on the protocol, and the answers will affect Lara's work, too. We're anxious to get these final trials out of the way and thought we'd kill two birds with one stone."

"Okay, go ahead and ask."

Dr. Barnes looked down at a typed list on his desk. "Any headaches lately?"

"I get them occasionally," Steve said.

"Have you noticed them increasing in either frequency or intensity?"

"Not really."

"Can you be more specific?"

Steve hesitated, trying to think of what to say. "They do seem more intense. I don't think they happen more often, though."

"Describe the difference."

"It hurts more. It takes longer to go away. I take four Advil now instead of two, like that."

"But not more often?"

"No."

"Are you having any vision problems you didn't have before? Any blurring or double vision?"

"No, nothing," Steve said. Concern was creeping into his consciousness. His brow creased.

Dr. Barnes noticed his discomfort. "Just a few more questions, Steve, and then we'll talk."

"Are you experiencing any loss of balance or coordination, facial tics?"

"I have noticed a feeling of vertigo sometimes when I walk. I stop for a moment and it goes away."

Dr. Barnes made another note and continued. "That's good. Any nausea or vomiting?"

"No more than usual," Steve said.

Gina interrupted. "That's not true. I hear you throwing up in the morning, Steve."

"I'm just clearing my throat from sleep."

"Bullshit, put down a yes for vomiting."

"Any involuntary convulsions, difficulty with speech?"

"No, none," Steve replied. He threw a sideway glance at his wife. She remained silent.

"Any difficulty recalling words, confusion, like losing the thread of a conversation?"

"Not at all," he answered. Gina was still silent.

"Any weakness on either side of your body? Numbness in your fingers or toes?"

"My fingers tingle sometimes if that's what you mean."

"How?"

"Like that tingling feeling you get when your leg falls asleep and then wakes up, like that," Steve replied.

Gina stepped on the next question. "Okay, I've had enough. Please tell us what's going on."

Dr. Barnes said, "I'm trying to …"

And Gina finished his statement for him, "avoid answering my question. Stop it."

Lara said, "Tell them. They have the right to know."

Dr. Barnes issued a huge sigh. "The brain scan detected a large mass on the upper left quadrant of your brain, Steve. It wasn't present before the trials, which indicates a fast-growing tumor. I need to consult an oncologist and order a biopsy as soon as possible."

"On my brain?"

"Yes."

Chapter 48

After studying the results of Steve's MRI, Dr. Davies, the consulting oncologist, said, "This is a grade IV primary brain tumor, the worst type you can have."

Dr. Barnes said, "I thought so. Have you ever seen one grow this fast?"

Dr. Davies consulted the previous MRI, compared it to the current one, and said, "These are rare to begin with, and no, I've never encountered this fast a rate of growth. Did you schedule a biopsy?"

"Not yet, I wanted your opinion on whether it's operable or not."

"At this rate of growth, it would be a colossal waste of time. It has insinuated into the surrounding tissue and will impact several different cognitive functions sooner rather than later. The rate of growth suggests a malignant tumor, but a biopsy is the only way to be certain. In my opinion, based on the size and location of the mass, the rate of growth, and the unlikelihood of a successful resection, it would be best to leave it alone and make the patient as comfortable as possible until the inevitable occurs. In other words, there's nothing to be done here. I'm surprised he's still walking around."

"How much time does he have left?"

"There's no way to be certain, but I would venture a guess of between three and six months."

"And the surgeon concurs?"

"Yes, he agreed with the timeline. We talked at length last night, and he believes if this patient were operated on for even minimal resection, it would likely result in the severe impairment of several cognitive functions, and maybe even his eyesight. It would not delay his demise by any appreciable time. I'm sorry, Dr. Barnes."

Barnes felt like someone had punched him in the stomach. He couldn't imagine what to say when he faced the Wilsons. Lara would be devastated as well. "Thank you, Dr. Davies. I have to contact the Wilsons and give them the news."

"I don't envy you."

"Yes, this is a very special family. Someday you and I will share a meal and I'll tell you the backstory. Right now, I can't discuss it," Dr. Barnes commented.

"I'll look forward to it."

The two doctors shook hands, and Dr. Barnes walked him out. He came back to his office and dialed Lara's cell. She answered after only one ring. "How did it go?" she asked.

"Not well," Dr. Barnes said. "He's not operable."

"Oh no" was all she could come up with.

"I'm afraid so. Do you want to call them for an appointment, or shall I?"

"No, I'll do it. When are you available to consult with them?"

"The sooner the better," he replied. "Tomorrow at noon would work."

"I'll make the call."

Lara had to sit and collect herself. She'd only known the Wilsons intimately for the last six months. It felt like a lifetime. They were such caring, giving people. She shut her office door. She desperately wanted to remain aloof and professional. But no matter how hard she tried to suppress her emotions, tears gathered until she finally gave in to her personal feelings. Sobs racked her body as she lay her head down on her desk and cried.

An hour later, she composed herself and called Gina. "Can you and Steve come in and see me tomorrow at noon? There are some issues we need to discuss."

"Of course, Lara. Is something the matter?"

"There are some complications we need to address. It would be best if we all did it together at the same time. Is noon good for you?"

Gina knew she was avoiding her question. She said, "We'll see you then," and clicked off.

She knew if she told Steve tonight, he would most likely get no rest, so she decided to wait until the next day. She spent a restless night, tossing and turning. Sleep never came. In the morning, she approached Steve. "Lara wants us to come for a consult today at noon."

"Oh, when did this happen?"

"Last night, I completely forgot."

"Really?" he queried. "That's not like you."

She snapped, "Give me a break here, Steve. I'm trying to hold it together."

"Okay, sorry." He grabbed his Kindle and went outside to read. Everyone was getting touchy.

At ten to twelve, they drove to Lara's office. Neither spoke during the ride. When they arrived, a grad student ushered them into her office. Dr. Barnes was there, too. The atmosphere in the room was quiet, serious. They knew instinctively something was very wrong.

Dr. Barnes was sitting on a chair in front of Lara's desk. Two more chairs were positioned in a semicircle next to him. Lara came out from behind her desk and sat on the edge facing the chairs. "Have a seat," she said. "I have some unwelcome news to share with you."

"It must be bad if you're not even going to say hello," Steve quipped.

"I'm sorry, Steve. I forgot my manners." She hugged him and then Gina. "Please sit down."

Gina barely made it to the chair. She was overwhelmed with the possibilities. She sat heavily just in time to prevent herself from keeling over.

Steve sat next to her. "What is it?" he asked.

"This is very difficult for me," Lara began. She couldn't force any words out. Her eyes filled with moisture, and Gina knew. She knew with a certainty what was coming.

Dr. Barnes rescued her. "This is not your area of expertise, Lara. Let me talk."

Lara only nodded. She stared at the floor.

"Steve, I'm not here to offer platitudes or make this easy for you.

There is no easy way to say this. Some people go out with a bang, and some people go out with a whimper. You are going to go out with a whimper." He paused to let his statement sink in. "Your tests came back with the worst possible news. You have an inoperable brain tumor that is growing at an unprecedented rate. I've consulted with an oncology specialist and a neurologic surgeon, and we all concur. There's nothing to be done; there's no way to treat you. I'm sorry."

Steve and Gina were holding hands; neither was even aware they had sought out the other's grasp. They just stared, open mouthed, at Dr. Barnes. Words would not form.

Dr. Barnes continued. "We estimate you have three to six months to live, but no one can be absolutely sure of that timeline. It may be longer; it may be shorter, but certainly no more than a year. It would be best to start any preparations you deem necessary as soon as possible."

"There must be something we can do, someone else we can go to," Gina blurted.

"Of course, you can," Dr. Barnes said. "I would expect that reaction. I would react the same way. I've prepared a list of the best cancer specialists available." He handed Gina a folder.

Steve dumbfounded them all with his next question. "Does this mean the trials stop now?"

"Yes, I've canceled the remainder of the trials," Lara said. "I assumed you would want some time to digest this, get your things in order."

Steve ignored her comment. "I'll bet the parents were devastated. Is there any way we can treat the ones we committed to instead of just leaving them like this?"

"Are you nuts?" Gina almost shouted. She stood up abruptly. "What are you saying?"

"Honey, a few more are not going to make a difference to my outcome."

"No, Steve, we're going to get another opinion, maybe several others. You are not going to do any more of this, not today, not ever."

"Gina, I know what Dr. Barnes told us is true. I can feel it the same way I can sense when a child is not autistic. I just know."

"How long, Steve? How long have you known?" She loomed over him. She was fuming.

"Since the additional MRI," he said. "I knew something wasn't right before that. I didn't want to worry you."

"You didn't want to worry me?" she said. "Now I know you've lost it." Her voice rose several octaves. "You didn't want to worry me!"

Dr. Barnes turned to Lara. "Dr. Jacobs, let's give the Wilsons some privacy to digest this. Come on." He rose to leave.

"No," Gina interrupted. "You stay right there. We're leaving. Steve, I want to go ... now."

"Okay," he said. "Let's go." He shook Dr. Barnes's hand and hugged Lara. "This is not your fault, guys. You have to believe that." He turned to Gina, but she was already gone. He turned back to Lara and said, "I'll call you later." Then he left.

Chapter 49

They didn't speak on the way home either. Gina slammed the car door as she got out. She went into the house without a backward glance. Steve sat in the car and considered how these developments would affect his family. He'd been given a death sentence, but he was oddly at peace with it. Of course, he worried about the impact on his children and his wife, but he'd known all along what the trials were doing to him. He'd suggested as much to Sister Annette, and she didn't blink. She told him she would enjoy every moment of the experience and let nature take its course. Now that he'd received a formal diagnosis, he fully understood what she was trying to say. It was as if she already knew the projected outcome.

Steve knew now was not the time to discuss this with Gina. He exited the car and went for a walk. Twenty minutes later, he was at the chapel. He entered the small structure and sat down in his regular pew. He didn't pray for relief. He didn't pray for a miracle. He prayed for strength, for wisdom, for patience, and for endurance. Mostly he prayed for understanding from others. The coming months were going to be difficult. He would need every ounce of fortitude to get through them.

He turned at the sound of the door opening and was delighted to find Sister Annette pushing her bucket through the entrance. She smiled at discovering her old friend sitting in his usual spot. "Hello there, Steve. How are you today?"

"Fine, Annette, just fine," he answered.

"It's nice to find you in such good spirits," she said.

"I think I've found some peace in all of this."

"Do you want to talk about it?"

"Yes, that would be great. Just what the doctor ordered, in a manner of speaking," he said.

"I take it your doctors have given you some news?"

"They have, indeed, but I don't think my wife is happy about it."

"Well, what was the news?"

"Do you remember when I told you I felt like I was losing a bit of my life each time I treated one of these kids?"

"Yes."

"Well, it turns out I was right. I was diagnosed today with an inoperable brain tumor. I have a large mass growing in the upper left quadrant, whatever that means. Gina and I were told I have three to six months, certainly no more than a year, to live."

"Oh my, that is serious. How did Gina take it?"

"Not very well," he said.

"I can only imagine what she's going through."

Steve appeared puzzled by her response. Annette recognized the look and said, "What were you expecting? Did you think that would make her happy?"

"No, I just—"

"Didn't think about it?"

"I guess not."

"You sure guess a lot," she chided.

"Okay, okay, I should have known."

Annette remained silent.

Steve continued. "She's really upset with me. I should have anticipated this."

Annette remained silent.

"She hasn't come around to accepting this."

"Have you gotten second opinions yet?"

"No, I know it's true. I know it the same way I knew what to do with the kids. I don't need a second opinion."

"I wasn't asking if you needed a second opinion. I was asking for Gina."

"Uh-oh, I hadn't thought of it that way."

Annette said. "She doesn't have your frame of reference, Steve. She needs reassurance. She needs to do everything you would do for her if the situation were reversed. You can be awfully dense at times, my friend. And we haven't even discussed Alexis yet."

"Oh God, what was I thinking?"

"You weren't. Steve, you know by now that thinking of others is the way to heal yourself, but it starts at home. When you get wrapped up in your own problems without considering the impact on those closest to you, it pushes them away. Don't do that. Put your family first and everything else will take care of itself."

"How do you make the most complicated decisions seem so simple?"

"I don't. You figured it out. I just pointed out the obvious. Put yourself in Gina's shoes for a moment. What would you do for her? She needs her partner. What about Alexis? Have you given any thought about how to explain this to her? You should think long and hard before you make another mistake. She needs her father. They both need to understand your choices and the consequences."

"You already know what I'm going to do, don't you?"

"I've a pretty good idea."

"I want to make the most of the time I have left."

"You're planning to be of service to these children for the remainder of your time?"

"Yes," Steve answered. "I'd like to treat as many as I can before I go."

"And you're at peace with your decision?"

"Yes."

"That's admirable. Have you discussed your decision with Gina and Alexis?"

"Not yet," he replied.

"Then when?"

"Right now," he said.

"Good choice." She smiled. "I'll see you later."

215

Chapter 50

Steve found Gina in their bedroom, under the covers, her head turned away from him. He sat next to her on the bed and rubbed her back through the blanket.

"Don't," she warned.

"I came in to apologize," he said. "I wasn't thinking. I'm so sorry, Gina. Please turn around and look at me."

She sat up and rubbed the moisture from her eyes with the heels of her hands so hard Steve thought she'd rub the skin off. She was angry. He pulled her arms away from her face and took her in his arms. "You're my best friend, my lover, the mother of my children, and I forgot that for a minute. I am so sorry."

She wept while he held her. They stayed like that for a long while. Finally, she looked up at him with swollen eyes. "What are we going to do? I am so scared, Steve. I don't know how to live without you."

"Let's do what you suggested before we go there. Let's get those second opinions. There might be some treatment Dr. Barnes doesn't know about yet. Okay?"

"But you said you knew already. Why'd you say that?"

"Because I can be dumb at times," Steve said. "I wasn't thinking clearly, and I just blurted out the first thought that came to mind."

"So, you're not sure?"

"No, honey, I'm not. How could I be?"

"I don't know. This is all too weird."

"Well, we agree on that." He issued a wry laugh. He reached out and erased the tears from her cheeks with his thumbs. "I'm still searching for the playbook." He kissed her. "Come on, I don't want Alexis to see us like this when she gets home from school."

They made the bed together, and Gina cleaned her face in the bathroom. Steve stood by the sink while she reapplied her makeup. "I'll never tire of watching you do that," he said.

Gina smiled into the mirror. "I didn't know that. Did you know I love to watch you shave?"

"Nope, I guess we still have a lot to learn about one another."

That comment brought on fresh tears. Gina almost broke down but then recomposed herself. She took a deep breath and said, "Come on, Alexis and Taylor will be home soon." She took his hand and led him out to the family room.

Patricia led Taylor into the family room where they were sitting together on the couch. In his halting voice, he struggled to greet his parents. "Hi, Mom," he said.

"Hi, Taylor. How are you?"

"Fine."

Steve said, "Hi, Taylor."

Again, he struggled to get the appropriate response out. "Hi, Dad," he managed. "How are you?"

"I am fine, Taylor. How are you?"

"Fine." His duties were finished, so Taylor went to the kitchen in search of a snack. Patricia said hello and followed him.

Alexis came home ten minutes later. She knew something was wrong as soon as she cleared the entrance. "Hi, guys. What's up?" She hugged each of them in turn, Gina first.

"We've had some new developments we need to speak to you about," Gina said. "Come and sit down with us."

Alexis sat on the couch next to Steve as though she sensed this discussion would revolve around him. "Are you okay, Dad?"

"Yes, honey, I'm fine. We need to address a medical issue as a family, though."

"What is it?"

"I had another MRI and they found a growth on my brain that we need to examine further. Your mom and I are going to see some specialists, or rather we're going to bring some experts to the base to examine me because of the stir it would create for me to go off base," Steve explained. "We wanted to treat you like an adult since that's what you are."

"How serious it this?" Alexis asked.

"It's always serious when you're dealing with something like this," Gina said. "But plenty of families go through this, and we'll handle it. We don't want you to worry, but this is going to take some time to get through, and we'll need your help."

Alexis took Steve's hands in both of hers. "You're not going to die, are you, Dad?"

"Of course not, honey. I'm just going to need some additional treatment."

She searched her father's face for the truth. "Honest?"

Steve held up three fingers in a Boy Scout oath posture. "Honest," he said. "We're going to see the very best doctors in the world."

"You promise?"

"I promise. Now you promise me something. I need you to help out around here while we do this."

"Of course, Dad," she said.

"Thanks, Lex," Steve said. He squeezed her hands in his. "I know I can count on you to keep your mother in line."

She smiled at his remark, but she knew; she knew. He hugged her to him. "Don't worry, sweetheart; I'll be fine."

She just snuggled up to him and said nothing. Gina and Steve exchanged parental looks over her head.

Chapter 51

Dr. Barnes set up appointments with six of the best physicians he could find, three oncologists and three surgeons. Gina and Steve met with two per day, one of each discipline. The oncologists discussed the possibility of treating the tumor with radiation therapy, which presented the challenge of damaging the tissue surrounding the tumor. Since the size of the mass already intruded on several areas of the brain that controlled his eyesight and physical motor responses, radiation treatment was rejected. The necrosis that would develop because of such extensive radiation would most likely leave him in a vegetative state. Aside from the obvious nausea he would suffer, they counseled that the chemo would not properly address a mass of that size and the same considerations they faced with radiation presented similar challenges. They suggested a new treatment that entailed drawing his own blood and treating his red blood cells to exclusively attack the mutating cells that created the tumor, and then transfusing the treated blood back into him. All of them agreed this was the only treatment that held any promise of remission.

The surgeons, being surgeons, were more willing to entertain the possibility of surgery to reduce the size of the tumor and see if that resection would improve his quality of life. All of them cautioned the couple that there would be no guarantee of a positive outcome. It was a severe risk. During exploratory surgery, they would decide whether to continue the resection or to simply leave it as is, close the incision, and make him comfortable until the inevitable occurred. They suggested chemo to reduce the size of the mass before attempting surgery. All three surgeons concurred on both the treatment and the prognosis if surgery was going to be considered.

At the end of the week, they met with Dr. Barnes and Dr. Jacobs to discuss the results of the consultations. "Have you decided on a method of treatment yet?" Dr. Barnes asked.

"No, we wanted to talk it out with you first," Steve said.

"Good, I was hoping you would say that," he replied. "I've also discussed your case extensively with each of these doctors, and I would like to add my opinion to the mix."

Gina said, "Please give us your thoughts."

"Okay," Dr. Barnes said. "It is my opinion your only viable option is to try the transfusion. It is new, but it has a high success rate in some leukemia and non-Hodgkin's lymphomas. I do not believe surgery is an appropriate avenue to pursue. If you go to a surgeon for treatment, you are going to have surgery. That's what they do. Most of the doctors I talked with were surprised you were still upright. In my opinion, surgery would most likely make your situation worse, not better. Usually we use chemo to reduce the size of a tumor to make it easier to surgically remove what is left, then radiation to ensure it does not reoccur. In your case, we are far beyond that due to the size and location of the mass, not to mention the aggressive rate of growth. I do not believe you would survive the process."

There it was, out in the open. Steve and Gina looked at one another, waiting to see if the other would speak. Steve took the initiative. "That's the same conclusion we came to. We decided we had nothing to lose by taking this route, as opposed to surgery, radiation, or chemo. There really is no downside to this therapy, is there?"

"No, not really, other than the therapy may not arrest the tumor. But that's the situation you're in anyway. I agree wholeheartedly with your decision. And Lara concurs."

"I agree," Lara said. "You should start as soon as possible."

Steve slapped both knees with the palms of his hands. "Then let's do it."

"I'll make the arrangements," Dr. Barnes said. "You're doing the right thing."

"Do you have the equipment here?" Gina asked. "You know what will happen if we leave the base."

"Fortunately, yes," Dr. Barnes said. "We recently built the finest military medical facility in the country on this base, and we do have the transfusion equipment. I already confirmed that."

"Thank goodness."

"I'll make the arrangements," he said.

The following week, Steve was admitted to the base hospital for testing. It took two more weeks to schedule his treatments. During the interim, Steve asked Lara if she would meet with him in private to discuss the autism study. They met in her office.

"Thanks for seeing me," Steve said.

"Don't be silly, Steve. Of course, I would meet with you. You're the whole reason we're here. This is the most significant event of my professional life. The results of these trials will keep me busy for the foreseeable future, perhaps the remainder of my career. I should be thanking you."

"I want to ask your opinion on continuing the trials. It doesn't seem right to waste this time while I undergo transfusions. There is no pain associated with the treatment, just a lot of boring time invested while I lay there doing nothing. I'm going to go nuts."

"Gina warned me you would try this," Lara said. "I guess she knows you better than you think." Her smile softened the comment. "First, you clear it with her and Dr. Barnes; then I will consider it. I need to be sure the trials did not bring this on. I've seen enough strange developments associated with your peculiar condition that are difficult for me, as a scientist, to assimilate, let alone understand, to give you an answer right away."

"But I don't feel any worse than two weeks ago. In fact, I feel pretty good."

"And maybe that's because we stopped the trials," Lara countered. "How are the headaches?"

"They're still there."

"You're equivocating," she said. "You want to be more specific?"

"They're no worse than before," Steve explained. "I just take four Advil, and I'm fine in an hour."

"How often? How many per day?" she asked.

"Two or three times," he said.

"That means four or five per day based on my experience with you."

"Now who's being funny?" Steve joked.

"I'm not kidding. Look at how much weight you've lost. How much do you weigh now?"

"I'm only down thirty pounds. I needed to lose weight anyway," Steve said.

"Hardly," Lara scoffed. "I can see definition in your face, Steve. Your eyes are hollow, and your bone structure is apparent at first glance. You look like an anorexic distance runner. You weigh, what, about one sixty?"

"About that," he lied.

"Ask Gina and Dr. Barnes, and then we'll see," she said. "Until then, this discussion is tabled."

Steve left her office and walked slowly to the chapel. He sat in his usual pew and closed his eyes, hoping for divine guidance. He was dying and he knew it. He also knew there was a finite number of children he could treat before that inevitability occurred. He desperately wanted to impact as many as he could before he treated Taylor. Gina was very close to asking him to do just that. He could sense it. He'd been successful in avoiding that conversation thus far, but he knew it was just a matter of time.

Sitting alone in that cool, dark place gave him a sense of serenity he didn't experience elsewhere. He felt a calm presence surround him. It was a place where he could explore his true feelings, free from the doubt and recrimination of others, and just let his mind wander, unfettered by outside opinion. He thought it was something young people yearned for and couldn't put a name to. It was the freedom to pray, contemplate, meditate, or simply reflect on the truth they believed in without embarrassment. Organized religion did not fulfill them. It was the opposite of inclusion, with its rules for proper behavior and its requirements to pray on a particular day, in a particular fashion, to a specific God identified by those who peddled their version of redemption. It also promised eternal exclusion—exposure to a righteous and vengeful God who would punish you if you did not adhere to His tenets. Unspeakable punishment from a frightening deity if you didn't go along; what a concept!

Every human being, deep down, knew there was a power, a spiritual connection between one another that was greater than the individual. It was the principle that entire religions were based on, governments were founded on, and companies were incorporated on—an incontrovertible truth. In the early days, there were clans, tribes, or groups formed around a common goal, usually food or security. It was no different now. People had simply lost sight of it. They substituted their emptiness with drugs, alcohol, sex, music, and meaningless relationships, refuting anything that did not bring them immediate pleasure. When all these pastimes were exhausted, they were left with the same emptiness that compelled them to seek satisfaction from other trivial pursuits in the first place. Annette would have said they were in service to themselves, not one another. The result was no one was served.

His train of thought led him to another conclusion. His wife, his precious Gina, had always been in service to him, to their family. In her simple way, she'd taught all of them the meaning of life, without the benefit of religious dogma. Her inner peace was not an act, just the opposite. It was Gina. Most likely, that was why their children were so well adjusted. Sister Annette and his wife had a lot in common. He decided he would arrange for them to meet. He wanted them to become friends.

The fact that he was dying also brought certain clarity with it. He felt a wave of gratitude for that book by Dr. Wayne Dyer wash over him. It was the discovery of that prayer in Hawaii by St. Francis that led him to this train of thought. "Dying to one's self" was not a philosophical exercise for Steve. It was a reality. And it felt good; it was a mantra for living or dying. To him, it meant serving the common good, something larger than himself. He compared the value of some extra time on earth against the treatment of several more children and came to a decision.

Steve did not experience divine intervention, and Sister Annette did not appear. He trusted his inner compass and came to his own conclusion.

Chapter 52

Gina was waiting for him when he arrived home. In fact, she was sitting on the front porch, reading a paperback. She set the book aside as Steve mounted the steps. "Lara called," she said.

"I figured as much."

"She said you asked to continue the trials."

"Yes," he admitted.

"Are you crazy?"

"Not at all," he said. He sat on the rocker next to her. "I know you think I am, but I've never felt so sure about another decision in my life."

"Steve, we've already discussed this. It's not just your life we're talking about. You have a family, children, and a business. What are you thinking?"

"I'm thinking I lead by example, not with my mouth. What I do from here until my last day is what matters, not extending those days. What my children witness, not what they hear, is what matters. The good I can do while I'm here and not the length of time I'm here matters, especially to those children like our son."

"It matters to me," she said.

"I know, sweetheart, and it means everything to me, too. But we are not the only ones to endure the impact of autism as a family. We are not on an island. For reasons we'll never understand, we were given an incredible gift, the ability to heal. Not to use it is disgraceful. You know that. In fact, if you answer one question with complete honesty, you know what we have to do."

"And what's the question?"

"I don't want you to answer me. First, I want you to take your time and reflect on everything that's transpired since my hunting incident—the wonderful people we've met, the families we've helped, the children we treated. Then I want you to picture someone with the ability to cure our son, Taylor, walk away and refuse to help us. Then tell me how that feels, the utter helplessness, the total despair. Then answer this question for yourself. What would you do?"

"Okay, and while I contemplate that scenario, I have one for you," she countered. "Imagine there is a possibility, perhaps a very slight one, that this treatment can arrest your tumor and extend your life and, with it, the possibility of treating even more children. Why on earth would you jeopardize that with a rash decision?"

She got up from her seat and went into the house. Steve knew this conversation was over. She'd won again.

At dinner that evening, Alexis asked, "When do the transfusions start?"

"Tomorrow, Lex," Steve said.

"What about the children who were scheduled for treatment from you?"

"Your mother and I decided to postpone any further treatments until we see the results of my transfusions. We should know by next month."

"I'll bet they're really disappointed," Lex said.

"I'm sure they are," Gina said, "just like we would be. But they also know if this treatment works on your father, many more children, and families, will experience the joy of recovery. That's why we put off treating Taylor for the time being. Believe me, they understand."

"I get it," Lex said. "Thanks, Dad."

"For what?"

"For not doing what I thought you would do."

"Am I that obvious?"

The two women looked down at their respective plates. Huge grins appeared as they struggled not to laugh. An answer was not required.

Steve began treatment the following day. He was admitted to the hospital, and a nurse's aide escorted him and Gina to a small antiseptic room that resembled an operating theater. "Have a seat, Mr. Wilson," she said. He sat in a comfortable, padded recliner next to an electronic machine, the size of a small refrigerator, with several tubes extending from its interior. Dr. Barnes, accompanied by an oncologist and a nurse, entered. His escort disappeared. Gina sat to the side.

"Hi, Steve; this is Dr. Levine. He is going to explain the procedure, hopefully in layman's English, and then treat you. This is Nurse Joiner. She will assist."

"Hello," Steve said.

They returned the greeting, and Dr. Levine began the explanation. "We're going to insert a needle to draw your blood and pump it through this machine, which will supercharge your red blood cells and train them to attack only those cells affected by your cancer, without damaging the surrounding healthy cells. Then, after the blood has been treated, we return it to your bloodstream to do its work. It will take a few hours to accomplish, so get comfortable. Do you have a book, or shall we turn on the television?" He said this last with a grin to diminish any uncertainty Steve might be experiencing.

"I'm fine, Dr. Levine. My wife is right there."

"Good, then let's get started," he replied.

Nurse Joiner wrapped his bicep with a rubber band and began prepping the area where the needle would penetrate the skin. "Don't worry, Steve. This will be a walk in the park." She inserted the needle before he realized she'd done so. She inserted another catheter in his other arm and turned on the machine. The doctor inspected several gauges, adjusting some of them, and then announced they were good to go. "I'll be back in a while to check on you. Nurse Joiner will stay and monitor your progress from time to time. Just press that button if you experience any discomfort at all."

"Thank you, Doctor."

"See you in a bit," he said as he exited the room.

Dr. Barnes patted him on the shoulder and said, "I'll be back later. Call me if you need me."

"Thank you."

Chapter 53

Six weeks later, Gina and Steve sat in Dr. Barnes's office with Lara Jacobs in attendance. Steve had completed the course of treatment recommended by his doctors. "I've studied the results of your latest MRI, Steve, and it's not promising."

"What does that mean?" Gina asked.

"The tumor has not reduced in size; in fact, it's grown larger. I really don't understand why you're still ambulatory and not in the hospital."

Gina dropped her gaze to the floor. She couldn't force herself to look at the other occupants in the room. Steve looked directly at Dr. Barnes. "I guess that means the trials didn't have anything to do with my condition," Steve said.

"We don't know that for sure, Steve. The trials may even have precipitated your cancer. There's so much we don't understand about this entire situation that I wouldn't venture a guess," Dr. Barnes countered. "And, as you suggest, it may have nothing to do with it. We simply don't know."

"It would seem to me that's a moot point now."

"What do you mean, Steve?" Lara asked.

"Well, it doesn't matter what caused my condition. With or without the trials, my prognosis will not change. I have a limited time to accomplish whatever I need to do. Isn't that why we're here?"

Lara nudged Steve with her elbow and nodded toward Gina, who was still staring at the floor in an obvious state of shock. Steve understood immediately. He said, "Dr. Barnes, Lara, thank you so much for your help. I think Gina and I will need some time alone, if you don't mind.

Unless there's something you want to add, I think we understand what you are implying."

"To be clear," Dr. Barnes said, "you have a limited time to live. You should get your affairs in order and spend your remaining time with your loved ones. I'm sorry."

"Don't be," Steve said. "I've enjoyed every second of my time with both of you. I wouldn't change a thing. Thank you so much." He hugged Lara, and then he hugged Dr. Barnes. There were tears in all their eyes.

"Come on, sweetheart, it's time to go." He took his wife by the hand and led her from the office. She walked like an automaton overloaded on Xanax, head down, shoulders slumped. No one attempted to hug her or interfere in any way. They sat and watched the couple leave. Once they cleared the doorway and exited the outer office, both professionals came together in an embrace and cried.

Outside, Steve deposited her in the passenger seat, went around the car, and sat behind the wheel. He didn't bother to tell his wife he wasn't supposed to drive any longer. It wasn't important. He put the car in gear and drove home. They did not speak.

At home, Steve reversed the process. He escorted Gina into the house and took her to the bedroom. He put her in bed, removed her shoes, and pulled the covers over her. "Relax, beautiful; we'll talk in a little while. I have something to do." Gina didn't respond.

Once again Steve got behind the wheel. He drove to the school where Taylor attended classes, with Patricia as his aide, and parked. The school was adjacent to the shoreline, only one hundred yards away. Steve found Patricia and Taylor out on the playground and approached them. "Hi, Patricia; hi, Taylor," he said.

"Hi, Steve," Patricia responded. "What's up?"

Taylor struggled with his response and then broke through. "Hi … Dad," he managed.

"Patricia, I want to take Taylor for a walk if that's okay," Steve said.

"Of course, no problem. Go ahead," she said. "Is everything all right?"

"Everything's fine, Patricia. I just want to spend some time with Taylor."

"Okay," she said. "I'll be right here when you're done." She watched the two men walk away toward the ocean. She knew they'd visited with the doctors that morning. She had an awful feeling about it. A lone tear escaped and trickled down her cheek.

Steve and Taylor held hands as they walked on the sand. It was a school day, so the beach was deserted. There wasn't a soul in sight. Usually Taylor would get excited to be on the beach and jump up and down as he ran from the incoming waves. Today he just held hands with his father and walked along. He was quiet, subdued. It was as if he knew something important was about to happen.

Steve began talking as though Taylor would understand each spoken word. "Son, I love you more than you'll ever understand. I haven't released you yet, but I will. I want you to know you were the first person I wanted to treat, but inside I knew I would lose the ability to treat other children just like you if I did. I hope you'll understand some day and will forgive me. I was going to do it now and take you home to surprise your mother, but I changed my mind. I have some other children to see before I do that."

Steve stopped and looked out to sea, one of the cathedrals he prayed in all his life, and fought to arrest his emotions. When he regained sufficient control, he continued, "Taylor, I'm not going to be here much longer. Dad has to go away. I want you to promise me you will take care of your mother and sister after I'm gone. They're going to need your help."

Taylor held eye contact with his father as if he knew this was required of him. Steve was surprised and pleased with this brand of attentiveness that was rarely offered. He went on. "You're a big guy, Taylor, taller than me already. You're going to speak. You're going to understand others. You're going to have a great life. I want you to respect your family, your future wife, and those who are less fortunate than you. I want you to stand for those who cannot stand for themselves. I want you to be a good man. I want you to become all those things I wish we could have talked about. Most of all, I want you to smile. I want you to be happy." He looked Taylor in the eyes. "But I guess you already are. Your mother saw to that."

They started walking again. "Son, if you're ever sad, if you ever feel the need to talk to anyone, I'm here. I'm in the ocean. I'm in the mountains.

I'm in the streams. This miracle taught me we're all connected. Just go to one of those places and I'll hear you. I'm a part of those places, just as I'm a part of you. There's a place called Honeymoon Lake where all this started. It's a place where I found peace. I want you to ask Uncle Tim to take you there. Take Mark with you. They'll know why. And pray for me. Pray for others. And pray for strength, humility, and love. But most of all, pray in gratitude. Thank the collective spirit that is the human experience. We humans are special, son. We can manifest so much goodness in this world if we make it a priority. I pray someday we will all wake up and realize our true purpose in life is to serve one another. What a concept, huh?"

He stopped again and took Taylor's hands in both of his. The urge to hug him was so powerful he felt himself leaning in. He wanted so badly for his son to talk back, to become a part of this conversation. He knew he had to stop, to leave the beach now, or lose control. "Come on, buddy, we have to go." He turned abruptly and walked back along the sand, afraid to look at his son.

Just before they left the beach, Steve and Taylor shared one more family ritual he'd taught his son when he was young.

Steve said, "Am I your father?"

"Yes," he immediately responded.

"Are you my son?"

"Yes."

"Are we best friends?"

"Yes."

"Are you going to love me forever?"

"Yes."

"All riiiight," they chorused together as they both raised their fists in triumph, laughing. It was their most important ritual, one that Taylor never tired of, never hesitated in his response. They shared a high five, and Steve escorted Taylor back to school and to Patricia's care.

"Did you have a nice walk?" she asked.

"A perfect walk," Steve said. "Thank you. I'll see you later."

Chapter 54

Next, he drove to his daughter's school, a few blocks away. He parked in the lot until the dismissal bell sounded and then got out, stood next to the car, and waited for Alexis to appear. When he spotted her, he waved his hand in greeting. She approached with a puzzled look on her face. "How come you're picking me up? Where's Mom?"

"She's home. Can't I pick up my own daughter occasionally?" he joked.

"Cut it out, Dad. You're not even supposed to be driving. What's going on?"

"I wanted to talk to you in private, honey."

"Okay ..." Alexis knew something serious was about to happen. "Let's take a walk on the playground."

They walked to the playground and sat on adjacent swings. "Honey, your mother needs your help. She's home now, probably waiting for us." Steve hesitated, unsure of how strong his daughter really was. "We visited the doctors today, and we received some bad news. The tumor in my brain has grown. It wasn't related to the studies. It's just bad luck."

"What are you saying, Dad?"

"Honey, I'm terminal. I'm not going to get better."

"You're going to die?" The tears were already forming, threatening to spill over.

"Yes." He could barely get the sound out.

Alexis came over and folded herself into his arms. They stood there, immobile for several minutes, while the campus emptied around them. Alexis buried her face in her father's chest and sobbed. He patted her on the back and held her head in his palm to comfort her. Words wouldn't form. He scanned the sky, the school buildings, the departing students—anything but his daughter. He was close to breaking. He couldn't do that. It would envelop his entire family if he did.

"How long?" she asked.

Steve struggled to answer. He managed to modulate his voice and said, "Months. I'm not going anywhere for a while. We've still got a lot to do together."

"How many months?" she persisted. She would not be put off so easily. Steve forgot how grown up she was.

"Three to six, more if I'm lucky," he answered.

"We haven't been very lucky so far."

"Oh, but we have. I have an incredible wife, a talented daughter, and a son who brings me joy every day. We've been very lucky, sweetheart." He paused, enjoying the feeling of holding his only daughter. "We've built a profitable business, traveled, made wonderful friends, and had some very exciting experiences that no one else has had. I wouldn't change a thing."

"You won't see me graduate from high school. You won't see me off to college. You won't walk me down the aisle someday." He could feel her shaking in his arms now.

"That's true, Lex. I can't deny it. But think of this: your brother will. He will give you away. He will stand for you. He will take my place. Think of that. What a miracle!"

"I don't want Taylor to give me away. I don't want him to take your place. Why does this have to happen to us?"

"Bad things happen to a lot of people, Lex. There are no guarantees in life. You have to play the cards you're dealt. Come on, now. Let's enjoy the time we have left instead of concentrating on the things we may miss in the distant future."

"No so distant, Dad."

"All the more reason, Lex," he countered. "Come on, I really need your help. This isn't going to be easy for any of us. I'm counting on you. You're the strongest of us all."

He felt her stiffen and pull away. She looked up at him. "Dad, I need you, too."

He returned her gaze. "I know that, Lex. I know. I need you as well. So, I'm going to tell you the same thing I told Taylor, something I truly believe. We are all part of something greater than ourselves. We're a part of one another. During these trials, I've been blessed to be a part of, I learned a great deal from these children. I felt their pain, their despair, their experiences, their frustration, and I also felt their joy at their release from those bonds. It was the single most incredible emotional impact I've felt since you and Taylor were born. It was as if I saw them born, or reborn, I guess. I am connected to them but not as connected as I am to you. I promise you I will never leave you. I will be in the air, the water, and the trees. I will be in all the places we've loved to visit together. All you have to do to find me is go there and speak to me. I will listen. I will talk with you. And I will watch you graduate from high school. I will watch you go off to college. I will see you graduate with honors. And best of all, I will give you away to your future husband. I will be there … in your heart, in your soul. All you have to do is believe."

"You are so full of crap." She smiled up at him; his girl was back.

"Okay, Lex, no more lectures."

"More like a sermon," she said. She brushed back her tears and said, "Let's go home, Dad. I want to see Mom."

As they approached the car, he asked, "Do you want to drive?"

"Are you serious? I don't have a license. You could get into trouble."

"I don't have one anymore either. What are they going to do, give me a ticket?"

A big grin erupted on her face. "Then, yes, I want to drive. Give me the keys."

"Do you know what you're doing?" he asked.

"Relax, Dad. I've already driven with Mom while you were at the hospital treating kids. Buckle up."

Steve just shook his head and beamed back a smile to match hers.

"Okay, Parnelli."

"Who?"

"He was an old-time race car driver."

She mashed the accelerator in response, revving the engine. Her impish smile appeared for a moment.

Chapter 55

Alexis pulled into the driveway like she'd been doing it for years. Gina appeared on the tiny porch to greet them. "I see you've discovered your daughter can drive," she said.

"Yeah, it seems I'm not the only one with secrets." Steve laughed. He ascended the steps and hugged his wife. "How long has she been driving?"

"Since we arrived on base," Gina said.

"Are you okay, honey?" he asked her.

"I'm fine, Steve. I just needed a little time to digest all of this. We'll all be fine."

"Are you sure?"

"Is there another choice?"

Alexis joined them on the porch. She hugged Gina and immediately left them to talk in private. She was a smart kid.

"Come and sit down," Gina said. They took seats on the rocker bench and pushed off to set it in motion. "I'm sorry I fell out for a moment," she said. "I wasn't thinking."

"Are you kidding? Don't apologize. You've been great through all of this. I would be at a complete loss if the circumstances were reversed." He leaned over and put his arm around her.

"Steve, if you could do anything you wanted, anything at all, what would you do?"

"You won't like my answer."

"I already know what it is," she said. "You'd treat more kids."

"You know me too well."

"Why would you spend what little time you have left doing that? Why not hug Taylor right now and enjoy some time with him?"

"This is going to sound selfish to you," Steve said. "When I treat a child and feel the release, it is the single most enjoyable moment in my life. I can't put into words the feeling that comes over me. I get this physical jolt as all their pain, frustration, and confusion leave them in an instant. It's a rush that I wish everyone could experience just once in their life. There's pain, for sure, but I guess it's a little like childbirth; it's so worth it that I immediately forget about the hurt. The joy completely overwhelms me. Does that make sense?"

"I guess so."

"If I treat Taylor first, all those children I may have helped are stuck. Believe me, the desire to hug him is so powerful, sometimes I have to go for a walk and leave him before I blow it. I want to finish the kids I committed to, so those families don't have to live with 'almost' for the rest of their lives, and then I'll hug him so hard, he'll push me away."

"I doubt that." She laughed.

"Gina, I'm saving Taylor for the most incredible experience of my life. I get to release my own son from his prison. I get to feel what he's been feeling all this time. What a gift to receive! For me, it's only three weeks until the best Christmas I'll ever have. I'm savoring the thought every day."

"How can you be so positive at a time like this?"

"You taught me how," Steve said, "every day we've been together." He pushed his advantage. "So, are you okay with that?"

"Of course, I am, honey. How could I not be?" What she really wanted was to hit him over the head with a two-by-four.

"I want to cut back to only two kids per week on Tuesday and Friday. In three weeks, all six will have been treated, and then we'll do Taylor. Is that okay with you?"

"It's okay with me, but Dr. Barnes is out. He won't do it. You're going to have a hard-enough time getting Lara to participate."

"She'll do it. She knows I'll do it without her if she refuses. She won't let me down."

"How do you know that?"

"She's been in service to these children a lot longer than we have. She has dedicated her entire life to these kids. I think she's one of the most caring, giving persons, I've ever met. Haven't you noticed the look on her face after a trial when she thinks no one is looking?"

"No."

"She looks like she scored the last chocolate in the box. Watch her next time. It's absolutely precious."

"How unprofessional of her," Gina mused.

"And you get the same look," Steve said.

"I do?"

"You can quit pretending now. I've seen you, Gina. You get the same pleasure out of this that I do."

She leaned over and kissed him. "Why don't we keep that our secret," she suggested. "People will think we're nuts."

"A good kind of nuts," Steve said.

"I'll go call Lara. She's been waiting for me to call."

"What?"

"You heard me. You can be so dense at times."

As she entered the house, Steve overheard her mumble, "Like you didn't know …"

Chapter 56

Lara greeted them the following Tuesday. "You've made some people very happy, Steve," she said. "Are you certain this won't hasten your 'departure'?" She waggled her fingers in air quotes.

"Positive," Steve said. "The sooner we get these kids treated, the sooner I get to hug my son."

"Before we begin, you have to agree: it's only these six. There are no more scheduled. And I get to witness you hug Taylor," Lara said.

"Agreed," Steve said. "I wouldn't have it any other way. Let's get started."

The first one was a five-year-old boy with a history of biting anyone who approached him. Steve sat on the couch with the intention of outwaiting him, but the little guy backed into the corner, facing outward, and sat down. He began rocking back and forth with a glazed look to his eyes and ignored Steve. After ten minutes of this repetitive motion, Steve decided to sit on the floor near him. He was careful to avoid any eye contact. He mirrored the boy's lack of interest by maintaining focal concentration on the opposite wall. He edged closer to the child in minute increments until he was only two feet away. That's when it happened.

The boy clicked his teeth together in an aggressive manner, so loud that Steve knew what he was doing without looking at him. The sound was unmistakable. He was threatening to bite him as a defensive measure. Steve continued to ignore him. That was a mistake. The little guy launched his body when Steve least expected it. Steve reacted instinctively to protect himself. He jerked his arms up in front of him to prevent the boy's gnashing teeth from reaching his face. The child sunk his teeth into the outside edge of Steve's right hand and swiveled his head like a dog playing with a stuffed toy, shredding the flesh and opening a hideous wound.

Steve pulled him close to hug him and release the frustration and fear he could sense in the child, but the little boy fought his every move. He twisted away and bit down on Steve's right forearm. Steve ignored the pain and rolled over on top of the boy, pinning him to the carpet. He maneuvered his body into a hug by holding the child by the back of his neck with his left hand and creating a vise with his imbedded right forearm. Instantly the little boy released his hold on Steve's arm and went slack. He began to sob loudly. Steve could feel his little body quake with the effort. He pulled away and rolled off the child, still holding him in an embrace. Then he felt the boy hug him back.

A frigid wave of air washed over him, and then the pain came. Every joint screamed in protest at the onslaught. Steve rolled away and held his injured hand against his torso. He curled into a fetal position and tried to hide his agony from the boy. It didn't work. The child knelt over him and tried to roll him back over. "I'm sorry. I'm sorry. I had to. I had to," he repeated.

It took a little longer for Steve to respond this time. He looked down at his hand and noticed the wound had closed, but it was still red and raw with a raised welt in the shape of a small denture. His forearm bore no marks. He fought off the nausea and pushed his back up against the wall into a sitting position. "It's okay, son. It's okay."

"I bit you. I bit you," he cried.

"You sure did, son. But it's healing nicely. It'll be fine in a minute," he said. Steve held his wounded hand in the other and inspected it. The welt had already reduced in size, and the redness had disappeared. "Look, it's fine."

The little guy held Steve's hand in both of his miniature ones and kissed the wound. "It will get better now. That's what my mom tells me," he said. Steve felt his emotions threaten to spill over. The pain persisted, but he didn't want Lara and Gina to realize his body hadn't fought off the insult to his flesh like before. It didn't heal instantly. It took longer. He was weakening. He comforted the little guy by patting him on the back. "I'm fine, my little friend, just fine. Thank you."

Lara entered the room and addressed the child. "Tommy, how do you feel?"

"Bad," he replied. "I did something bad. I hurt the man."

"No, Tommy, you didn't do anything bad. You were scared, weren't you?" she said.

"Yes, but I'm not scared now. I want to see my dad. Where is my dad?"

"Come with me," Lara said. "I'll take you to him." She looked down at Steve on the floor with his back to the wall. "I'll be back," she said.

She escorted the boy out of the room. As he left, he said, "Thanks, mister. That was great!"

"You're welcome, Tommy. Bye."

"Bye."

Lara reappeared ten minutes later. Steve had felt strong enough to take his seat again on the couch before she returned. As she approached, Steve asked, "Where's Gina?"

"She decided to go home. I think the wrestling match was too much for her to witness."

"It's happened before," he said.

"Not like this," Lara countered. "It was obvious, Steve."

"What was obvious?"

"You didn't recover as quickly as before. How long did it take to get up?"

"I made it to the couch just before you entered." He knew the recording would make a liar out of him if he tried to conceal his reaction.

"That's appreciably longer than the others."

"I know, but I think this was a special case. That little guy was scared witless. He didn't know what he was doing."

"Why do you say that?"

"I felt it. In each case I've felt varying degrees of pain. I think it has to do with the history of the child, what they've experienced in their personal journey. This guy had a lot of baggage."

"You're right about that. Let's get you home." She helped him up.

Chapter 57

Lara drove Steve home. He didn't feel strong enough to walk. When he entered the house, Gina was reading in the family room. "How did it go?" she asked.

"Fine, honey," he said. "But this little boy was quite a challenge. There was such darkness surrounding him." He sat down on the couch next to her.

"What does that mean?"

"Each of these kids has a history. In some cases, they've been treated with love and care by their caregivers. In some cases, like this one, not so much."

"And you can feel that?"

"I can feel the degree of fear or frustration in all of them, sometimes the actual abuse that took place."

"Wait … wait, these kids have been abused?" Gina was incredulous.

"Not all of them," Steve explained. "Some of them most certainly."

"How do you know that?"

"I feel it; the release from pain goes right through me."

"You're absorbing all this?"

"Yes, I thought you knew that," Steve said. "Anyway, it's more like a conduit than a sponge. It leaves through me; it doesn't stay with me."

"And you don't think this affected your health?"

"No, I don't, and it's a moot point now anyway," Steve said. "Come on, Gina, we've already been through this."

"I wish you'd told me this a long time ago. I never would have agreed to any of this if I had known. I wouldn't have let you treat anyone, not even Taylor."

"Gina, please …"

"No, Steve, I don't want you doing this anymore. You're killing yourself. It isn't right."

Steve sat down next to his wife. He put his hand over hers and said, "Gina, it's too late to regret the past. It's done. Come on, I know you're worried. I know this is hard for you. You've been so good, so kind. Please help me get through this. I can't do it on my own. Please!"

"I try, Steve. I really try, but when I think of living without you, all that goes out the window."

"Think of talking to Taylor, of having him by your side. Think of all the things we can teach him now. It'll be a whole new world for us."

"For me, maybe; you won't be here."

"I'll always be here."

"Cut it out, Steve. I don't want to hear that right now."

"It's what I believe," he said. "I would never have done this if I didn't. In fact, I don't think this would have happened at all if I didn't believe in this connection to one another. You'll see, Gina. Someday you'll realize how much we're all connected, and not just us. Everyone is connected somehow. Race, religion, nationality—those are only name tags we wear when we try to impose our will on others. One day, humanity will wake up and realize how much power we have when we serve one another. And whatever time I can share with Taylor, I'm going to enjoy thoroughly. Trust me. Taylor will show us both."

"And I suppose you know this the same way you know everything else. You feel it." Her doubt was obvious.

"That's right. Gina, let's not waste the time we have left together. It's too late for recriminations. Come on, I need you."

Gina melted into his arms. They stayed that way for a long time.

On Friday, Steve treated an eight-year-old boy. There was no assault, no resistance at all. But it took a similar length of time for Steve to recover. In fact, it was another minute longer before Steve could sit up. When he did, he had to run to the bathroom to vomit, a first. The chills were more pronounced. The ache in his joints was almost unbearable. And now the nausea had taken center stage. It washed over him in a wave whenever he sat up.

By the end of the following week, Steve had treated two more kids with positive and rewarding results, but the nausea ramped up each time. He repositioned the couch near the bathroom door to facilitate a quick escape to the bowl after he treated each of them. Gina returned to the trials and began timing each recovery. She was not at all pleased with the decision to continue but resigned herself to the process because of his commitment to finish the children he'd promised to treat.

He was now forty pounds lighter than his usual 190 pounds. Gina thought he resembled a scarecrow. His clothes hung off him as though he were a mannequin dressed in clothing four sizes too big for him. The debilitation was just as obvious. His eye sockets were reminiscent of Lurch from *The Addams Family* movie. His facial skin was taut, stretched over an exaggerated bone structure. The veins in his hands bulged outward to create a raised spider web of dark blue ink on parchment. His hair had turned white. His skin tone was pale. He did not look well.

There was only one more week until he finished the trials and treated Taylor. Gina begged for a miracle. She wanted her husband back.

On Tuesday of the final week, Steve treated an eight-year-old boy. He appeared to suffer from a particularly profound case of autism. He didn't speak, and there was no eye contact, ever. He avoided any physical contact to the point he would scream and flee if anyone attempted to touch him. He watched Disney tapes 24/7 and screamed in protest if the television was shut off or failed for some reason. He slept only when he became so tired that he simply passed out. He ate only macaroni and cheese to the exclusion of any other food, and he drank only water, no ice. He was impossible for the family to keep in the home. They brought him to Steve from a lockdown facility in nearby Orange County, with his arms restrained in a garment that resembled a straitjacket.

Steve was sitting on the couch when the boy was ushered into the room in his jacket and unceremoniously left alone with Steve. He began screaming as soon as the door closed. Steve rose unsteadily from the couch and approached the child. The boy, still screaming, backed away until his backside was pinned against the door. Steve bent over and picked him up. He held him against his torso and whispered in his ear, "I know. I know." Gradually the little guy relaxed. His rigid frame softened, his head drooped onto Steve's shoulder, and he melded his frame to Steve by locking his ankles around his waist.

Steve set him down and turned the newly compliant child around. He unbuckled the jacket from the rear and peeled it off him. He didn't have to turn the boy back around. The child spun around and reached up, grabbed Steve by the back of his neck, and pulled him into a fierce embrace. He was crying so hard; his voice was unintelligible but plain enough to realize he was using words to communicate. Steve could make out "so good, so good, so good," but little else made sense.

The sensation of cold was overwhelming. The pain buckled his knees, and he fell back onto the couch with the boy still attached. Bile rose in his throat, threatening to erupt. Steve no longer ate before treating the children, but the gag reflex persisted nonetheless. Sweat broke out on his forehead, and he began shivering with the cold at the same time. His body was betraying him. He released the child.

"Mister, mister, are you okay?" The little guy perched on the arm of the couch and held Steve by the hand. He caressed the back of his hand, alternately patting and rubbing the paper-thin flesh as though the act would restore some warmth to it.

Lara and Gina rushed in. Lara took charge of the child. She said, "He's fine, George. He just needs some time to get better. Come with me." She held out her hand to escort the boy from the room.

"No, he's not. He's hurt," George said. "I could feel it. He's hurt."

Gina intervened. "He'll be fine, George. Help me get him to the bathroom." Together, the three of them raised Steve from the couch and supported his weight while they walked him through the adjoining door. As soon as Lara ushered the child from the room, Gina shut the door and Steve collapsed onto the tile floor. "Let me lie here for a while, honey. The cold feels good. I don't want to get up."

She hit the stopwatch function on her iPhone and opened the window curtain. George's parents and a teenage girl, presumably his sister, were all crying, sharing a communal embrace with their recovered family member. She witnessed the emotions displayed outside until she could no longer bear to watch. She closed the curtain and sat on the closed lid of the commode. There was nothing she could do but wait.

Thirteen minutes passed before Steve sat up. He grasped the edge of the sink and pulled himself into a standing position with Gina's assistance. He felt light-headed and disoriented for a moment and had to sit on the commode to regain his equilibrium. He held his head in his hands for a few minutes and then lurched out the door to the couch and collapsed. "Damn, that one hurt," he said.

"Steve, you're scaring me," Gina said.

Steve smiled up at her. "It was worth it, totally worth it." The smile persisted. "That little guy, George, was as bad as I've ever felt. In that facility, strangers had to restrain him to brush his teeth, to cut his hair, to cut his nails, and to bathe him. His life was awful. They buckled him into that straitjacket to put him to bed every night. They had to force him to eat. He spent twenty-four hours a day alone in his room. The only human contact he had was when force was applied to him. The Disney tapes were his only escape. It's why he spent so much time in front of the television. He needed it to escape."

"You could actually feel all that?" Gina asked.

"Yes, and I never want to again. Hold me for a while, honey. Just hold me."

Gina could feel him shaking as he lay there.

Chapter 58

Gina needed assistance to get Steve into the car. He was so weak that she put her arm around his waist and supported as much of his diminished weight as she could manage. They took slow, tiny steps until they reached the curb where she left him to retrieve the car. She pulled up and guided him into the vehicle. He fell into the passenger seat with a grunt, put his head back on the rest, and closed his eyes. Gina buckled him in and started the car. She drove slowly while he fell into a deep sleep. By the time they arrived at the house, he was snoring. She parked the car in the shade, lowered the windows, and left him to sleep in the front seat. She was glad the kids were in school so Alexis did not witness this. She called Lara.

"I'm a little worried, Lara," she said. "He's still out front, sleeping in the car."

"I'll be right over."

When Lara arrived, Steve was still asleep in the car. She watched Steve breathe for a while, took his pulse, and then she and Gina sat in the shade of the carport and discussed their next steps. "Do you think it's time to take him to the hospital?" Gina asked.

"Maybe. Let's wait until he wakes up so we can discuss it with him. I'll know better once we talk. His breathing is normal, and his pulse is strong. I don't believe he's in any danger. Has he been like this since he treated George?"

"Yes, he fell asleep as soon as he got in the car. He's been exactly like this ever since. Lara, I'm worried." Tears formed and snaked down her face, unbidden and silent. She stared out at nothing. Then she caught herself and angrily brushed the tears away. She would not quit, not now, not after all they'd been through.

Lara put her arm around her shoulders. "You've been the strong one all this time, Gina. It's okay to let it out occasionally." She massaged her back.

"I know. He's just so stubborn, you know?"

"I do. He is one of a kind. What kind I don't know, though."

Gina managed a pitiful laugh. It came out as more of a bark. "I don't know what I'm going to do without him," she said. "It seems like we've always been together. I don't remember where I left off and he began."

"Let's not fall into the melancholy yet. You've got a lot of time left, Gina. Come on," she cajoled.

"You're right." Gina recovered her composure. "Let's wake him up."

Gina opened the car door, and to her surprise, Steve opened his eyes at the sound. "We're home?" he asked.

"Yes, Lara's here." Gina smiled.

Steve looked around his wife and spied his friend. "Hey, Lara, what are you doing here?"

"Checking on you, Steve. You didn't recover so well this time. Can you get yourself out of the car?"

Steve swiveled his hips and pulled his body out with help from the ceiling handle. When he was upright, he said," See? I'm fine." He walked a bit unsteadily like an inebriated driver taking a sobriety test at the side of the road. Once inside the house, he slumped into his easy chair and smiled. "All better now," he said.

"Steve, stop pretending," Lara said. "That was not your usual reaction, not even when you're tired. What happened in there?"

Steve decided this was too important to pretend it was a fluke. He said, "Lara, I've never felt anything like that. That poor child has been mistreated in every sense of the word. I could feel the cruelty he was exposed to, the lack of compassion, the loneliness. He's had an awful life."

"And you think your reaction was a direct result of feeling all of that?" she asked.

"I'm sure of it. It's not something you could experience and then forget, not ever," he answered. "Maybe it's because I'm not as strong as

I was. It might be that I'm not able to fend off the sensations I receive when I treat these kids. I don't know. Where did he come from? Doesn't he have any family?"

"He did once. They were poor and homeless and had no resources to treat him. They were forced to relinquish his custody to the state. The lockdown facility he was confined to is not a place I feel should even exist, but in today's economy, it's the only alternative. This only confirms my original opinion."

"What do you mean?" Steve asked.

"The epidemic of autism has already exploded. If we don't begin developing homes for these children before they become adults, the mental health community is going to be overwhelmed. You'll see hundreds of thousands of these human beings relegated to being shelved for the remainder of their lives without any chance of recovery or a normal existence. It's not just an embarrassment to the American people; it's a disgrace. The lowest among us deserve much better."

"I'm disgusted."

"You should be, but that's not why I'm here, Steve. You had a serious episode. I'm not comfortable with the outcome. You need to be examined by a doctor. I already called Dr. Barnes. He agreed to see you."

"When?"

"Now," Lara said.

"I don't think …"

Gina cut him off. "As soon as you feel up to it, we're going to the hospital, Steve. Don't waste your breath. We are going!"

"Okay, okay," he relented. "Just give me a half hour."

"Half an hour," Gina said, "and then we go."

Lara got up and said, "I'll see you there. Don't disappoint me, Steve."

"I'll be there."

After Lara left, Steve said, "Honey, can we stop at the chapel on the way? I just want to spend a few moments alone before we go."

"Okay, maybe I can finally meet Sister Annette. I'd like that."

"Me, too," he said. "I think you'd like her."

Chapter 59

Gina assisted Steve into the chapel and helped him to sit in a pew. She went back to the car to allow him some privacy. He was too weak to kneel and offer his gratitude, so he settled into his pursuit of the perfect prayer while he sat. He knew how weak he was, how big a toll the last child took. He prayed for acceptance, for strength, for endurance. He offered his gratitude for a life well spent. He had one more child to treat, and then his son would be next. Just the thought brought a smile to his face. He could feel his facial muscles rejoice at the idea he would soon talk to his own son. Just one more.

He kept one ear alert for the sound of the door opening, the familiar bump and squeak of the bucket wheels over tile. He dearly wanted to see Annette one more time—to see her welcome smile, to hear her simple counsel, and to thank her for her friendship.

She never appeared.

Gina entered the chapel and said, "Steve, it's time to go. Dr. Barnes called my cell and wants to see you now."

Steve looked up and sighed. He was disappointed he wouldn't see his friend. "Okay, honey. Help me up."

Gina escorted him to Dr. Barnes's office. She was surprised at his ability to walk unassisted after visiting the chapel. He appeared to regain his energy and balance after his spiritual detour. He wasn't back to his old self by any stretch of the imagination, but he was stronger. She surmised he still retained the ability to heal himself. It just took longer.

Dr. Barnes greeted him with a gentle hug and held him at arm's length. "You look like crap," he said.

"So, do you," Steve joked. "I thought you weren't going to have anything more to do with all this."

"I said I wouldn't take part in the trials any longer, not that I wouldn't treat you," he explained. "I want to examine you."

"Okay."

They went into his examination room alone and returned twenty minutes later. Dr. Barnes approached Gina and Lara and said, "I want to admit him to the hospital for observation. I don't like his reaction to physical stimuli. His strength and balance are seriously impaired. A fall or an accident is likely in his current state."

"He seems to have recovered already. Is this really necessary?" Gina asked.

"I think it is. Look, Gina, if he's stronger in two days, he can treat this last child and then we'll catalogue his reaction to the treatment and decide your next steps from there. It would be in your best interests to admit him."

"Okay, if you feel that strongly about it."

"I do."

"Don't I get a say in this?" Steve asked.

"No," both women answered in unison.

Gina helped him through the admittance process and settled him in a private room. Once he was comfortable in bed, she announced she was leaving to explain their situation to Alexis and ask Patricia to watch Taylor for a while longer. She stopped at the chapel on the way home and entered the tiny building. She'd never gone to a Christian church to pray, unless Steve asked her to join him, and even then, she didn't understand the importance he attached to his solitary visits. She sat in the very spot Steve occupied when he came there and closed her eyes. The reality of losing her partner of three decades hit her hard. It was here. It was now. She began to cry softly.

Without conscious realization, she asked the ether for the strength to assist her husband, the endurance to raise her children alone, and the grace to accept the inevitable. She begged for a peaceful transition for the love of her life and the attainment of his goals. She prayed for the wisdom to explain their decision to their children. And in that perfect moment she understood what her husband must have felt: the peace, the forgiveness, the acceptance. It enveloped her, holding her in a warm cocoon of unconditional love.

She secretly hoped Sister Annette would appear while she was there. She wanted to meet the woman who had provided Steve with a level of comfort and acceptance in his decision to continue the trials. She wanted to experience what he had in those conversations. God knew she could use it now.

No one appeared.

Chapter 60

Gina gave the news to her daughter, Alexis, and Patricia agreed to stay and look after Taylor for as long as she was needed. Gina and Alexis returned to the hospital to find Steve awake, alert, and refreshed. Alexis, however, burst into tears upon seeing her father hooked up to monitors and an intravenous nutritional feed. He held his arms out and pulled her to him. "I'm fine, little one. They're just being careful. I'll be out of here in a couple days. This is just for observation."

Lex buried her face in Steve's chest and sobbed. "I don't want you to be here at all," she managed. "I don't like this."

"Me neither, but your mother made me," he joked. "You know how she gets when we don't pay enough attention to her."

"You still think you're funny, don't you?" Gina said.

"Of course, I've kept you entertained for over twenty years."

Gina joined the banter. She knew Alexis would benefit from witnessing how her parents handled a difficult situation. "Or so you thought," she quipped. "I was faking the whole time."

"What do you think, Lex? Do you think she was faking?" Steve asked.

"We all were, Dad. You're just not that funny."

"Uh-oh, be careful. You'll wind up just like your mother," he warned. Then he added, "If you're lucky."

They exchanged playful insults for a while. Then Steve asked, "How's Taylor doing?"

"He's fine. Patricia is going to stay and watch him until we get home," Gina said.

"I am so looking forward to this weekend. I can't help wonder what he's been thinking all this time, what he'll tell us," he said.

"He'll probably say you're not that funny, Dad." Alexis laughed.

Steve reached out to grab his teenage daughter, and she easily eluded the attempt. His lack of coordination was obvious. He covered his failing ability by saying, "You're just too fast for me, little one. You're not so little anymore, are you?"

"No, Dad, I haven't been little for a long time." She was five feet seven inches tall.

"Well, I'm still going to call you that," he said. "Is that okay?"

"It's okay," she answered. She fell into his arms again.

Two days later, Steve was back home. His ability to heal had diminished, but he still generated the strength to get out of his hospital bed the next day. He'd recovered sufficiently enough to walk around the corridors and make a nuisance of himself. By Thursday they had no choice but to release him. The next day was Friday, the last day to treat another child, and then, on the following day, Taylor. He was so amped up he couldn't rest. He asked Gina to drive him to the chapel. He wanted to express his gratitude one more time before he treated his son.

Gina drove him to the chapel and remained in the car while he trudged up to the door. He entered the familiar confines that had given him so much comfort and sat in his usual pew. He closed his eyes, settled into a meditative state, and concentrated on the feeling of gratitude that overwhelmed him each time he thought of conversing with Taylor. He remained motionless and gave in to the feeling of warmth and peace that came over him.

Twenty minutes later, he heard the front door open, and he turned in the hope his old friend had arrived. He found his wife staring back at him. "I was just checking on you, honey. How are you doing?"

Steve hid his disappointment and said, "Fine, sweetheart, I'm all done here. Come on, let's go home."

They spent the evening with Alexis and Taylor, watching Taylor's favorite Disney movie, *Cinderella*. Taylor could recite every word, song, and inanimate noise on the disc. Steve had taught him to use his "quiet voice" when watching films in public, and he was overwhelmed with emotion watching his son move his lips and silently speak the characters' lines. He felt his eyes water at the thought that this would be the last time they had to watch movies this way. He held his son's hand and enjoyed the communion while he still could.

The only Wilson who slept that night was Taylor. Steve, Gina, and Alexis watched television, read into the wee hours, or stared at the ceiling. The next day would change their lives forever. Maybe they could even resume a normal life somewhere—off this base, of course.

Gina forced Alexis to attend classes, promising to pick her up immediately after the dismissal bell sounded. Taylor and Patricia went to his day program where he practiced daily living skills for perhaps the last time. The anticipation was so rampant it was difficult to concentrate on any task.

Steve and Gina arrived at Lara's office and entered as usual. They found Dr. Barnes waiting for them along with her. "I was hoping you'd be here. It wouldn't be right to do this without my favorite doctor in attendance," Steve said.

They all exchanged embraces and Lara said, "Ready?"

"You bet," Steve said. His face erupted into a wide grin. He couldn't help himself. He went alone into the treatment room and sat on the couch, still wearing a smile. "Let's go, Lara. Time's a'wasting."

The door opened and a twelve-year-old boy entered. He had long, dirty, brown hair and deep-set brown eyes that darted everywhere at once. He wore mismatched, green plaid walking shorts with a wrinkled, yellow Hawaiian Aloha shirt. His feet were sheathed in the dirtiest pair of black sneakers Steve had ever seen. They looked like you could peel them off his feet rather than unlace them. The aroma of an unwashed body followed him into the room.

Steve waited patiently for the young man to notice him. Five minutes passed before he gave up and approached the passive child. He was just standing by the door and staring off into space, as though deliberately ignoring Steve. He was nearly the same height as Steve's six-foot frame and probably outweighed him by fifteen pounds. Steve positioned himself directly in front of the boy's face, forcing him to acknowledge his proximity. That was a mistake.

The boy lunged at Steve without warning. He grabbed him by the shoulders and emitted a hideous, unintelligible scream directly into his face from only inches away. Steve wrapped his arms around the young man's waist and pulled him close. The boy rushed forward spilling them both onto the tile floor and cracking Steve's head against the unforgiving surface. The sound was sickening to hear. It resonated like a basketball rebounding off a wooden floor. And yet Steve held on.

Dr. Barnes, trailed by Gina and Lara, rushed into the room. Steve still held the preteen close to him like a drowning man clinging to a life raft. The boy was no longer struggling. He was lying atop Steve and crying, his body rising and falling in great heaves.

Dr. Barnes gently peeled him off Steve to examine him. Blood was leaking from his right ear, and his eyes had rolled up into his head. He was unconscious. Barnes checked his airway and breathing, and then took a quick pulse reading. "Get an ambulance here right now," he said.

Lara rushed into her office to call. Gina directed the boy away from her husband. He said, "I'm so sorry, so sorry. I couldn't help it. I thought he was going to hit me. I thought he was like the others." He was sobbing uncontrollably. The words were barely audible.

Lara came back and said, "They're on the way, two minutes out." She heard the boy apologizing and took charge of him. She knew how he'd been treated in the facility she'd rescued him from. When he wouldn't, or couldn't, listen to oral instructions, an orderly would position himself in his line of sight and repeat his instructions. If the boy continued to ignore his commands, he would slap his face to gain his attention. She'd witnessed this brand of ignorance only once when she was assigned oversight to this particular lockdown facility. She'd arrived unannounced one evening and walked in on the exchange. She'd terminated the orderly on the spot and spent the evening taking his place. That was why she decided to include Michael, the preteen, as the last treatment. He'd been through hell in his short life.

"It's okay, Michael. It was an accident. It's okay. Shush now. It's okay." She took the young man into her arms and caressed his back. He continued to sob as she held him. The embrace was a first for both.

Dr. Barnes held Steve's head still to protect him from any further injury and looked up at Gina. "He'll be fine, Gina. They're almost here. He'll be fine."

Gina could only stare. No words would come.

Two navy medics entered the room with a gurney and gently laid him on the portable bed, wheeled him outside into the ambulance, and drove off with Gina and Dr. Barnes in the back with Steve.

They didn't hear Michael, the young man, say, "I hurt him. I hurt him bad."

Chapter 61

They wheeled Steve directly to the X-ray room to assess the severity of his head trauma. Monitors and a saline drip were already attached to him. The technician positioned the gurney so his head was directly beneath the crosshairs of the machine. Dr. Barnes stood by the display to survey the damage in real time. After viewing the X-ray, he called for a surgical team to meet him in the operating room stat. Gina stood in the hall desperately trying to control her horror.

Two surgical nurses appeared and wheeled Steve out of the X-ray room and down the hall to the operating room. Dr. Barnes stayed with Gina for a moment. "He has severe bleeding of the brain. We need to alleviate the pressure as soon as possible. We have some of the best surgeons in the world here with a lot of experience. He'll pull through." Then he left to consult with the surgeon.

While she was waiting, Patricia appeared, holding Taylor's hand and leading Alexis down the hall. Both females were already crying. Taylor was his stoic self. Nothing registered. They fell into a group hug. Taylor stood by.

When the broke apart, Gina asked, "How did you know to come?"

Patricia said, "A woman came to Taylor's school and said we should pick up Alexis and come to the hospital."

"Was she short, with curly brown hair?"

"Yes."

"Where is she?"

"I don't know. We left her there. She hugged Taylor like she knew him and told us to go right away. It was the oddest thing—"

"What?"

"Taylor hugged her back, a real hug. You know how he just stands there, limp, when you ask for a hug?"

"Yes."

"Well, she didn't even have to ask for a hug. And when Taylor hugged her, he hugged her like I'd never seen before … like he knew her well. I was jealous."

"When was this?" Gina asked.

"A half hour ago," Patricia said.

Gina looked at her watch. "That's not possible. It's only been twenty minutes since the accident."

"Maybe I lost track of the time," Patricia replied. "I had to stop and pick up Alexis on the way."

Five minutes later, Dr. Barnes and Lara made their way down the hall to the waiting group. The look on his face told Gina all she needed to know. Her husband was gone. She slid down with her back to the wall until she came to rest on the floor. All her strength left her. She was empty. Alexis collapsed next to her mother and held her. They barely heard Dr. Barnes say, "I'm sorry, Gina, Alexis. He didn't make it. The added trauma and the mass on his brain were too much for him. We didn't even open him up. He passed without regaining consciousness. There was no pain. I'm so sorry."

Lara, Patricia, and Taylor held hands while Gina and Alexis stayed locked together on the floor, holding one another. It took them ten minutes to regain their composure enough to ask, "Can we see him?"

"Of course, I'll take you to him," Dr. Barnes said. He helped Gina up and hugged her and then hugged Alexis. "Your father was a brave man," he said.

"I know," Alexis said. She didn't lift her eyes to the doctor. She didn't trust herself.

He led the five of them down the hall to a room near the operating theater and held the door open. "I'll watch Taylor. Go ahead," Patricia said.

"No, he's coming with us to see his father. You, too, Patricia. You're a part of this family, too," Gina said. She scanned the group. "I want all of you with us."

All six of them entered the small room and crowded around the bed. Even Taylor seemed to understand the solemnity of the occasion. He stood by the bed, gazing down at his father. Steve's face was calm and serene as if he was asleep. Everyone, except Taylor, burst into a fresh round of tears at the sight of him lying there with his eyes closed. He seemed so small, so frail, like all the air had been let out of the balloon. Gina reached out and took Steve's hand. She didn't know what else to do. Alexis took the other.

Alexis bent over and kissed her father one last time. Her tears fell onto his face as she did so. She spun around into her mother's arms and buried her face in her shoulder. Gina held her while the others looked on and cried with them.

Then Taylor did a curious thing. He sat down on the bed next to Steve and kissed him on the forehead, just as his father had done to him countless times. Then he lifted his father, limp and lifeless, away from the gurney and into an embrace. He took him in his arms and held him like that for a long time. Everyone froze in place.

After what seemed an eternity, he gently released Steve to recline on the mattress. He said, "I love you, Dad."

He turned to Gina and said, "Don't worry, Mom. I'll take care of you."

Epilogue

Two weeks later, Steve was laid to rest in a private ceremony; only his immediate family, Lara, and Dr. Barnes attended. The next day, as the Wilsons were preparing to leave the base, Gina decided to visit the chapel one last time. This was where her husband found peace. She wanted to experience this place once more, as he did. She entered the tiny structure and sat in his seat. She thanked God for the gift of such a special man and the recovery of her son.

When the door opened, she swiveled in her pew, hoping to finally meet Sister Annette and thank her for befriending her husband. She was disappointed to find an elderly priest who smiled when he saw her. "You must be Mrs. Wilson," he said.

"I am."

"I'm Father James Foley."

"Did you know my husband?"

"No, but I used to see him come here from time to time. He didn't seem like he wanted company, so I never intruded. I made sure no one else intruded on his privacy. You develop a sense for these things. I heard he was a wonderful man, though. I'd like to offer my condolences."

"Thank you, Father." She hesitated and then asked, "Do you know where I can find Sister Annette?"

"I'm sorry," Father James said. "I don't know a Sister Annette."

"She cleans the chapel occasionally," Gina said.

"Mrs. Wilson, the chapel is cleaned by volunteer soldiers. There are no nuns on this base. I'm sure I would know if there were."

"But my husband …" Something stopped her. "Thank you, Father. I was confused for a moment."

About the Author

Lawrence Williams is the father of an autistic child born in 1988. Tyler was born before the age of the internet, smart phones, appropriate education choices, and the development of effective intervention methods. The prospects for a fulfilling life for his son has been his primary focus.

Lawrence lives in Southern California with his wife of 31 years.

Tyler now lives in a group home of adult autistic young men and is a flourishing, happy, delightful person, quick to smile and eager to engage others.